GRANTA BOOKS

WHEN THE WORLD WAS STEADY

Claire Messud

When the World was Steady

GRANTA BOOKS
NEW YORK

GRANTA BOOKS
250 WEST 57TH STREET, SUITE 1316
NEW YORK, NY 10107

Published in the United States by Granta USA Ltd.

First published in Great Britain by Granta Books 1994 in association with
Penguin Books

1 3 5 7 9 10 8 6 4 2

ISBN 0-9645611-3-1

Library of Congress Catalog Card Number: 95-77366

Printed in the United States of America

For M.R.M., for F.M.M.;
and, of course, for J.W.

Is it lack of imagination that makes us come
to imagined places, not just stay at home?
Or could Pascal have been not entirely right
about just sitting quietly in one's room?

Continent, city, country, society:
the choice is never wide and never free.
And here, or there . . . No. Should we have stayed at home,
wherever that may be?

(from 'Questions of Travel' by Elizabeth Bishop)

PROLOGUE

THE GRASS AND the damp soil oozed up between Melody Simpson's toes as she picked her way to the bottom of the garden to watch her children sleeping. It was a summer night, but brisk, and she clutched her dressing-gown around her as she went, patting at her hair although it was past midnight and there was nobody to see.

The clear quiet sang, almost, in Melody Simpson's ears: it was the first summer after the war, the first summer of a new life, when—battered and bruised though He might be—God was in His Heaven and all was right with the world. Melody Simpson did not believe in God, of course, except as a figure of speech. Only at moments like this she was tempted. Before she remembered the rest.

Virginia and Emmy had built themselves a tent from two large sticks and an old sheet weighed down at the corners by bricks from the wasteground up the road where the end-of-terrace house had been bombed out. The tent had been Emmy's idea, but at five she was too lazy or too young to execute it, and only when Virginia, a responsible if timorous nine-year-old, had taken on the project had it become real.

Melody Simpson had to squat to peer in at them. Awake, the girls were always squabbling, their natures at once as fluid as air and as fixed as concrete and, above all, eternally opposed to one another. But asleep in their singlets and knickers, beneath a tartan blanket, their small, pale arms overlapping, they seemed to share their dreams and to be content.

Melody Simpson could not have described the emotion she felt in this small hour of this free summer morning. She would not remember it, or not specifically. There may have been birds singing, and the breeze may have been full of the honeysuckle that grew along the wall, but Melody Simpson did not notice. What she felt was a longing, in her limbs and her belly and in her spirit, for her daughters' futures, for every joy or triumph that swirled in their dormant imaginations as well as in her own. Was this love? Or greed? Or selfishness? Or pain? Or the anticipation of certain disappointment? Had she believed in God, she might have deemed it a moment of prayer. But she didn't, and didn't. And being the sort of person who thought such reflection a tedious waste of time, she tugged a little at their blanket, by way of maternal rearrangement, and then tiptoed back across the lawn and up to her own solitary bed.

BALI

BALI IS NOT a big island: it is fifty miles wide at its widest, and at most ninety miles long. But it is big enough to get lost on. Kuta Beach, the tourist resort on the island's south coast, must only be a couple of miles in diameter, but one can get lost there, too, amid crazy alleyways of bars and brothels and pirate tape shops, or along the crowded hillocks of sand patrolled by hawkers and deal-makers and old women offering massages. The Balinese, remarkably adaptable, have simply severed Kuta Beach from the island, like amputating a limb—in their minds, of course. To go to Kuta Beach is, for a Balinese, to leave Bali. It is so simple.

The real Bali, then, is to be found higher up or further out, along narrow, winding roads or in emerald rice paddies or over on the destitute, lava-scarred eastern plain where the tourists never go. In all these places that are 'really' Bali, the watchful, angry mountain Agung dominates. There are other, smaller mountains—Abang for the devout, Batur for tourists. But Agung is the mountain of the gods, fierce, unpredictable givers and takers of life. Everything depends on Agung, and everyone is situated by it.

Not to know where you are, not to know where the mountain is: in Balinese there is a word for this, *palang*. To be *palang* is to be paralysed: not to be able to work or to dance or to sleep.

Orientation and order are everything. Everyone has a place.

Emmy Simpson Richmond, at forty-seven years of age, was *palang*. She stopped at the stall in the bend of the road and pointed at a bottle of 7UP. She would have preferred a slice of green mango with salt, or a rambutan, but there was none of the latter and the mango was being sampled by three large black flies. Before Emmy could stop her, the woman stallholder dunked a greasy glass in the drum of water at her side to rinse the dust, and poured the soda into it. The woman was smiling, it would have been rude not to accept, but Emmy wasn't pleased: her stomach had been holding out so well, despite everyone's warnings, and it seemed a shame to risk it for a drink she didn't really even want.

Thick and sweet and fizzy, the 7UP sucked any moisture she had left in her mouth as it went down. She turned her back on the woman and the stall as she drank, looking instead at the great drop on the far side of the road and the view beyond. She was halfway between Penelokan and Kintamani, or so she thought, having decided to walk the eight kilometres rather than pay the cost of a hotel room to ride in a *bemo* bus. The drivers had laughed at her and, it was true, she now worried that she wouldn't get to Kintamani until after dark. Already the sun was falling low in the sky.

She was looking at two mountains, Batur and Abang, different worlds on either side of a lake. The lake had glistened, earlier, but now emanated darkness, as though with the passage of the sun the spirits rose from its depths to skim across the surface.

Batur, directly in front of Emmy, was how she imagined Hell to be: a barren, blackened cone of lava, rising in relentless symmetry from the lake's west shore. Nothing grew on its slopes, except the curving tracks where tourists passed daily to the summit. Emmy hadn't been there and would not go, but she could imagine the soft black sand and hard black rock against which the climbers had to struggle, without a single shrub for shade.

To the east of the lake rose Abang, or what one could see of it. All afternoon, although the sky had been otherwise unblemished, a hazy cloud mass had shrouded the holier of the two mountains. Abang was said to be lush with vegetation, a tropical rainforest even, and in the wet season inundated with spilling rivers that prevented climbers from reaching the ancient temple at the top. Now, however, in the drier months of June and July, Balinese and some Javanese students made pilgrimages to the temple, to make offerings and to pray.

Emmy was determined to make the climb. Very few tourists did, although Emmy wasn't sure why not. No doubt the Balinese were more reluctant to take tourists there than to Batur: the Balinese, Emmy had discovered, had a strong sense of the sacred.

A Frenchman in her *losmen* in Candi Dasa, a man alone like herself, and with the same forlorn air of one suddenly deserted by life, had given her the name of a flute-playing guide in Kintamani who would, the man promised, take her wherever she wanted to go. Which is how Emmy found herself at this bend in the road an untold number of kilometres from Kintamani, with the tropical night, deeper and blacker than other nights, preparing to fall.

Using two words of her guidebook Indonesian, she turned back to the woman at the stall and asked her how far it was to the village: the woman raised a hand: five fingers. When Emmy had asked the girl selling postcards over an hour before, she, too, had raised a hand. Emmy felt a fool for the money she hadn't wanted to spend, and also, suddenly, for the caprice that had brought her to this pass in the first place. She thanked the woman and set off up the empty road.

There was no traffic at all, except for a pair of gaunt and

hungry-looking dogs with patchy fur, headed in the opposite direction with an apparent sense of purpose. Emmy heard the *bemo* coming up behind her before she saw it, the rattling blue carcass of a truck, with wooden benches on its bed and a makeshift roof, a wall-eyed ticket collector dangling precariously from the back running-board. Emmy flagged it down.

The benches were full, and a mother took her son on her lap so that Emmy could sit down.

'*Teri makasi*,' said Emmy. 'Thank you.'

'English?' a man opposite asked. He was Western, in his late thirties, clean-cut, obviously not English himself.

'Yes and no. Used to be. I've lived in Australia so many years now . . . ' she trailed off, smiled.

'I see.' He smiled back. His teeth were very pointy, and this, combined with the close cropping of his hair and the unusual breadth of his skull, gave him a devilish air. 'I am German, myself.'

Emmy nodded. She didn't know what to say to that.

'You're going to Kintamani.' He said it as a statement. 'To climb Batur.'

'No,' she said. 'Abang, actually. I hope.'

He raised an eyebrow. 'That is adventurous of you. Have you a guide?'

'The name of one.'

'I've been living a month in Kintamani,' the man said, 'and not one expedition has gone up Abang. Batur, daily. Abang, no.'

'I know. That's why I want to. That's not the only reason, of course, but . . . '

'You do much sports, yes?' He looked her up and down. Emmy put her hands over her bare knees and glanced around the bus. The others, although they doubtless understood little or no English, were watching the exchange intently. 'I say this,' said the German, 'because it is quite a difficult climb. It is three hours.'

The *bemo* bounced to a halt. 'This is the centre,' the German said. 'If you want a *losmen*, this is where you should get off. I live further along, past the playing-field on the way out of town. Goodnight.'

'Yes, thank you. Goodnight.'

The village was unlike the seaside towns that Emmy had seen; unlike Ubud, even, or the smaller villages through which she had passed. It could not have been less like Penelokan, its neighbour down the road, where whitewashed cottages nestled on a shelf above the lake, and Western-style restaurants with resident *gamelan* orchestras welcomed busloads of visitors daily.

Kintamani depressed her. Stained concrete buildings with little windows lined the dusty street. Bali's ubiquitous dogs sniffed at trodden peel and cabbage leaves, and stick-legged children with high spots of colour on their cheeks scuttled from doorway to doorway, rather than playing boisterously in the road as they did elsewhere. And in the moments that she stood looking, as the *bemo* jostled on up the hill, Emmy noticed that it was getting cold.

Finding the three *losmen* huddled in a row was not difficult, except that then Emmy had to choose one. Although she had, until now, sought out places on the island with few tourists, she had not been anywhere where there appeared to be none, save the sinister German—whose reasons for settling in Kintamani for a month she didn't want to know.

The *losmen* looked not like guest houses at all but like typical Balinese households: there were no guests in sight. Emmy couldn't help but think, despite guidebook assurances about the Balinese love of Western tourists, that in truth she was despised. So she was afraid. Afraid, too, to be a woman alone, here; the horrible question, 'You married? You married?'—to which Emmy had to restrain herself from saying, 'Not any more'—had been asked everywhere she had been on the island. Here, nobody came up to her and asked; nobody approached her at all, not even to sell the oranges they carried in piles upon their heads. For the first time in her two weeks in Bali, she felt alone. More than that, she felt divorced. By and from everyone.

In the gloom of the third *losmen*, Emmy discerned a Western man, missed at first because his back was to the doorway. He was playing with a child. The game consisted of her running across the room to him—a stumbling little run; the girl was not more than two or three—and his lifting her off the ground. Each time he lifted her he said, soothingly, 'There's my pretty little one, there's my beauty.' And the little girl would squeal.

Emmy crossed from the dusk into the unlit salon, and the child's mother emerged from the shadows. Yes, there was a room; would Emmy like to see it? She led Emmy back behind the sitting-room, where two more children sat eating their supper, to a courtyard that served also as a garage. Off it were half a dozen rooms, one obviously larger, with the door ajar. Emmy saw a grandmother sitting there, chewing betel, and assumed it was where the family lived. The woman unlocked the door next to it and handed her the key.

The naked bulb hanging from the ceiling revealed a concrete box, slightly longer than the bare and mouldy mattress on which Emmy now sat, and about twice as wide. Once painted pale green, the concrete was flaking in places, and the corners were festooned with cobwebs. There was no window, other than a slatted opening above the door.

As she examined the two scratchy blankets at the base of the bed—for lice? for fleas?—Emmy thought of home, of her comfortable bedroom and of the crispness of her newly washed linen. This room, this whole experience, was for someone Portia's age, surely? How ironic to think that she, Emmy, was here, while her daughter basked in the comforts of Emmy's house in Double Bay. Even now, while Emmy sat shivering beneath a bare lightbulb, watching a centipede ripple earnestly across the floor, Portia was doubtless reclining in her—Emmy's—bed, with Pietro at her side. They were probably, Emmy thought, crossly stamping on the centipede, soiling the sheets.

She put on long trousers and a cotton pullover and ventured out to the sitting-room. A lamp had been lit in one corner, shedding a dim light. The man whose presence was responsible for her own was still seated with his back to the door. He was reading an ancient copy of *National Geographic*, left by some other traveller, some other year. The woman was not in evidence, nor were her children; rather, an Indonesian couple with a baby sat at the table where the children had been eating. They were talking quietly, but nodded as she passed.

Emmy installed herself in the armchair opposite the man and picked up a magazine from the table between them.

'Good evening,' she said, in what came out as her primmest Sydney society tone.

'Yes, quite right.' His voice was distinctly cockney, she could hear it now. He poked his head around the side of the magazine, which he had been holding unusually close to his face, and eyed her half-suspiciously. 'Quite,' he said again, and put the *Geographic* down.

He was at least sixty-five, possibly more, and had a dissipated air: pouchy skin sagged in folds beneath his jaw; a spread of broken blood-vessels reached from the bridge of his nose across his cheeks; his yellow-white hair, wispy, appeared to dance around rather than grow out of his head. He struck Emmy immediately as a pervert of some kind, hiding his pederasty or his opium addiction in the tropics. This impression was only enhanced by his crumpled, spotted linen suit, complete with panama hat neatly tucked beneath his chair. He seemed to appraise her with equal intensity.

She wondered what he saw: she had not caught sight of her reflection in days and did not know how much she might have changed in the course of her rugged meanderings, her sun-filled hours out of doors. Usually, she knew herself to be well-groomed, a plump but pleasantly solid figure with a youthful face. She had large dark eyes, enhanced, she felt, by their creeping crows'-feet; she had a small forehead and a strong, slightly curved nose; her cheeks were still sprinkled with girlish freckles, her jaw was still strong, her dark, straight hair was thick, and her downy cheeks, she knew, were browned rather than burnt. In Sydney, among her friends, she was considered to be ageing well. Until recently, she had always taken pride in her appearance; she had thought of herself as attractive.

After a moment he said, 'You don't quite look the type. A bit old, aren't you?'

'I beg your pardon?' The Sydney society tone again.

'Well, for this whole thing.' He gestured limply at the air. 'Batur?'

'No, Abang. I could say the same of you.'

'He's a guide, you know,' he said, jerking his head towards the back of the building, presumably in the direction of the woman's husband. 'But he won't take you up Abang. It's not worth their while for one person.'

The woman came in with a tray of steaming food: dinner for the Indonesian family. Both Emmy and the man—whose name, it transpired, was Frank—waited until she had left to speak again—a futile silence, seeing as she spoke little English.

'Have you been here long?' Emmy asked.

'In Kintamani? On the island?'

'Either. Both.'

'Here, I arrived today and will leave tomorrow. I go around the islands every year—Bali, sometimes Java, sometimes Lombok, Sumatra. Other bits of the region too—Thailand, you know. Always Bali. The Last Paradise.' He winked. Lewdly, Emmy thought. 'Such friendly people. The only Hindus, you know, in

Indonesia. Makes them more hospitable.'

'Does it?'

'And I love the little children. Such beautiful little girls.'

Emmy wasn't sure what he meant, but she didn't like the sound of it. When she remembered his eager game with the owner's daughter, which had drawn her in the door of the *losmen*, Emmy felt certain that this winking, grinning, flaccid apparition was a seasoned child molester. Worse than that, he was the only Western gauge the *losmen* owners had besides herself. Which meant the smiling woman, the earnest Indonesian family, they would all think she was cast from the same mould. He was still smiling.

'Are you from England?' she asked. She herself rarely felt English any more; she could perhaps wedge a gap between them here.

'Used to be,' Frank said. 'My daughter's gone back. But I've been out in Australia for years, couldn't live in Britain again, not now.'

This was worse: this was *her* life. It was only a matter of time till Portia set off for London. She decided not to ask more.

She got up and went to the street door to observe the night. A few distant lamps winked in the darkness, and somewhere dogs howled at the moonless sky. The air was cold; there was a breeze, not soft and salted as by the sea, but bitter and somehow dangerous. There was no patter of feet along the road; no hushed singsong of voices in the dark; no wafting strains of *gamelan* music.

Supper consisted of a plate of fried rice filled with lethal chili peppers, and beer. She and Frank ate in semi-silence, he slurping greedily and reddening, eventually sweating, from the chilis. Emmy picked fastidiously at her plate, careful to avoid the vermilion flecks; but there were so many that the process was lengthy, and the rice soon cooled to a glutinous and unappetizing mass. She offered it to Frank, who downed it with swigs of beer that splashed a little and dribbled down his chin.

'You should speak to him.'

Emmy looked puzzled.

'Oka. The guide. The owner.'

'You said he wouldn't take me.'

'He probably won't.'

'Besides, I have a name. I'll ask the woman where I can find him.'

Frank shook his head. 'I wouldn't do that. Rivalry. Ask outside, in the morning. In the market. But if Oka *would* take you,' he said, leaning forward confidentially, 'you could go tomorrow at dawn, and be out of here by noon. You could come with me to Singaraja. It's not too friendly, as villages go, this one.'

'Why not?'

Frank shrugged. 'There are rumours. People—Western people—get robbed here, or cheated. There was even a murder once, although it was never proved. A death under mysterious circumstances, shall we say.' He sat back in his chair and belched, waiting for Emmy to take the bait. She decided not to. After a moment he said, 'What would you say to a bit of fun?'

Again, she did not know what this meant. It flashed through her mind that he might be propositioning her. 'No thank you,' she said.

'A game of cards?' He pulled a worn pack from his jacket pocket. 'A quick one?'

'No thank you. I've had a long day.'

'As you like.' He looked disappointed. As she left he was dealing himself a hand of patience.

As a child, Emmy had known exactly what she wanted and how to get it. Born with the echo of bombs in her ears, she had felt special from the start. Her sister Virginia had been old enough to spend the war doubled over in fear, but as the two of them crouched with their mother in the shelters, tiny Emmy would continue to hum or mumble to herself, oblivious, not missing a note when all around her gasped and shuddered.

She herself had no memory of this. And she had no memory at all of her father, a sacrifice to the enemy early in the war, a pilot shot down before Emmy's singsong took on any tune. What was for Virginia a tragic first loss was not even a hiccup to her younger sister. It wasn't until much later, when she felt for some reason that she should, that Emmy began to miss her father.

Her first and eternal belief was in the creation of one's own luck. More than that, there was for Emmy a distinct morality to luck, an interrelation between good and bad luck and virtue and vice. Throughout her life, Emmy always took it very hard if things went badly for her.

When, at twenty, she announced to her mother and sister that she was leaving their modest home in south London in order to marry a dashing Australian named William and head for the Antipodes, they were not surprised. Emmy was in the brief flush of her beauty, between the sloppy plump child she had been and the handsome but formidable matron that she fast became. As Mrs Simpson pointed out, what better place for her to make her own luck than in the newest of the new worlds? And who could stop her?

Virginia was perhaps even a little glad. From the day of her birth, Emmy had never ceased to terrorize her older sister, or at least that was how Virginia saw it, and she attributed her pinched, shy nature to that unplanned birth amid the whistling bombs: all her dread born at once. That Virginia would probably have been the same without Emmy was not something she recognized on that damp spring morning in 1960 when Emmy said she was leaving.

Emmy felt her sister saw the world upside down. Virginia

believed that things just *happened* to one, and Emmy saw this not merely as a mistake but as evil. Her final advice to Virginia was to pray. As they weren't then religious believers of any sort, Virginia, surprised, asked to whom Emmy would have her do so.

'To yourself, silly,' Emmy said. 'That you'll have the gumption to *live.*'

Emmy and William had sailed to Australia, to William's home in Sydney, and there Emmy had discovered her luck to be greater, even, than she had imagined. She had married into a family of aspiring publishers, whose empire was small but flourishing, based on a solid ground of working sheep-stations.

Emmy would always tell Portia of her joy when, early in her marriage, she and William had made a tour of those outback stations. She had been greeted at homestead after homestead by women with their sleeves rolled up and dust in the creases of their skin, women with their arms outstretched, all of them weeping, weeping at the sight of Emmy, because they lived alone among men and she was water in the desert, balm on an aching wound. She heard about their cramps and labours and miscarriages, she heard their recipes for biscuits and the lists of supplies they couldn't get hold of. She heard about their worries for their children—those who had them—and their problems with their men. She took down titles of books that they longed for, hesitant requests for feminine luxuries. Some hadn't spoken this way for years, one for almost a decade. And as she left each woman to climb into the buzzing shell of the plane, Emmy would throw her arms around her and weep with that woman, these tough Australian labouring mothers and bright-eyed, primly English Emmy.

During this trip, Emmy felt more blessed and good than she had imagined possible: her luck was at a pinnacle, she was needed and envied and loved. She clung to the memory always, and disregarded the fact that, back in Sydney and hurled into a whirlwind of social and wifely obligation, she had somehow neglected the lists of books, of luxuries, then lost them, then forgotten them altogether. When she did recall this, with a quickly stifled pang of shame, she would remind herself that she had been young.

But that was just the first forgetting, and it seemed, somehow, when much later all the perfect luck had soured, that it had been only the first step in a mammoth self-deception. Thinking that her life was in her hands, Emmy had ordered her days with lunches and receptions and had eventually borne a child. She had launched a career writing about restaurants and society, gleeful impetuous pieces about places that delighted her, published in the papers and magazines of her husband's family.

'Be like me,' she would tell Portia as her daughter grew older. 'Be sure your life is your own, your happiness in your control.'

And then, a year and a half ago, things started happening to her, pulling the pins out of her life, revealing . . . what? That she had been blind and a fool all along. William, whom she had barely considered a factor, more a presence, a part of herself that was at times irritating but was, above all, a part of herself, left her. He left her for her friend Dora, the wife of his friend Andrew. At Emmy's outcry over the selfishness of two divorces (not one but *two* families ruined!) William replied, calmly, almost generously, as if explaining to an uncomprehending child, that he was merely taking control of his own life.

Six months ago, Portia had informed Emmy that she was dropping out of university to study sculpture at art college. She had, at the same time, changed her Christian name to 'Pod', so that she truly was no longer the daughter whom Emmy had nurtured and created. And this mysterious Pod, who still hung clothes and ate food and slept in Emmy's house, had recently brought home Pietro, a fellow sculptor, the son of an Italian labourer from the far western suburbs of the city, from the rows of little bungalows that stretched for ugly multicoloured miles and looked, not very much but oh-so-slightly, like the drab terraced houses of south London that Emmy had so triumphantly abandoned many years before.

Emmy was forced to concede that things did just happen. But still, she insisted to herself and to her one dear, remaining friend Janet, that if things did indeed just happen, it was only because you let them.

She took on the full weight of responsibility for the changes in her life. She felt that perhaps the very adaptability she had considered a virtue had brought about her downfall. Shedding selves like skins, she had also shed their emotions—or rather, her own. This mutability had led to a loss of herself and, Emmy had to conclude, to a loss of her luck. And it had been so easy—until she was called upon to play 'divorcee'. Divorcee wasn't in her repertoire. It was not, to her mind, a lucky opportunity. Not an opportunity at all.

She found the burden of her failure so great that she was suddenly, and for the first time in her almost fifty years, incapable of making any decisions at all, of taking any action. What if she were deceiving herself? Playing into the hands of the enemy? She had been so blind, William and Dora's affair had gone on for years. She couldn't see their old friends, she was a laughing-stock. She remembered that she was English, he Australian, their friends somehow thereby his. As for her work, she could not write for his magazines, it was too great a blow to her pride; she could not write for the opposition, it would be too public a betrayal.

She spent an entire month leaving her small house in Double Bay only to go to the supermarket or to walk Aristotle, an Afghan hound and the sole remainder of her pulverized existence, along the thin strip of beach at the end of their street. The alien Pod did not count, a fairy changeling dropped in her darling Portia's place. Emmy grew broader than she had ever been: unable to decide what to eat, she ate everything, hoping something, some potion ingested, would restore her life to her.

She did not decide, really, to go to Bali; she chose Bali only when Janet had decided that Emmy had to go somewhere. Janet had got on the phone to Qantas, had decided on the date, had given Emmy's credit card number and had then turned, in the by now cockroach-infested kitchen, to ask Emmy where she wanted to go. She had to say something, or Janet would, she threatened, pack her off to London, to her mother and sister, whom Emmy hadn't seen for six years and found dreary in the extreme. At that moment, her head in her hands at the kitchen table, Emmy had said, for some reason, Bali. Perhaps not for *any* reason, but rather because, on the table beneath her eye, one of her ex-husband's magazines was open at an article entitled 'Bali: The Last Paradise'. What, after all, had she left to lose?

That afternoon, in a moment of exuberance, Pod's Pietro had backed her car—yes, her, Emmy's car—into and over the unsuspecting Aristotle. He too, last and most cherished, was gone. Emmy had no life left to be lucky in. It was time for something.

If only she didn't catch herself adapting again, moulding herself. In this tiny cell of a room, there was not much to mould to, and, Emmy assumed, it would be the same on the mountainside. The real island, which she sought, would bring out her real self. It would provide answers and a new beginning. Looking around her she felt certain, suddenly, of her changing fortune, of her soon-emerging soul. As William and her daughter and her sister all proved, the arbiters of luck and opportunity were not things but people: flesh and blood. And in their absence, she might be free.

As it turned out, the flute-playing guide, whose name was Gdé, was taking an expedition up Abang in five days' time. It was very rare, he insisted, that he should go at all; he was the only one, he assured her, who would take tourists; he suggested very strongly that she wait. He was a round-faced man with a goatee, and he had the disconcerting habit of laughing whenever he spoke. The people he was to take were Australians, he giggled. They were 'especial friends'; they were, he implied, inhabitants of the island rather than tourists. Would they mind if Emmy joined their party? Oh no, Gdé laughed again: they were very hospitable people.

Which left her with four days: it was Tuesday morning and they would be gathering for the climb before dawn on Saturday. Emmy didn't want to stay in Kintamani for that time. Fifteen minutes walking with Frank among the pyramids of citrus fruits and mounds of cheap clothes and chickens in baskets that constituted the morning market, and Emmy had seen enough. Even the early morning mist that should have rendered the scene magical could not change her grim impressions of the evening before. Besides, for breakfast there had been *nasi goreng* again, the same fried rice with chilis, and if she stayed on in the village, Emmy was certain she would starve.

Already someone in the market had pointed at Frank—who must have slept in his clothes; he looked more bedraggled than ever—and said in English, 'You husban'?' When she said no, the youth grinned, stuck out his tongue and said, 'Yes, you husban'! You husban'!' So when Frank suggested that they ride to Singaraja in the same *bemo*, Emmy figured she might as well accept.

Frank was headed north to a resort called Lavina Beach, where, he whispered in her ear, they had flush toilets in the *losmen*. Emmy did not commit herself to going there, although she could tell that Frank thought she had.

This *bemo* was a newer model, an enclosed van that had once been carpeted floor to ceiling in ochre shag that was now peeling away in strips. The vinyl on the seats had cracked and popped, allowing obscene sproutings of greyed foam. Frank sat beside Emmy in the row behind the driver, and two Balinese men managed to squeeze in next to him. The combined girth of Emmy and Frank would, under normal circumstances, have been considered to fill the space, but the pock-marked driver was unwilling to let go of a single potential fare.

They sat in the van for almost an hour before it was full, an hour during which the morning mist cleared and the sun grew strong, so that even with the windows down, or those that would open, the *bemo* became a pungent stew of spices and grease and hot vinyl and, above all, the sour smell of unwashed flesh.

Sitting so close to Frank, the fat of their buttocks closer than touching, almost mingling, Emmy felt it was indeed high time he made it to a world of flush toilets and showers. He had removed his linen jacket for the freedom of his lightweight shirt, which was missing a button, allowing aggressive stray chest hairs to poke through. It was dyed a deep, varying yellow in the circles of his armpits, where days, perhaps months, of perspiration had gathered.

Through this hour, Emmy and Frank didn't really converse. They behaved like a long-married couple, each in a reverie, sometimes noticing something outside the van and pointing it out to the other, with a tap or a nod.

When the *bemo* set off, they were launched into even greater intimacy. The road was narrow, steep and winding, but the driver wasn't about to slow his pace for such minor impediments. Emmy found herself in Frank's lap, then he in hers. She was so miserable that she almost missed the sudden and spectacular transformation from arid mountain landscape to the swollen fertility of terraced paddies, deep green boxes flooded with muddy water, in which men, women, buffaloes and ducks waded in the distance.

To be back in this safe world—what she had known and expected of the island—was a source of relief to Emmy. With that relief came the realization (although she had known it all along) that she wanted no more of Frank's company. He, like the village of Kintamani, depressed and repelled her.

At the bus station in Singaraja, he reached and took her hand as they got out of the *bemo*.

'What *are* you doing?' she hissed, reclaiming it. Her 'viper-tongue' tone, Portia would have said: Emmy at her most forbidding.

'Well, we've got to hurry. There might be a bus leaving for Lavina Beach right now. We don't want to miss it.' His eagerness, from another, might have been touching, but Emmy was too indignant to be charmed.

'We? *We?* What are you talking about, *we?*' She raised her voice. In the flurry of the station some of the people stopped to stare.

'Well, I mean, I thought you said—'

'You mean, you thought I'd provide a "bit of fun", did you? A little diversion?'

'No need to get riled up,' he said, huffy now, offended. He was gripping his battered little suitcase tightly, with both hands. 'I don't believe I ever suggested or implied such a thing. And . . . ' he faltered, then went on, 'And if such a thing ever crossed my mind, it was only because of *your* behaviour.'

'My behaviour?'

'Following me through the market this morning, cuddling up against me in the bus—'

'I beg your pardon?' By now there were a dozen people around them, smiling, sucking their teeth, pointing, whispering. 'As if there was anywhere else for me to put myself. Listen, Mr— Frank—I've had quite enough of this. I'm not going with you, to Lavina Beach or anywhere. Goodbye.' She hoisted her pack on to her back and walked out of the circle that had formed around them. The crowd laughed and cheered.

After a moment she heard Frank asking repeatedly, loudly, 'Lavina Beach? *Bemo?* Lavina Beach?' and a chorus of drivers replying. A man tapped Emmy on the elbow and said, 'Missus, you husban', going, *jalan jalan*, you husban', look.'

Frank was indeed stuffing himself into an already crowded *bemo*. Emmy felt a flash of regret at having been so rude to him. 'He is not,' she said to the man at her side, who was obviously perplexed, '*not* my husband. No husband.' She showed him her bare ring finger. He shrugged and turned away.

What to do now, where to go? Singaraja, like Den Pasar, the capital, was bustling and urban, with billboards and neon signs and a dirty, hot smell. She didn't want to stay there. Lavina Beach now seemed appealing, the prospect of a cabin by the sand and the soughing of the water beyond. Not to mention the luxury of plumbing! But having lost her temper with Frank, and all for effect, really—she hadn't known how else to be rid of him—she couldn't risk the humiliation of running into him again. All she knew for certain was that Lavina was to the west of Singaraja, and that she would, therefore, go east.

When she found a *bemo* destined for Amlapura, at the southeast tip of the island, she got in and went.

It was well before dawn on Saturday morning when Gdé came to waken Emmy. She had arrived back in Kintamani only the evening before, after dark, having had difficulty finding a bus out of Singaraja. She had spent the week not ten miles from the city, paddling in the freshwater pools at Air Sanih, walking alone along the stretch of black sand beach, wandering to the *warung* down the road, where two old betel-chewing women served up *saté* and where the crispy prawn crackers called *krupuk* were kept piled in jars on the plastic tables.

Several tourists, on motorcycles and bicycles, stopped for meals at the *warung* and spoke to Emmy. To them she seemed a fixture, installed on a bench near the road, sunburnt, drinking Coca-Cola with a paperback novel in hand, in this spot where Westerners usually only rested an hour.

'Do you live here?' they all asked, wondering whether they had perhaps come across an uncharted celebrity, settled in the back corner of the island, one the guidebooks had not yet mentioned. 'Are you a painter?' Looking at the novel: 'Do you write?'

To which Emmy daily said 'no' or 'I live here *this* week' or 'I've written *letters*,' or some equally tired joke, leaving the adventurers to pass on, disappointed.

The guest house at Air Sanih was peopled by Javanese tourists mostly, small, modest women in large black bathing-suits who would poke a finger or toe into one of the pools and then dart backwards, squealing, until at length a husband or a brother would push them in with great splashing and fanfare.

When Friday came, Emmy was loath to leave. Her resolve to return to the mountain had evaporated, and the vigorous ascent of a peak draped in wet cloud seemed less and less appealing to her ever browner and softer body.

She cursed when Gdé woke her, pounding on the door of her cell, the same one as at the beginning of the week. The same experience, minus Frank. Minus the breakfast of *nasi goreng*, too, she discovered when she fumbled her way out into the pre-dawn. The innkeeper and his family were still asleep, waiting for the cock's crow.

Gdé was, to Emmy's mind, unnaturally lively. He wore shorts despite the chill, and danced a small jig there in the courtyard at the prospect of the climb.

'Very good, very good, now you up. You waiting for me out front. I coming back.'

'Where are you going?'

'I am going to make offerings. Offerings for a successful climb. It is a good day, I have checked before with the priests, this is why we are going on this day. I make offerings for seven people, we will be seven people. Before I make offerings but the day was not good, the climb is not successful.'

'Not successful?'

He shrugged and opened his hands, which shone pale in the darkness. 'Today is . . . auspicious day, yes? Today will be successful. I coming back.'

When he returned the beginnings of light were filtering through the swirling air. Emmy could see that Gdé carried two small banana-leaf dishes with rice cakes and flowers in them. She felt anxious. 'Is something wrong? Couldn't you make the offerings?'

He laughed. 'Oh yes. Very good day for climbing today. These are for the mountain.'

'The top?'

'For the first temple. Halfway. For the second half of the climb.'

Emmy and Gdé then sat in silence, awaiting their companions, who didn't come for the better part of an hour, during which time Emmy wished herself back in bed many times. The market, like the day, was growing around them, the noise and traffic picking up, half-naked children appearing in alleyways, everything in soft-focus like the opening of a film.

Before they arrived, Gdé seemed to know they were coming. There were loud cries in rapid Balinese, and then a horrendous sound of scraping, out of sight down the hill.

Gdé got up and motioned for Emmy to follow: less than fifty yards down the road towards Penelokan, in the middle of the market, they came on a bus—but a *real*-sized bus, or almost, certainly much bigger than the vans and trucks that Emmy had grown accustomed to. White, monstrous, growling, it had run aground on just such a van in an attempt to avoid a pile of cabbages on its other side. The van owner stood by, yelling, but the bus driver was unfazed.

When the tirade ceased for a moment, he put the bus in reverse and pulled the two vehicles, groaning, screeching, apart.

The van was scratched and dented, it was true; but already so decrepit that it was difficult to tell which scrapes were new and which dated from months or even years earlier. The bus driver did not stir from his seat, high above the van owner, who was still complaining. Gdé darted among the crowd to the door of the bus, as if from stone to stone across a stream. Emmy had slightly more trouble making her way behind him.

'Eh, K'tut!' he greeted the driver, who curled half his lip in the semblance of a smile. '*Selamat pagi!*'

'G'day Gdé!' boomed a voice from the depths of the bus, a thick Australian accent that prompted titters from within. He said the two words in exactly the same way.

'Hello, Buddy.'

Hello Buddy? Emmy was surprised by the name. Buddy? Had she landed a sheep-shearer for a climbing companion? She tried to peer in the bus window and only then did she realize that the windows were hung with batik curtains and that those curtains were drawn.

Gdé waved his arm at Emmy, half smiling, half impatient, urging her on to the bus. She rounded the corner into the cave-like gloom, to a sight for which she was wholly unprepared. While some stiff benches remained in front, the entire back half of the bus had been stripped of seats, and in their place was installed an immense and many-cushioned bed.

Sprawled in the middle of it, propped up by cushions, was a small, barrel-chested man slightly older, Emmy thought, than she herself, although it was difficult to tell. He was dressed from head to toe in various clashing batiks, which all in turn jarred with the prints of the cushions and the bed itself.

On either side of him, more awkward and tentative, perched two young women not much older than Portia, one big-boned, with cropped, bleached hair, and the other with a long, smooth, hennaed tress and a heart-shaped face. Emmy sensed that the women were related neither to each other nor to Buddy, which made her wonder how they came to be there. Then she noticed, slumped in the last row of seats, his back to the others, a boy of about seventeen or eighteen, a longer, thinner version of Buddy, with the same faintly bulbed nose and indulgent mouth.

Gdé, like Emmy, had been looking the group over. 'Mr Buddy,' he said, with evident alarm, 'You say five people plus me and Emmy—this is Miss Emmy—' (that was all the introduction she was to get; Buddy barely nodded) '—but there are only four of you. K'tut climbing?'

'Nope, Gdé. Just us. That a problem?'

It obviously was. Gdé turned and spewed a stream of near-hysterical Balinese at K'tut, who opened the bus door for him. 'I coming back.'

He reappeared moments later pushing a small boy in front of him. 'Wayan wants to climb too. OK, Buddy?'

'Sure, OK.' Engrossed in conversation with the platinum blonde, Buddy was as indifferent to Wayan as he had been to Emmy.

The young Wayan and Gdé sat together on the bench behind Emmy, and K'tut the driver proceeded to back the bus down the road until they could turn around.

Everyone focused on Buddy except the boy Emmy took to be his son, even if this meant craning or twisting uncomfortably. Not that Buddy said or did anything significant during the drive. He merely lolled, his thick body loose to the bumps and rolls of the road. He was explaining his import–export business to the blonde—artwork, batik, baby shoes, it seemed—in a fairly offhand way. Emmy tried again to guess at the relation between them: they spoke the words of strangers, and yet their manners with one another were so intimate.

Buddy's son, arms crossed and knees up against the seat in front, was fiercely feigning sleep, the only concrete indication that this woman was perhaps closer to Buddy than some would have liked.

The bus came to rest in a dirt clearing, a sort of car-park at the base of Abang, itself rising invisible above them. Here, as at all other odd and unexpected spots around the island, a thatched kiosk offered dusty bottles of Coca-Cola, Fanta and 7UP to the rare passers-by.

It occurred to Emmy that she was in no way mentally prepared for this expedition: she had no idea what to expect. Someone, somewhere, had said three hours; she had neglected to ask whether it was three hours up and down, or three hours up. There was something about Buddy's smug but solemn look that made her fear the latter.

'I've been up here twice now, Junior,' he was explaining to his son, in a voice that seemed to Emmy both strained and condescending. 'This'll be the third time. And believe me, it's a rare Australian who's been at all.'

The boy merely nodded. His thin, burnt arms swung a bit, and he toed bullishly at the dirt. He did not look his father in the eye.

The young Wayan had run ahead, following the gently sloping trail into the woods. Gdé was obviously eager to follow, waiting only for Buddy who, in turn, waited for his reluctant son. K'tut the driver stood at the edge of the clearing and spat melon seeds over the long drop towards the lake.

Nobody had spoken to Emmy since she had joined their party, a fact which both relieved and alarmed her. She did not particularly *want* to converse with these people, who seemed to her an unsavoury, not to say vulgar, crew. And she was alarmed for two reasons, the first being that one of them was bound to say something to her sometime, and anticipating that awkward moment was worse, possibly, than the moment itself would be; and the second that supposing—such rudeness hardly seemed possible, but just supposing—that none of them did make any effort to chat, then the coming three or possibly even six hours would be fairly awful.

The first hour or so was pleasant, a brisk upward walk amid solid trees, along a path that occasionally afforded glimpses of the lake below. The sunlight fell dappled through the branches, not strong, and although she was a little warm, Emmy felt quite comfortable. She dawdled a way behind the others. Deep in conversation, the two young women walked together, not far ahead. They were English and their accents were shrill. Buddy soldiered on in front of them, pausing to point out fungi or flowers or the view. Beyond him, Gdé picked out the path—for although there was a distinct way to follow it was in some places obstructed by a fallen log or large rock—and Wayan and Junior had scrambled far ahead, out of sight.

Emmy picked leaves and put them in her pockets. She walked with her head back, watching the skipping rays of light falling towards her and the occasional waltz of branches in the windless air, when a bird alighted or a seed dropped; or with her head to the ground, examining the colours that sprouted among the roots and damp debris, the glinting sweet-wrappers and discarded bottles left by other climbers.

Because her eyes were down, and because nobody thought to alert her, straggling behind as she was, Emmy came abruptly to the base of what she would later, with a clear conscience, call the cliff. Within a matter of feet, the path turned into a wall of mud. At the same time Emmy became aware that no sunlight filtered down to them any more. More than there being cloud between them and the sky, there was cloud between them and the earth below. At the gaps in the vegetation, Emmy looked down and saw only more nothing.

She squinted up at the mud. The two young women were clawing their way halfway to an apparent ledge, created by a tree-trunk, where the rest of the group waited. Emmy realized she would have to say something.

'Hey there, Gdé!' she called. 'What am I supposed to do?'

Gdé's voice wafted down to her. Not, Emmy thought, the way a stone would fall. She was almost certain she heard Buddy say, 'Shit.'

'It's a river bed, Emmy. Muddy. But is plenty of places to hang on. Grab hand hold and foot hold and go slow. We waiting. And don't look down!'

The redhead turned towards Emmy long enough to say, 'It's not so bad really.' She had a grey mud smear on her cheek.

To Emmy, the slope might as well have been glass. She looked down at her feet, tiny in their white tennis shoes and impossibly far beneath her. She tried to imagine them holding her up on the vague mossy outcroppings she could discern above, and she felt her knees twitch. 'I can't stay *here*,' she said aloud.

'You saying something? Hold on, Emmy.' Gdé slid down from stone to stone with his arms flung out like a child playing at aeroplanes. In moments he was reaching out his strong hand, the same hand that had loomed so pale and fragile in the morning darkness, now so much more capable than her own.

'Put your foot here,' he pointed. He held her by the wrist. No longer smiling, he grunted as he bore her full weight on the first leg-up.

'Thank you.' Emmy heaved, and reached her arm up again. But he, too quick, had sprung to higher ground and squatted against the mountainside, beckoning, almost taunting. The voices of the others broke the air far above.

'Come on, Emmy, you can do it,' he pleaded. He had made offerings, after all, for seven. Buddy might be impatient, but for Gdé Emmy was essential to the success of the climb. And Emmy, looking at Gdé's anxious face—not taunting at all, when she focused clearly—had some small sense of his urgency.

She grabbed at a root that snapped under her weight, but not before it gashed her palm, a smooth line from forefinger to thumb along which red beads began to blossom. Tetanus, Emmy thought. But everyone was waiting, Gdé with them now, and as if for her he had taken his flute from his pack and coaxed an eerie, melancholy tune from it. The spirits were urging her on. Emmy slapped her bleeding hand around a stone embedded in the dirt, closed her eyes against the fears that assailed her—of heights, of slipping, of many-legged crawlies and poisonous insects—and hauled herself to a second foothold.

In this way, eyes shut for the most part, she scrabbled and slithered up the mud face, brushing her hair from her forehead with black fingers and thereby painting her skin a dull grey. It felt like innumerable unending heavings, unbearable. Emmy thought of the first land animals tearing themselves out of the water, up, along the shore. Everything was dripping: the sky, the sickly, caressing foliage, her own skin.

When she grasped the trunk she couldn't believe she had arrived. She couldn't believe she had made the climb, as she turned for the first time to the near vertical drop.

'Bravo, Emmy!' The blonde clapped her on the shoulder. Emmy sat on the log, dangling her feet, half-expecting the trunk to dislodge and barrel back the way she had come.

'It is not so hard, yes?' Gdé was encouraging. Buddy strained at the bit. His son sat down next to Emmy.

'You 'right?'

'I'm OK. Thanks.' She looked at him carefully for the first time. Somehow he had escaped the grey bath. His small nose gave him a calculating air that his pouty lips belied. He was freckled, skinny, gawky; but would, in time, be handsome and more distinguished than his father.

'You're white as a ghost. D'you want some water?' He offered her a plastic bottle, wiping the rim for her on his T-shirt. Emmy was just putting it to her lips when she heard Buddy behind her, not speaking to her, but so she would hear: 'Mobilize the troops! Can't sit here on our arses all morning, we'll never make it that way.'

The cold water had a strange effect on Emmy. She felt it on her teeth and in her throat and all the way down to her stomach. It made her forehead hot, then cold, and she grew suddenly dizzy. A sweat, cold and profuse, erupted over her temples, under her arms, down her back.

Gdé was leading everyone away, up on their stomachs through more muck. Everyone but Junior.

'I don't know if I can make it,' she said. And by way of explanation, ruefully, 'No breakfast.'

'No worries. I'll wait.' He seemed ready to go, though, pacing across the ledge, eyeing the backsides of the climbers. Emmy, embarrassed, waited for the weakness to pass, looking neither up nor down as that could only make it worse.

'Go ahead.'

He hesitated. 'You gonna wait here? The *whole* time?'

Emmy thought of the eternity since they left the bus. The miles between her and K'tut in the car-park. The crawlies and the silence. Alone, here, she might start to scream and be unable to stop. She might roll down the mud and break her neck. Sacred Abang made her wary. It gave her the willies. The boy was impatient, fidgeting, curious about the others.

'I guess not. I'd *like* to go . . . but I can't go very fast.'

'That's OK.' He sounded doubtful.

'I also can't do it alone. I'd have to ask you to wait for me.' Emmy was humbled. She didn't like to ask for help, especially not from a child. But it had an unexpectedly good effect.

'No worries. I'd just as soon go with you. Otherwise, I'm alone. I'm not with them.'

'Your dad?'

He shrugged, dismissive.

'I'm Emmy.'

'I know. The way Gdé was calling you . . . ' He sniggered.

'Junior?'

'That's not my name. My dad calls me that. Ego gratification. But at least I was spared *his* name!'

'Buddy?'

'That's his nickname. No, Horace.'

'Horace?' Emmy laughed. The little man was much less daunting as Horace. 'So what are you?'

He grinned. He had a crooked front tooth that gave him an impish aspect. It was endearing. 'I'm Max.'

'Who thought of that?'

'I did. I was actually christened Christopher. But I prefer Max. Please call me Max.'

'My daughter's done that.' Emmy tried not to sound annoyed.

'What was she? What is she?'

'Portia. Pod.'

'Not much to choose between, eh?'

'Maybe.'

'Do you know,' said Max, 'In Bali there used to be only four names? It didn't matter what sex the kids were: first child, Wayan or Gdé; second child Madé; third, Nyoman; fourth, K'tut.'

'And then? Fifth child?'

'Begin again. So my new secret name is Madé. What about you?'

'Is that the second one? Then that's me, too. Madé.'

The next section of the climb was much easier, both because Max was with her, and waiting, and because some earlier travellers had left a braided rope of vines attached to a boulder at the next ledge. Emmy clambered only a few feet upwards before reaching the vine and then it was simple, fun even. Max let her go first, waited till she tossed the rope back to him from above.

Gdé, Wayan, Buddy, Sasha and Sylvia (as Max told her they were called, Sasha being the blonde one) disappeared not only from sight but from earshot. Occasionally Emmy thought she caught strains of Gdé's flute, but Max did not hear them, didn't believe that was what she heard. 'They wouldn't stop long enough; Dad's in too much of a hurry to get to the top. For him, it's not worth it till he gets to the top.' He made an exasperated face. 'I think you're hearing the spirits.'

Emmy blushed. The thought had occurred to her but she wouldn't have said so.

'Honest. This island is teeming with them. Even Buddy believes.'

'Horace, you mean?'

They giggled.

Not all the way was so steep and treacherous. There were passages of mild slope where they could walk upright, the damp cloud kissing their faces, leaving their hair limp. At one moment, on such an easy stretch, the mist cleared around their feet and they could see the brilliant lake miles below. Emmy almost fell to her knees to cling to the earth, to hold on for dear life. It was like the childhood sensation, when lying flat in a field gazing at the night sky, that one might fall off the earth into the void; only now, with the void in the direction that gravity was pulling her, Emmy felt the alarm was more immediate. But the white blanket of air closed around them again, fast and comforting.

The fog was at its thickest when they came across the shrine. They were almost in the middle of it before they realized. Carved stone huts on pedestals loomed on either side of the path, their shelves scattered with offerings in various stages of decay. Some had been upset, by wind or birds or spirits, and had shed their petals and sculpted bits of fruit underfoot. Gdé's two banana leaves, with their colourful treasure, glowed among the rest, as yet untasted by the gods.

'I think they'll wait,' Max said. 'Until we've gone back down. I don't think they're far, I mean, they're *watching* . . . '

'Do you think so?'

'Oh, I think they're benevolent enough. But I wish *we* had an offering; I don't like riding through on Gdé's, you know what I mean? Have you got anything? A button, a bead? In your pockets?'

In her pockets, Emmy found the mottled leaves, many-shaped, that she had plucked in the foothills. Max took them from her and arranged them in a fan shape on one of the platforms. She watched while he shut his eyes and appeared to pray.

'Is that how a Balinese would do it?' she asked when he was done.

'I don't know.' He laughed. 'I've never really watched. I've been to a couple of ceremonies, tooth filing, cremation . . . But I've never watched people really *praying*. Worshipping, I mean. Whatever.'

'Me neither.'

They resumed their climb, almost swimming through the chill air. Emmy, overheated from exertion, was grateful for the cold. It kept her from feeling faint. Max explained himself, his father, his life, as they walked.

Horace 'Buddy' Sparke was, in fact, the owner of a sheep station near Canberra. Until recently he had lived mostly on the estate, overseen it, and then spent part of the year travelling and part in a house in Queensland. Max was sure that, had Emmy's family—her ex-family—maintained its connections to the land, they would, by necessity, have come across Buddy Sparke.

A year previously Buddy had, after some thought but not, Max assured Emmy, too much, put the station in the hands of his trusted manager, set about building himself a house in Bali and moved full-time into the import–export business which had, until then, been a hobby. There had been complications, because

Indonesian law did not allow a foreigner to own land, but somehow, ever the businessman, he had built a house overlooking the gorge just to the north of Ubud, facing a sacred ridge on which nobody would ever raise so much as a hut.

Buddy's life was not without difficulties: he was a man of many women wherever he went—although, according to Max, neither Sasha nor Sylvia was of his harem—and recently there had been feuding among certain of these lovers, accusations flying, harsh words, a slap. Buddy had informed his son that in the matters of the fair sex, 'East and West, like oil and water, don't mix.'

Max, formerly Christopher, had grown up in Sydney with his mother and older brother, his parents having divorced when he was still a baby. Now eighteen, just out of school, he was uncertain of his next move. He knew he was looking, he was just not sure what for. Since his arrival in Bali a month before, he had spent more time with his father than ever in the course of his remembered life. It wasn't getting easier, he told Emmy; what he had seen as freedoms in his father's lifestyle proved, unsurprisingly, to be just another set of rules, another game.

'We had a fight last night,' he explained. 'He came close to bashing me one. I still don't know if we're speaking. In private, I mean.'

'What was it about?' Emmy wanted to know.

Max didn't want to tell her. Instead, he explained about Sasha and Sylvia, university students from England, travelling. They, like many others, had met Buddy in a restaurant in Ubud only a few days before and, recognizing a good thing when they saw it, had moved their luggage at once from their *losmen* to the house on the hilltop.

'Nothing sexual yet,' said Max, 'but it won't be much longer. Not if they stay in the house. Which one do you think? I bet you think Sasha, because she's so . . . you know. But it'll be the mousy one. Ten to one. I'm getting pretty good at telling.'

Most of this conversation went on while Emmy was either above Max or below him, engaged in physical exertions that had her complexion turning purple, so he remained unaware of the extent of her discomfort. She was quite sure, by now, that William would not have crossed paths with Buddy Sparke. The parameters of Sydney society were such that they couldn't seem comfortably to hold Emmy as a divorcee, let alone someone like Buddy, a loose and selfish man who took advantage of women his son's age and . . . and yet, Emmy had to concede, whose luck seemed to be holding out pretty well.

'He's riding for a fall,' she said sagely, panting as she rested for a moment against the mountain face.

'D'ya think?' Max squinted. He was standing, slipping his heels backwards in the mud, ready to fall off Abang, and unconcerned. 'Ruby was a blow, but not a *fall*, exactly.'

Ruby, now three, was the product of a holiday in Thailand; Aimée, her mother, drifted in and out of Buddy's life, but they weren't still together. Another child was on the way, to Suchi, an Ubud widow. For her it was Wayan, for Buddy, K'tut, so they hadn't yet decided on a name.

'I don't know what they'll call it,' Max said, 'But the older he gets, the more exotic Buddy likes things. Everything, from what I understand.'

Emmy ignored this last comment. The vines and trees around them were thinning. Still they could see nothing above. Emmy crawled ahead in terror that the mists would part, even for a moment, to show the distance they had come. Max, foolhardy, made his way as upright as he could. He was ahead of her, suddenly enfolded in the whiteness.

'Max, wait! How much further do you think?'

'Dunno.'

'I'm not feeling too good. Can you hang on?'

'Come on, Emmy!' He sounded like his father. 'Don't give

up *now*. If you want to stop, well—'

'OK, you go ahead.' Her buttocks, her thighs, her shoulders aching; the cut hand filthy and stinging; her hair clutching stringily at her forehead, her neck: the tears were inevitable. Of course he would leave. Of course she couldn't do it. Of course she had deluded herself and was now a nuisance. The tears were hot amid the cold sweat on her skin. They were salty. One dropped between her legs to water the dirt.

'Emmy! Hey, Emmy! Em-my!' Max sounded far away. 'Emmy, listen!'

She heard nothing but her breathing. Then the flute. Indisputably the flute.

'I'll wait. I'm waiting up here. Come on. It's not far, it can't be!'

It wasn't. The last ten or fifteen yards were the worst, though; the only vegetation was spidery tufts of grass amid the rubble and dirt. When she reached for them, they snapped off, handfuls of something like desert spinifex burning her hands. Emmy, with Max behind her now, looked upwards, only upwards. She whimpered, did not even care that she might be heard. She had forgotten her size; she felt very tiny, a pebble in the vast ether, trying to hold on. No past, no future, just a strong sense of her grave mistakes, the certainty that she could roll backwards and down, as far as the lake. And the flute ahead. The flute and the sound of voices.

'Welcome to the heavens ' Gdé grinned as he hauled her over the last hump, on to the flat ground of the temple. Sasha, Sylvia and Buddy slouched around the temple's ruined inner sanctum, peeling rambutans and bananas. Buddy called out to her. It seemed a blasphemous thing to do.

'Good on ya. We'd given up. Gdé here was upset, kept insisting he'd have to go get you. Offerings for seven and all that. Junior with you?'

'Right behind.'

'Happy now, eh Gdé?'

'Yes, Buddy. I told you, it's auspicious day.'

'Suspicious day, eh?' Buddy laughed, his mouth full of banana.

'Been here long?' Max asked, swinging a leg on to the remains of the temple's stone floor.

'Oh, twenty minutes, not long,' Gdé said, rushing with his pack to offer Max fruit. He didn't give a banana to Emmy until Buddy's son had been served.

'Is it disrespectful to eat in the temple, Gdé?' she asked.

He looked puzzled, then amused. 'Everything is OK. I make offerings before we came.'

As if in protest, it started to rain. Buddy had young Wayan take their picture, all of them including Emmy, on the temple steps; Gdé with his flute, Buddy with an arm around Sasha and the other around Emmy, oddly not touching her, Max squatting at the front, brow furrowed, lower lip sagging sulkily. Everyone but Max was smiling.

Emmy felt strangely pleased that Buddy had an arm around her shoulder. She didn't like the schoolgirl leap her stomach took, but his unwillingness to speak to her earlier, and her new knowledge that he was a womanizer, made his most minute attentions seem flattering. Max's thwack on her back was less rewarding, although given his help it should have been more.

They set off back down the mountain almost at once, everyone but Emmy and Max having rested. Emmy couldn't help feeling disappointed even in her triumph. A veil of soggy cloud, some tumbled stones, a snack: was this all? Or had the others experienced something she had not, in those precious minutes before she reached the summit? Why would the spirits, or luck, or whatever there was, not speak to her? For a time, Emmy, who had sweated so much of herself away in this climb, felt diminished, but in the course of the descent, the feeling was put aside and forgotten.

Going down, it was not difficult to keep together. In the steepest places, either Buddy or Gdé helped Emmy, holding her by the hand. Max and Wayan crouched and slid on their heels, leaving everyone behind them and the river bed more slippery in their wake. There wasn't much conversation, although Sasha and Sylvia sometimes whispered to each other. There was something about the way Gdé and Buddy took her arm, something about the certainty with which Emmy placed her feet, that made her feel regal.

When they came to the end of the river bed, she thought the car-park could not be far. But the path through the bottle-green woods went on forever, and the gentle slope was more difficult for Emmy's exhausted body to negotiate than the sheer drops had been. Her knees buckled at every step. Her trousers caked to her legs with drying mud and sweat. And back in the sunlight, it was hot.

As they neared the car-park, Buddy picked a small, velvet blue flower. 'Your reward,' he said, pressing it on Emmy.

Instead of the agitation his attentions had provoked on the mountaintop, Emmy now felt like slapping him. When he turned away, she crushed the flower underfoot.

Max was in the car-park before them, gulping Fanta. He was talking to K'tut the driver, who blew smoke rings into the noon air.

'Emmy, you'll have lunch, yeah?' Max asked.

'I don't know. I guess.'

'You don't have anywhere to be this arvo?'

'Not unless I want to.'

'Great. Buddy, Emmy's coming with.'

His overtures to Emmy clearly at an end, Buddy twitched in barely perceptible assent, and climbed on to the bus without a word.

On the road, everyone slept. K'tut steered the rolling, lumbering bus like a glass ship, careful not to disrupt slumber. Emmy dreamed she was still climbing, but not afraid; the lake, instead of far below her, was all around. She was climbing through a silent azure sea and she was at peace.

Only K'tut and Wayan were awake when she opened her eyes. Even Gdé was dozing, bolt upright, his head snapping with the bumps in the road. She did not know how long she had been asleep but she could see clearly that they were no longer near Penelokan or Kintamani. Everything was different; richer, greener. The dirt was black. There were paddies in the distance, and sometimes right next to the road. She made her way to the front of the bus.

'Excuse me, K'tut, but where are we?'

He chewed on an unlit cigarette. 'Almost home. Almost at the Monkey Forest. We stop for lunch in the Monkey Forest, Buddy says.'

Ubud, then. She could have smacked Max: he must have known. Spoilt child. Spoilt children, father and son both. Even as Pod, her daughter wouldn't have behaved this way. Or maybe she would; Emmy couldn't be sure any more.

She sat back down and watched the forest grow up around the bus and heard the screaming, chattering of the monkeys' assault coming from all sides, and then the thud of one landing on the roof. It wasn't, perhaps, so bad. It wasn't, perhaps, wrong just to let things happen.

The sun was already casting long shadows: it was well into the afternoon. All her muscles tingled and some twitched of their own accord. She was famished. She shut her eyes and imagined all the things she would like to eat for lunch, starting with *saté*.

London

WHEN VIRGINIA ROUNDED the corner on to her street, she saw her mother hoisting the evening paper up to their second-floor window in a basket on a rope. A young man stood on the pavement, awaiting payment, or thanks, or something; but as soon as Mrs Simpson had the basket in hand, she flipped it inside, withdrew her grey head and slammed the sash.

Virginia didn't like it when her mother imposed on neighbours, but foisting errands on to unsuspecting strangers was beyond the pale. And then not paying for her paper! Besides, Virginia had a copy of the *Evening Standard* in her bag, a little oily, perhaps, with the remains of her lunch, but perfectly readable.

By the time Virginia got upstairs, Mrs Simpson was settled at the kitchen table with a cup of tea and the tabloid spread in front of her. She didn't look up as she said, 'You're late tonight.'

'I walked.'

'Your ankles will swell, with this heat.'

Virginia looked down at her thin stovepipe calves. She didn't really *have* ankles. Never had. Couldn't matter if they swelled.

'Busy day, Mum?'

'Are they ever?'

'I bought some haddock.'

'I've been in all day, you know. And I had biscuits for tea just now.'

'Mother, you're not *supposed* to.'

'Supposed to, supposed to! Virginia, I could die tomorrow. Aren't you out this evening?'

'The meeting's not till nine, because Angelica's working late this week. She's on holiday from next Monday.'

'Speaking of holiday?'

'I've told you. I just don't know. Simon's off starting next week, Selina the week after, which has the office almost empty . . . '

Mrs Simpson sucked her dentures loudly and rustled the newspaper pages in exasperation. Virginia noticed that her mother's bosom was uneven.

'Mum,' she said, reaching out to adjust the prostheses through her mother's silky blouse, 'they're lopsided.'

Mrs Simpson slapped her daughter's hands away. '*I'm* not going out, thank you very much. And I don't believe we're expecting company. So if I choose to have one breast rakishly higher than the other I would thank you to leave me alone. Now go and water the plants.'

Virginia took the key to the downstairs flat and left her mother rocking slightly in the fading light, glasses slipped to the end of her nose, arms crossed protectively over her chest.

It was Mrs Simpson who had volunteered to water their neighbour's flowers while the woman and her boy were visiting family in Sweden, but of course it was Virginia who had to do the work. In the unusually hot summer, Mrs Simpson—Melody to her friends, an oddly soft name for so hard a woman—barely moved from her chair. She had even given up on the shopping. All the neighbours were asking after her. She had taken to accosting passing acquaintances and even strangers, from the window, and sending them on errands, the proceeds of which she hauled up in the basket. She had even set up a little winch on the window-ledge to facilitate ups and downs.

Mrs Reece from two doors down had told Virginia that her mother was now lowering Bella, the tabby, in the basket, and then lowering the keys to stunned pedestrians in order that they might let Bella in again. It was only a matter of time, Mrs Reece pointed out, till Melody let the keys into the hands of hooligans who would take advantage.

Was it the heat that was making her mother so eccentric? Virginia's mother had rarely made scenes in public, a fact for which Virginia had always been grateful. She wasn't sure how she felt about living with a local oddity.

She considered these things as she doused the houseplants. So many worries clamoured for her attention. Her mother's sudden insanity wasn't the only thing. There was this issue of the summer holiday. Mrs Simpson had always been content with a week of having Virginia at home and possibly a couple of days with cousins in East Anglia, or at the most a weekend in Hastings or Brighton—and once, in a time of great daring, Cornwall. Now she had taken it into her head that she wanted to go to Scotland for a week. And, not one for half measures, she insisted that Edinburgh was very nice but barely Scotland: she meant the Hebrides. She wanted to go to Skye.

Her people—Virginia's people too—were from Skye on her mother's side, and Melody wanted to see the place again after more than forty years. Virginia didn't know how to respond. She thought at first the whim would pass, but it didn't. Like the other strangenesses, it grew in her mother over the weeks, and hardened. Whenever the subject came up, Mrs Simpson's eyes got a glitter to them and her chin set itself tight.

And then there was the office: everything there was in a state of disarray, initiated in part by Virginia's half-formed decision—taken after three halves of cider in the pub around the corner on the occasion, two months previously, of Martin, the assistant's birthday—that she was infatuated with Simon Ramsbottom, her colleague for over seven years, her direct superior for six months, and a married man.

How or why she had allowed this to happen she could not now recall. Love—or its shadow—had been excised long ago from the range of her emotions, after the trouble, the bad time in her youth. She had, for all of a decade now, settled her substantial share of love on God, to whom it rightly belonged. That a smidgen of it, however tiny, should have slipped from her control and latched on to Simon was bewildering and regrettable, and not simply as a point of principle. She knew that Simon could sense her growing confusion, and she knew also that her behaviour was distinctly unprofessional. Sometimes she would be discussing forthcoming interviews with him, or the progress of new staff, when suddenly she would picture him naked in his chair and imagine that she heard him crooning softly to her to climb over the desk. Whereupon she would lose track of the conversation and blush violently, whether more from the titillation or the horror of the fantasy she was never sure. Truth be told, she had never found Simon in the least *physically* attractive: he was squat and runcible and slightly foolish. Which made it all the more upsetting that she couldn't get him off her mind.

She had not sinned in anything but thought, and had been praying hard for the restitution of her reason. Everyone—or at least all the women—in her Bible study meetings had been praying too. She had contemplated talking to her minister about it, but felt there would be something odd about a woman of her age and prominence in the church discussing love with the timid Reverend, whose fire was only for God and only in the pulpit, as it should be. Her mother, if she told her, would only hiss and roll her eyes and say 'poppycock' to the lot of it, torments and all, the way she said 'poppycock' and 'balderdash' to God.

'If there was a God,' Mrs Simpson would say when asked and

only then, 'You, Virginia, would be married, and Emmy would still be married, and your father would still be living, and the world wouldn't be warring and starving to death.' She always said this with a certain amount of satisfaction and sucking of her teeth, as though to imply that she was perfectly content that all these things were so and that she would rather have them that way than contend with her Maker.

As things stood, Virginia confided very little in her mother. Summer always prompted irritation and distance between them, but this month of June, so hot and anxious, was particularly bad. And not half over yet.

The television was, as every night, audible on the landing when Virginia got back upstairs. Her mother now sat bathed in the set's blue light with a tumbler of whisky against her knee.

'You're not *supposed* to,' Virginia almost said, but what was the point? Mother was right, she might die tomorrow, and what would the comment do but cause friction? She was resigned to her mother dying unsaved, as resigned, that is, as a good Christian can be, but she did not like the thought that her mother might die while she and Virginia were in the midst of a tiff. For this reason bad terms were to be avoided as often as possible. This said, Mrs Simpson had not shown any signs of ill health, not a day of it, since her double mastectomy many, many years before, for what had proved to be benign tumours anyway.

As she fried the haddock, Virginia alternated between anticipation and despondency: anticipation at the prospect of her meeting, and a feeling akin to despair over her mother's silence, a despair she knew to be unreasonable—her mother had always been and would always be moody—but couldn't help.

'It's not a fish I much like, haddock,' was the first thing Mrs Simpson said. 'Fish does make the flat smell.'

This was too much. 'If you would do some shopping, Mother, which you are perfectly capable of, you might find—'

'I was going to say, if you had let me finish, that for all that you've cooked it very nicely. I'm quite enjoying it.'

'Thank you.'

'It's odd about smells,' Mrs Simpson said. 'They're so strong in the heat. I've never thought of old Bella smelling, but lately there's a real animal smell around. Have you noticed?'

Virginia waited. It was bound to be a complaint about something.

'No? It's mostly in the daytime of course, so you wouldn't. When the sun streams in. I thought maybe there was a dead mouse somewhere.'

'Don't be absurd! We've lived in this building ten years and we've never had a mouse. In south London, after the war, we had mice. But not here. Unless you think they're crawling out of Regent's Park or down from the Heath and climbing up our stairwell? Maybe cadging a ride in the basket?'

This was Virginia's first real remark about the basket, and her mother chose to ignore it. After a pause she said, 'The other thing I thought, Virginia, is that maybe the smell is *me*. I don't know whether suddenly, with all this heat, I haven't begun to smell *old*. The whiff of death on me, you know? Like old people's homes or flats where old ladies live alone. Old ladies like me.'

'If that's what you think, maybe you'd better start bathing more often.' Virginia said this as lightly as she could. But her mother's comment seemed a breach of the decorum that kept them both going. Mortality was not an open subject, or certainly Virginia had always assumed it was not. 'I'll believe in the dead mouse before I can accept that kind of nonsense. I've got to go, Mum, or I'll be late.'

'Your book's by the front door,' Mrs Simpson said. She never called it a Bible, always 'a book', or 'the book', with no hint of a capital letter. 'I'll do the washing-up.'

The Bible study group to which Virginia belonged met once a

week on Wednesdays in the flat of a secretary named Angelica Trumbull, just up the road from Chalk Farm tube station and only a few minutes' walk from the Simpsons' in Primrose Hill. Although it was ostensibly an ecumenical meeting, everyone who attended regularly was affiliated with the Church of England, and, more than that, with St Luke's church in Belsize Park. The exception was a young Hindu student who had arrived in Britain less than a year before; he lived downstairs from Angelica and occasionally sat in on the meetings just for company. In his mid-twenties—like Angelica—he was subject to some scrutiny by the others in the group, several of whom were convinced he was paying court to his hostess.

Virginia, who had actually taken a little time to talk to Nikhil, was not of this contingent. She found in him a sensitive and lonely soul and she entertained hopes of awakening him to the miracle of Christian fellowship, although she did concede that to date he was more interested in the general conversation and the cakes and coffee than in any discussion of the gospel.

Not that they always discussed the Bible itself: sometimes they discussed particular teachings or leaders—John Wimber, say, of whom Angelica was an avid follower, or Billy Graham—or even particular sermons. On evenings when the Reverend couldn't make it, they talked about his sermons and whether they, as representatives of the congregation, agreed with them. Usually they did, unanimously, but they refrained from holding these conversations when he was present for fear of embarrassing him. Reverend Thompson, a slight, balding man in his late thirties, was unflappable about the Lord and his beliefs, but easily flustered in his person.

As for the regulars, besides Nikhil and the Reverend there were seven of them, sometimes eight. There was Janet, a Christian counsellor; Janet's husband Alistair, who could only make it sometimes, being a doctor and often on call; Mrs

Hammond who, though much older than Mrs Simpson, was brave and unflagging in her attendance; Stephen Mills and Philip Taylor, two theology students at the University of London, slender, excitable young men with sharp senses of humour; Frieda Watson, a strong-minded divorcee of about Virginia's age; Angelica; and, of course, Virginia herself.

It was an odd collection of people. They themselves marvelled openly at their diversity in age and occupation. Almost weekly Mrs Hammond could be counted on to open the meeting by saying, 'Blessed are we who allow our Lord Jesus Christ into our hearts! Where else but through the Lord could an old woman like me still be growing and learning and sharing with people like you?'—at this moment she clasped her gnarled hands with great fervour—'Let's start by offering the Lord Jesus a prayer of thanks!'

To which the Reverend, when present, would say, 'Quite right, Mrs Hammond, quite right.' Occasionally one of the theology students would throw out an 'Alleluia' or an 'Amen' in the background to reinforce the general enthusiasm.

But in fact, Virginia was not so optimistic about the harmony of their group, and didn't feel the Lord was doing his bit to smooth things out. The Lord was testing her, it seemed, on the very ground where she should feel safest.

It had to do with the occasional 'Alleluia'. That background affirmation always sounded false, sarcastic even. Virginia was upset by the theology students.

Stephen and Philip had appeared together, out of nowhere, one Sunday just after Easter, at St Luke's. They were inseparable, almost interchangeable, disconcertingly similar in their mannerisms and their affectations. It hadn't initially occurred to Virginia to think of them as 'that sort', although Angelica had whispered something about it almost the first time she saw them in church. But knowing this (as by now she felt she did), and aware that if they knew anything about the word of the Lord (which as theology students they must) then they were condemning themselves to damnation—in the light of all this, Virginia had a hard time accepting their presence.

'But Reverend,' she wanted to say but couldn't, 'they are emissaries of Satan.'

He would have said only that affectation was not necessarily any indication of sin. He would have said they were taking the first step towards the salvation of their souls and were to be encouraged rather than shunned.

But Virginia—who had turned to God precisely because her distressing experience had revealed human nature to be fallible, sly and, well, *fallen*—was less trusting. She had observed them, both at church and in the group, and she didn't think they were taking any steps towards salvation at all. What she had observed was that the group—herself included—was being observed. Mrs Hammond's heartfelt call to prayer was being recorded as a sociological phenomenon for some assigned essay at the university on evangelism within the Anglican church. Virginia was almost certain.

She had talked about it with Angelica, who understood her distress at finding the seeds of Satan in the one secure corner of her life. Angelica was Virginia's closest ally and dearest friend in the group, and for Virginia, Angelica was the truth of harmony through the Lord that Mrs Hammond praised so. For although the two women were similar in many ways, and Virginia sometimes thought she saw in her friend her own younger self, only worldlier and better equipped to cope, it was difficult to conceive of any purpose other than the Lord's work that could have brought them together.

Angelica Trumbull, at twenty-eight, twenty-three years Virginia's junior and technically young enough to be her daughter, was a source of true inspiration. Like Virginia, she had behind her a veiled tragedy, to which she occasionally referred, but some years ago she had found God, and this oblique evil had lifted, leaving a heavyset but attractive young woman with the face of a cherub and a cascading mass of blonde curls, who shouldered the responsibilities of her single life with a quiet eagerness. An eagerness, indeed, that Virginia, who often felt defeated despite all the Lord's blessings, would not admit even to herself that she envied.

Angelica was utterly nice. Or perhaps, Virginia thought as she climbed the hill in the fading heat with her leather-bound Bible in her sweaty palm, 'utterly' was not the right word: she had too much fun with Angelica for either to be utterly nice, and there had been conversations after which she felt sullied and repentant. But then, it was not always possible to be both truthful and nice, and her friendship with Angelica was about God's truth.

When Virginia reached Angelica's house, she saw that there was no light in the window of her friend's flat. She looked at her watch: it was ten minutes before the hour, and obviously Angelica had been delayed at the office. Dusk was upon the buildings and trees and the rows of parked cars like a fine powder, and Virginia stood at the foot of the house steps unsure of where to go. At the corner there was a pub with frosted windows, from which faint strains of music and a hubbub drifted back towards her. Behind the glass, the light wavered, jostling shadows like a tempestuous sea. Virginia didn't want to go there. She turned a full circle, slowly, peering into ordered living-rooms and bright kitchens where people mimed the acts of real life: a couple standing in front of the television, the woman absently drying a dish with a striped tea-towel; two young people waving their hands in argument, mouths flicking open and shut soundlessly; an elderly man reaching up to fiddle with curtains and pull them shut. He stopped to look back at her, and Virginia felt conspicuous and forlorn.

She had somehow hoped that in this moment of turning, Angelica would have been spirited home, and that there would now be light and suggestions of bustle from the top of the house, but there was nothing. The old fellow was still staring, from one house over, and under his gaze Virginia climbed the steps and pressed the Trumbull buzzer. She imagined that she heard the echo of it, and then the silence that followed in the empty flat above. It was almost nine now, but none of the others were visible along the street—not even Philip and Stephen, who were always prompt, unwilling to miss a sociologically important minute—and so Virginia pressed the buzzer beneath Trumbull, marked 'Gupta'.

His 'yes' was wary, and as she explained herself, Virginia found she was patting nervously at her flat, greyed hair, and leaning perhaps too close to the intercom. But Nikhil buzzed her in at once, and when she reached his landing she found him already standing, arm outstretched, in the doorway of his flat.

He was awkward, and his large ears were almost pink as he welcomed her. Virginia found his discomfort in some measure reassuring and relaxing. 'Of course, of course,' he said to nothing at all. 'Sit down. Come in. We will wait together for Angelica to return.'

His flat was the same as Angelica's, but while hers was her own, peach and yellow and elegantly appointed, Nikhil Gupta's was rented and spartan, with only a hideous vinyl suite and Formica table. His books and papers were scattered in disarray across all flat surfaces, and the only personal item in sight was a large framed photograph on the mantel. Virginia examined it, while Nikhil cleared a place on one of the vinyl armchairs, which proved, beneath the papers, to be peeling and stained.

'Lovely flat,' said Virginia, for lack of any better conversational gambit. 'Just like Angelica's.'

Nikhil looked pained and said only, 'Tea?' and then, 'Do sit.'

'Yes, yes . . . ' Virginia turned back to the picture. 'I'm sure the others will arrive any minute. And Angelica, of course.'

From the kitchen came an unexpected crashing of dishes and pots by way of reply. Virginia imagined cramped squalor, and regretted agreeing to tea.

The photograph was a black-and-white posed family portrait that looked ancient although it could not be, for to one side, among several other youths, stood a stern but only slightly younger Nikhil. There were about a dozen people in all, in front of a large tropical-looking tree, with a snowy-haired patriarch and a distinguished older woman in a sari seated in the centre.

'Are these your parents?' she asked as she accepted a chipped mug of boiling black tea.

'No milk, I'm afraid.'

'Doesn't matter. Are they?'

He appeared closer to emotion than she had yet seen him. 'My grandparents,' he said. 'And cousins and brothers. And parents, my father'—pointing to a round, balding man—'and mother'—a tired, gaunt woman with an expression of marked displeasure—'and my sister.' He said this last very softly, and allowed his finger to linger on the tiny celluloid chest of his sibling. She, an adolescent of perhaps sixteen at the time of the picture, was by far the most perfect figure in the rows of family members: dark-eyed and clear-skinned and . . . the word that came unbidden to Virginia's mind was *luscious*. Just looking at her moved the stiff Nikhil almost to tears, which seemed to Virginia unhealthy and possibly suspicious.

'You miss them a great deal?'

Nikhil's nod was dutiful. 'But it's more complicated with Rupica. Will you sit?'

Virginia perched gingerly on the arm of the sofa and surreptitiously inspected her tea for bugs. With the same effort with which she had—unsuccessfully—willed Angelica into her flat, she willed one or all of the group into the hallway downstairs. She strained to catch a footstep or a tapping on the building's front door, and imagined that they were all even now gathered comfortably on the steps, Mrs Hammond leaning against the railing with the others grouped around her, placidly passing the time about the drive to raise money for prayer books or the forthcoming summer retreat . . . Virginia very much did not want to hear about Nikhil's sister Rupica, although she could not have said why not, except general residual bitterness about all very good-looking people and an unacknowledged fear that she was going to hear something unsavoury.

But Nikhil was speaking. ' . . . Eight months ago.'

'Pardon? I thought I heard them coming.'

Nikhil would not be diverted. 'I said,' he said, 'that when I first came, for my studies in international relations'—a wave at the books and papers—'my family came with me from Delhi, the three of them. This was eight months ago. My father is a civil servant and took a month's leave. Rupica is now of university age, nineteen. She is as beautiful as her photograph, and we have all wanted the best—for her to study and then marry well and be happy. But she'—a limp, helpless gesture. Nikhil reddened. 'She has never had a studious or orderly temperament. She does not accept the inevitable.' He paused, began again. 'My parents are very educated people. My father, too, studied in England.'

'I'm sure,' said Virginia, rueing her decision to ring the Gupta bell.

'They are not backward or provincial. But Rupica . . . so when we came, all together, for a month in September, we were staying first in a hotel in Bloomsbury, and Rupica and I shared a room. In the night, after the first week, she would wait until she thought I was sleeping and then she would dress and go out.'

'In revealing clothes?' asked Virginia, in the tone that prepares to be scandalized. She listened less now for sounds from the landing.

'Jeans. A pullover. Her hair in a plait down her back.'

'Where did she go? Poor girl, led astray, was she—she wasn't—

'She had met a man. I did not tell our parents. I thought she would tire of him, that there was nothing in it. Before, in Delhi, she had met others. She was reckless, as I say. But I was wrong, and it was a grave mistake.'

'She wasn't—'

'On the morning before they were all to return to Delhi, Rupica did not come back to the hotel. I was forced to tell my parents how she had gone every night and forced to say I did not know where to.'

'Odd you didn't ask?'

'Perhaps. But in the afternoon she came back, and brought the man. I was at the university and did not see him, but my parents said he was very old. As old as they are, perhaps. And they were married. They had married in the morning while we worried. And my parents did all they could, but they are married. Rupica is nineteen and can do as she pleases here. They live in Scotland, and we have broken with her.'

'He's Scottish? How interesting.'

'I don't care what he is. My beloved sister is lost. And perhaps I come to your meetings to try to understand. Your meetings with Angelica.'

'Sorry?'

'Rupica insisted that he was, in his way, a very religious man. A Christian. So I try to understand him. And her. Until I do, I cannot see or speak to them. And it is not easy.'

'Have you spoken to Angelica about this? I'm sure he's not one of us. Not a Christian. Some sort of nut, perhaps. But no truly religious man would behave the way he has. And against your parents' wishes!' Virginia was thinking, 'And no true Christian would marry a Hindu. A heathen. No matter how beautiful she was.'

'I think they are here now,' Nikhil said, resuming his distant manner. In the stairwell, Angelica's heavy, even tread was followed by other, more eccentric gaits, and the sound of voices and of Mrs Hammond's cane. Then there was the click of the key in the lock, and the shuddering of floorboards overhead as half a dozen or more bodies settled themselves in, scraped furniture about the hardwood floor. That racket alone would have been enough, Virginia thought, to make her join the group. Better the fellowship than the sound of their feet.

'Shall we?' Nikhil stood in the hallway, waiting.

On her way out, Virginia managed to dart into the kitchen to put down her empty mug; to her consternation, she found the tiny room was spotless, the earlier clamour caused by the washed dinner dishes on the draining-board: one lonely plate, one bowl, one glass, and two battered but impeccably scrubbed pots.

Upstairs, the meeting was already well into its opening ritual: flopped in the most comfortable armchair, dress hiked, cane between her knees, Mrs Hammond was praying aloud, eyes upturned and shining. The others were more sedate, heads bowed and eyes shut, and Alistair the doctor was scratching at a spot on his chin while he spoke to God. In the corner, one of the students was actually kneeling. Angelica was in the kitchen, and alongside Mrs Hammond's encomium to the Reverend and his flock came the intermittent rustlings of cake wrappers and the packet of tea, the burble of water, the soft chink of porcelain cups. Virginia and Nikhil surveyed the sitting-room. For the first time, she saw it a little as he must, and it suddenly looked peculiar and not cosy and familiar at all. She quite hated him for spoiling her evening.

Angelica brought the tea tray through as Mrs Hammond wound up her prayer and Philip—was it?—shouted a hearty 'Alleluia'. He had a small, forgettable face and little round spectacles and it was surprising that his lungs were so strong. Angelica, on the other hand, was radiant, her large, oval face glowing pink as the Laura Ashley lamp at her elbow, her blue eyes wet-looking and innocent, her dimpled forearms dispensing the necessary in deft, graceful movements. Her attractiveness was felt by everyone, Virginia was sure. It caused a hush, an admiring look from Stephen (or was it Philip? the same face, only dark instead of blond, and without glasses), and a light smile even from Nikhil, who strode forward to accept his cup as though he hadn't drunk tea in days instead of minutes.

'I thought, everyone,' said Angelica, never stopping the circulation of food and drink and never spilling a crumb or drop, 'Sugar, Mrs Hammond? I know I was to prepare an analysis of the reading Frieda suggested last time . . . but—milk, Philip?'—with the glasses, Virginia noted—'but this week has been *awful*. I *am* sorry, Frieda—' Frieda, her wiry hair askew and her face furrowed, slumped back in her chair and scowled at the plate of Madeira cake. 'But I thought it might be apropos and maybe easier, seeing as I've made us all late, if we just had a little talk about Reverend Thompson's last sermon. I mean, especially seeing as he's not here?'

'Oh, goody,' said Stephen, in an unappealing way.

'Which was it again?' from Mrs Hammond.

'I was so looking forward to discussing the reading,' grumbled Frieda.

'On what, again?' from Mrs Hammond.

'Revelation, chapters five to eight,' offered Janet.

'The sermon?'

'No, no dear,' said Virginia, patting Mrs Hammond's exposed, bony knee and endeavouring to pull the old woman's dress down a little as she did so. 'The reading. That was the reading Angelica didn't prepare. You must remember the sermon, dear. It was on the sins of the flesh.'

'Of course, of course. Very strongly worded, a fine sermon.'

'*So* relevant, I thought,' said Janet, stirring her tea.

'Is that all right then, shall we just do that?' Angelica smiled hopefully.

'Yes dear, fine. We'll do the reading next time,' said Mrs Hammond, who, by virtue of her seniority, was able to decide any such issues without consulting the others.

Virginia only half-listened to the discussion that followed. For the first time ever, she was watching instead of participating, and it was as if she couldn't will herself back into her body, back into herself; she had to sit on the outside, painfully aware of the absurdities Nikhil must see and hear, and painfully aware, too, of Nikhil. He was physically separated from the others, sitting on a straight-backed dining-chair outside the plush circle of sofas and armchairs. Stephen and Philip were almost outside, but not quite, and they were together. Nikhil sat with a coffee-table book of the Sistine Chapel on his lap (a gift from Virginia to Angelica the Christmas before, when the latter had gone to Rome for a week), and he looked alternately from the magnificent representations on glossy paper to the eager faces of the group. He had a strong hooked nose, which seemed to incline even further earthwards when particularly evangelical or extreme comments were made. Then, when Alistair spoke (which was rarely), or Mrs Hammond (who, despite her energy and commitment, was also a fairly modest contributor to discussions), Nikhil would turn abruptly back to Michelangelo, as though he could glean more about his sister's choice from the vision of Judith bearing Holofernes' head than from the timid, dithering remarks of those present.

The conversation turned to communism, and thence to extreme politics, to the Americans, to AIDS and to homosexuality. Nikhil was aware of the heat generated by the topic: Virginia saw him shut the book of photographs altogether.

'I think they deserve it and I'm not ashamed to say so,' said Frieda, crossing her arms and glaring at the window. 'It's a sin, it's in the Bible, it's very clear. Ask the Reverend. And the Church of England, they're always pussyfooting around the issue because half the ministers are pansies, groping up each other's frocks in the vestry before services—'

'Frieda, *please!*' Angelica made a rapid eye gesture at Mrs Hammond, who hadn't heard all of the tirade but enough to pique her interest.

'What about women?' said Philip with a smirk. 'It's not so clear about women, is it?'

'Well,' said Virginia, in as icy a tone as she had ever used, 'I can't imagine it's an *issue*. It's just not an issue.'

'It exists, you know,' Philip insisted.

'God's retribution isn't seeking out *women*, because women aren't guilty. We only have to look at who is being struck down. It's *men*,' she hissed, with such venom that Angelica made a chiding face, and Nikhil leaned forward in his chair, biting his lip.

'Virginia dear,' said Janet, in her soothing, counsellor's voice that made Virginia bristle down the back of her neck, 'You mustn't *simplify* so. I do think we're taking rather a reductive approach. I really do not believe that AIDS is caused by God in that way. If it were, God would stop it, in the repentant.'

'Does He?' asked Stephen, from the kitchen door, where he had gone to ferret for more food. 'I mean, in all the crusades, Billy Graham and Swaggart and Bonker and even less massive gatherings, has *anyone* been healed of AIDS?'

Everyone looked up, or down, or at their hands and tried to think of an instance they had heard of, or better yet, had witnessed. At length, Mrs Hammond said, 'There must be *someone*. It's just that in our church, our congregation, we don't have such problems, so we don't know.'

Virginia looked from Philip to Stephen and back again; she could have sworn they exchanged glances, significant ones.

'Rotten fruit. Can't repent properly, can't be healed,' muttered Frieda.

'Madeira cake?' Angelica passed the plate, depleted now, to Nikhil.

He stood up and rubbed his trousers with his palms. 'Thank you, no. Thank you, Angelica, this has been most interesting, but my books are calling.'

'I can't hear them,' said Stephen.

Nikhil frowned. 'Yes, well, goodnight to you all. And to you, Virginia.' He bowed and left the room. Virginia could hear his lonely trail back to the vinyl lounge suite.

'What was that all about?' asked Frieda.

'He does seem sweet. Oddly silent though. Never know what he's thinking,' said Janet, as if, reflected Virginia, those whose minds were not illuminated by the gospel thought and felt in mysterious, dark ways.

'Were you with him, then?' prompted Angelica.

They were all watching. Virginia stretched her neck to its full length. 'Well, *you* weren't here, and I couldn't stay out on the doorstep—the neighbours were staring.'

'So what's his flat like?' Alistair had woken from apparent slumber to ask.

'Rather grim. It's rented. It's—'

'You don't suppose—I mean, he didn't take offence, he's not—' bubbled Angelica.

'If he is, it's a damn good thing. He should know where we stand.'

'Don't be ridiculous, Frieda. Of course he's not. He's had a hard time. A difficult year.' Virginia spoke sharply. 'And there's no need to swear.'

'But did you, I mean, what did you find out?' Angelica had her wet velvet eyes open as far as they would go.

'What do you mean?'

'About why. Why us, why *here*.'

'Because you live here, my dear. Because his sister has married a Christian.'

There was a murmur all around and then everyone tried to speak at once. Virginia picked up the Sistine Chapel book and slammed it on the coffee table. 'One thing I found out,' she said, as all eyes turned again to her, 'is that noise in this building carries dreadfully. So if I were you I would save my unpleasant speculation for another time and place.'

When the others had gone home, Virginia stayed to help Angelica with the washing-up. The small kitchen grew steamy from the torrents Angelica wasted—she didn't fill the sink but washed and rinsed each dish individually—and Virginia felt soothed for the first time that evening. There was great intimacy in the act of drying Angelica's plates, in the two women brushing against each other as they made order. Angelica was so generous, physically, that she all but filled the kitchen on her own, and Virginia had the impression of moulding her sparer self into the spaces that were left for her. Such a sense would, in other circumstances, have grated, but with Angelica, she believed it was a harmonious compromise, an expression of God's love.

'Did he really say that?' Angelica asked, as she swizzled soapy water in the teapot.

'Who? What?'

'Nikhil.'

'Oh yes, apparently his sister, who is younger than he, if you can believe it—'

'No, Ginny, about coming up here because of me. Because *I* live here.'

'Not in so many words, I suppose.'

Angelica looked disappointed.

'But he implied it. I'm sure he implied it. Do you—you don't—'

'Don't be silly. I just wondered, because you said.'

'Of course.' Virginia dried the cutlery energetically. The moment was spoiled. She had to keep talking to cover the annoyance she felt—annoyance at Nikhil's intrusion even into this private time. 'About his sister, it's extraordinary, as I say, she's younger than he, a child really, and she's gone and married a *much* older man, a Christian apparently, and she's—' And then Virginia stopped suddenly.

'She's what?'

'Nothing. He told me stories about it. In confidence. It's not for me to repeat them.' In fact, Virginia found, with the words on the tip of her tongue, that she was as jealous of her time with Nikhil as of her time with Angelica, and that particularly given the interest the latter displayed in the former, she didn't want to give anything away. By way of changing the subject she said, 'He is, they are Hindu. The family. He said.'

'Yes I know. Quite a peaceable and delightful religion, I always think.'

'Honestly, Angel! And them off knifing each other by the dozen in the back alleys of Calcutta!'

Angelica furrowed her creamy brow and said, sternly, 'I do think you fall prey to stereotypes *too* much, Virginia. Just too much. It's backward and intolerant of you, I sometimes feel.'

Virginia could not move. It was as if every pore had begun to seep moisture or tears and it was all solidifying into a cold, horrified casing around her. Her friend had never spoken so harshly to her before. She heard the little gasping sobs her throat made, and set all her strength to not crying in earnest.

'I'm sorry, Ginny my love. I didn't mean it.'

Virginia leaned against the sink, and Angelica stroked her grey hair away from her steamy face, resting a young, full cheek against her older one. Angelica's skin was inexplicably cool, as if the altercation had not affected her at all. Angelica kissed her ear and her chin and put an arm around her shoulders, but Virginia felt strangely detached.

'Are you all right, pet?' Angelica asked, so close that her lashes fluttered against Virginia's skin.

'I must go home. Mother will be going to bed and she gets

annoyed.'

'Oh silly, come off it! Ginny, don't let this be something between us. I just thought now and earlier, about homosexuals, you were more . . . well, you just didn't have much patience. That's all.'

'And you feel differently? I never knew!' Virginia sounded more sneering than she wanted to. She couldn't help it.

'You *are* sulky. Ginny, love, don't go off in a huff, please?' Angelica kissed her again. 'Please, pet? I suppose I do feel differently, a bit, because of my age, maybe, and my family.'

Virginia turned her prickling eyes full on her friend's face and said nothing. But the frozen feeling went away, and she was very attentive.

'Which I don't want to talk about, Virginia Simpson, as you well know. So let's talk about something else. Like the fact that Mrs Hammond's withered thigh was *very* visible above her stockings. From where I was sitting, anyway.'

'Yes, it's true, it was, wasn't it? And I could swear that Alistair was eyeing her leg when he pretended to be sleeping.'

'Ginny, he wasn't!'

'And Philip and Stephen, not to argue on the subject, but they *were* blushing.'

Angelica giggled. 'Stephen *particularly*. Beet red! He had to come and scrounge in the fridge so we wouldn't see his face.'

Virginia felt she had said, at last, the right thing.

'I guess we should pray for them, really.' Every so often she suggested this to alleviate her conscience.

Angelica flapped at Virginia's shoulder in mock rage. 'You turncoat! You *really* think just like Frieda and you know it.'

'I don't. You know I don't. I try to think the way God wants me to. We can't do more than that.'

'Too true.'

'I must head home, Angel, love. But I will pray for those

69

boys. And I'll certainly pray for Nikhil.'

As Angelica waved her friend out, she said, 'So, Virginia, will I.'

The walk home was downhill, smooth and quiet. It was past eleven, and Virginia strode as swiftly as she could without appearing nervous. There was no moon, and the trees and cars cast black shadows in the blue night. Virginia hummed a hymn as she went, and tried to understand the evening.

She had never felt so torn before, so self-conscious about her religious life. Knowing a little how Nikhil felt—certainly more than she had gleaned during brief silences in Angelica's flat on earlier evenings—made her retroactively self-conscious about all the times he had been there listening to them and judging them all. Only now, quite suddenly, did it seem extraordinary that he had never volunteered anything about his beliefs, because only now did it strike Virginia that he actually *had* a spiritual life. In his flat, it had been clear that he felt passionately about his faith and about his sister's disregarding it; which didn't make Virginia question her own, exactly, but it made her wonder.

And it reminded her that she had made a choice, that she had joined the church ten years before from a spiritual vacuum, in an act as drastic as Rupica's abandonment of her family. In that decade, she had never thought about it as a choice; rather as the Truth washing over her in a wave and showing her an absolutely Right life. Not perfect, obviously, but Right. She hadn't ever thought—not consciously, only dismissively—that others, like Nikhil, had different lives that to them were Right too, and that they might (and this was the worst of it) see hers as wrong. Then a thought came to her that she dismissed almost immediately, turning instead to practical matters and fumbling for her house-key: the thought was that Rupica, whose behaviour was so patently wrong and whose husband could not be a *real* Christian, might nonetheless have been moved by an experience as cataclysmic to her young mind as Virginia's conversion had been for her; that is, that Rupica, misguided though she obviously was, might have seen her clandestine marriage and her departure for Scotland as the only possible path to the Right life.

All in all, Virginia thought as she slipped into the darkened Simpson home and registered her mother's whistling snore emanating from the front bedroom, the evening had been most distressing. Nikhil was now more troubling to her than Stephen and Philip combined, and she felt more strongly than ever that the one safe and joyous haven in her life was under siege.

It was only a little later, as she slid between the taut sheets of her single bed and reached to the bedside-table for her leather-bound Bible (from which she read every night before sleeping) that she realized the Book had been left behind, dropped, like a textbook on the EC or contemporary Latin American politics, among the papers and scribblings on Nikhil's sofa. In penance, she recited all the psalms she could remember and prayed for guidance and forgiveness. But it was a very long time before she finally found sleep, and as she drifted off she could hear the earliest morning birds between her mother's snores.

Melody Simpson began banging pots shortly after eight. The crash and clatter was so dramatic that Virginia thought her mother must have fallen to the floor carrying half the fitted kitchen with her. In fact, when Virginia made it to Melody's side, nightgown askew and big toe stubbed on the way, she found her mother sitting at the table, comfortably slapping two frying-pans together like a child playing with cymbals.

'Are you completely mad? What will I do with you? Are you mad? Mother?'

Mrs Simpson stopped and looked up, knowing and amused. 'Good morning, dear. I hope you slept well? I didn't want to waken you, but I couldn't find any coffee beans. You *did* buy some? And you did, I hope, have fun painting God's town red? It must have been midnight—'

'Oh crumbs, Mother, look at the time!'

'I know. As I say, you were in so late I didn't want to wake you.'

'Come on, I'm not twelve, I'm half a century old. And I've got to go to work today like any other, so you can keep swilling your coffee, or your whisky for that matter . . . You did this on purpose.' Virginia was frantically scanning the cupboards, the fridge, the freezer, for coffee, but knew as she did so that there wasn't any left. Mrs Simpson just smirked.

'Tea. Tea, Mother. Tea it is. That's all we've got. You could've at least put the kettle on. I've only got half an hour.'

'The world won't end and Ramsbottom won't choke if you're a little late. But you go and dress, and I'll do the business.' She hauled herself up and shuffled to the sink, practically pressing her daughter out of the room as she did so.

As Virginia scrubbed her torso, combed her hair, flossed her teeth, she cast a quick glance at her long face, with its noble profile but slightly buck teeth and protuberant, heavy-lidded grey eyes. Her chin, despite her slimness, was beginning to wattle. Her hair, always fine and straight, was frizzing and coarsening with age to thin steel wool.

She could hear her mother muttering and organizing next door. What, she wondered yet again, was going wrong? But when Virginia emerged, dressed and tidy, Mrs Simpson was looking out of the window at the morning bustle, and the breakfast was impeccably laid as always. There was no clear indication that Melody Simpson was losing her wits; it seemed rather as though she was letting her nature loose a fraction more

72

each day, allowing her sly and spiteful facets fuller range than in the past. Madness or senility might have been more benign.

Mrs Simpson watched as Virginia gulped her tea and stuffed toast into her mouth, registering pleasure at the crumbs and drops of marmalade her daughter scattered on the table, her lap, across her chin. The older woman sipped daintily from her cup, fastidious as a cat, and even in her haste Virginia could tell there was more of her mother's private joke to come. Sure enough, as Virginia stood to leave, Mrs Simpson spoke.

'It's such a fine day again today, Virginia dear, I thought it would do me good to get out.'

Virginia raised an eyebrow.

'I thought, if you weren't doing anything, I could come and join you for lunch. It's been years since I saw your office.'

'Oh *Mum!*'

'Of course, if it's a burden and you don't want me, I can just stay here like every other day . . . '

'Don't be silly, it's not a burden, it's just that—'

'No, never mind. I'm sorry I—'

'Come. Come then. I'd love it. One o'clock. Take a taxi. And be on *time*. I've got to run.'

'I'll bring a picnic!' Virginia heard her mother call as she dashed downstairs.

Virginia worked for the University, in an administrative—or rather, executive—capacity, and her office was one in a warren of cubicles on the third floor of the University's austere central building. She was not important enough to have a window on to the street, as Simon Ramsbottom now did, but she did have a window on to a courtyard with a view of other windows, and she did not aspire to more than that. Her title was Deputy Director of Personnel (Temporary), which did not mean that she was to hold the post temporarily (she had been in it for years), but rather that she was responsible for the hiring (and occasional firing) of temporary staff. She had discovered over time that most people outside of her particular niche of puce and olive paintwork had no idea of what this post entailed. When considering the function of the University, outsiders did not stop to count the secretaries, janitors, security guards, cooks, bottlewashers, switchboard operators, maintenance staff and chambermaids the continuing well-being of the institution demanded. And because of this oversight, they could not conceive of the seasonal swellings or contractions in overall numbers, of the unforeseen illnesses, maternity leaves or deaths in the family, or of the weeks of carefully planned holidays that left posts vacant for anything from a week to six months. All these jobs still needed to be done: Virginia was responsible for the people behind the people behind the scenes.

For years Simon had been her direct counterpart, Deputy Director of Personnel (Permanent), but his recent promotion meant that he no longer bothered himself with printers or drivers or even secretaries, and was involved instead in the recruitment of big-shots: accountants, business managers, the occasional assistant to the director of a department. (This week, she knew, Rams-bottom was trawling for someone to fill a post in Tropical and Infectious Diseases around the corner, thus far with little success.) He had moved from two doors down on her side to directly across the passage, and even with her door shut she could hear him chortling with his secretary, a boy named Martin who, at twenty-seven, looked a decade younger than he was: his suits were sharp, his glasses tinted, his laugh a little too loud. In her more dour moments, Virginia had been known to say to Mandy, the secretary she shared with Simon's replacement Selina, that they would see the day when Martin, laughing with the boys, would bypass the lot of them to take Simon's job. And that, Virginia always finished with a sour flourish, was the day she would resign.

So in the enclave there were Simon and Martin, Virginia, Mandy and Selina. A happy family, Simon liked to say, but it had its hidden disruptions. While Virginia suffered from her recent and inexplicable attraction to Simon, it was nothing next to Mandy's naked adoration for the man. Simon was typically oblivious and thought Mandy 'charming' but insignificant.

Rather, it was Martin who paid Mandy undue attentions, fawning and placing a careless palm on her shoulder or her waist. Virginia had half a mind to tell him to stop it, but loathed him so much she could barely speak to him. This loathing was born of the fact that Martin seemed intent on stealing her job, a little at a time. She had mistaken his overtures for helpfulness at first, but was soon able to see clearly.

For years, as well as interviewing and recommending all temporary applicants, Virginia had been obliged to compile the bi-weekly internal newsletter of posts available, both temporary and permanent, one on blue paper, one on gold. It was an unrewarding task, and Virginia had always complained about having to do it. When Martin arrived, shortly after Simon's promotion, he had offered first to take the typing off Mandy's hands, to which the latter readily agreed. Then he offered to do the lesser listings— janitorial, say, or works department, just the temps at first. But now he was doing more and more—as the listings all went through Simon's office before coming to Virginia, Martin saw them first—and whenever Virginia said, 'About the newsletters, I'll have them done by tomorrow,' Martin would grin his sinner's grin and reply, 'Oh, Miss Simpson,'—never had she heard such a pointed 'Miss'—'they're just about done. I thought you wouldn't want to bother with them.'

It was unspeakable. She had practically stopped saying anything about them at all, and she was certain of his triumphant sneer on Thursday mornings when the newsletters went to press. This was such a morning, and Virginia was determined not to clap eyes on

Martin until after lunch. Or at least not for a while.

She was shuffling papers and drinking the tea Mandy had left on her desk before she arrived, when she heard the secretary outside her door, rattling the knob.

'I can't understand it,' Mandy was saying. 'She's *always* on time. I thought I left this door unlocked. She may have been held up, or . . . it's not like her, it's most unusual. Don't worry, we'll find her.'

Virginia hesitated. She knew at once who it was: her first appointment of the day, an American student named Calvin Jones, over for the summer on a temporary work visa and dying for one of the University's ill-paid menial placements. The Americans always were—Virginia loved them. But she didn't feel like seeing one just now. She could simply lie low, drink her tea and wait for Calvin to give up; an equally avid substitute would soon follow. But she heard Mandy babbling on: 'Just a minute,' she was saying, 'I'll run and get the key. You can wait in Miss Simpson's office, it's more comfortable. I'm sure—'

'Mandy, is that you?' Virginia spoke loudly and tried her best to sound surprised. 'What *are* you doing out there?'

'But Miss Simpson,' Mandy said, 'It's locked. I had no idea you were here.'

Virginia stepped across and smoothly turned the key. 'Silly me,' she said, smiling at an alarmed Mandy and a scrubbed youth in a button-down shirt, 'I'm so used to locking it when I leave at night that I must've done it this morning when I came in.'

Mandy, dim though she was, didn't believe a word of it. 'Right. Well,' to Calvin, 'I told you we'd find her. Miss Simpson, Calvin Jones.'

'I was expecting you.' She sat the boy in the vinyl armchair opposite her desk and returned to her seat.

'Calvin Jones,' she began.

'Yes ma'am?'

'You have a permit, I assume. Did you bring it? Good. And your passport? Thank you. I'll have Mandy take copies in a minute. We have to, of course, to protect ourselves.' She laughed, to make Calvin more at ease. The ruse did not appear to work. 'So, three months?'

He nodded.

'We might have just the thing. A post is coming up next Monday, for three months, or almost.' She looked from the list of jobs on her desk to the boy's square, callow face. 'You said on the phone that you can't type, am I right?'

'Well, not *can't*. Just not fast. But I can type.'

'Yes, of course, all Americans can, more or less, can't they?' She smiled again, and this time drew a response. 'But never mind, the point is, for this one you don't need to. Do you have any filing experience?'

'Um . . . '

'I'm sure a bright fellow like you would have no trouble. Are you methodical?'

'Yes ma'am.' He seemed quite certain of this, and added, as if by way of explanation, 'I major in History. It's on my resumé.' He pointed at the folded piece of paper he had passed her along with his passport and working permit. A cursory glance told her at once that he was grossly overqualified for the job. But he wouldn't mind: the University looked good enough on the CV, if he didn't tell the truth about what he'd done.

'Yes, well,' she said. 'Very good. We've got an opening in the mail room, for a clerk. Not perhaps the most fascinating work, but quite varied. You learn a lot about how the place works, and where everyone is.' She fixed her eye on him to see whether he wavered, but his eager, nervous expression remained unchanged. 'Do you think that might suit? Thirty-five hours a week, four pounds eighty-three an hour?'

He nodded, fidgeted, signed the contract. Every time she saw an American signing, Virginia felt a little remorseful. Unlike her sullen, knowing compatriots, adolescents like Calvin could not foresee the scrimping, the nights of greasy cafeteria meals, the exhausting monotony that awaited them. Some British adventure! But Calvin seemed ready to seize it and run.

Virginia had two more interviews before lunchtime, both recent school leavers galvanized into feeble job-searching by their parents—three out of four of whom were already themselves in the employ of the great University. With such 'legacy' cases, it was always advisable to place the offspring somewhere, however briefly, no matter how moronic they seemed, to avoid the ire of their fathers and mothers.

This morning, Rosemarie did indeed head for the kitchen; and young Franklin was sent to join his father driving trucks for the works department. Because of their visits Virginia managed to miss Martin altogether, but she could not escape Simon's watchful eye: he called to her from behind his desk as she showed Rosemarie, the last one, out.

Ramsbottom was a small, thick man, and even when seated he found it difficult to look imposing. But he tried. He was a judo aficionado and had decorated his walls with snaps of himself and his mates (other balding, sagging fellows in their forties and early fifties), robed in white, kicking up their heels. On the wall behind his swivel throne—above his head, for all visitors to see and remark upon—glittered a gilded plaque announcing some minor judo triumph. It had been in this office and the one before for some years, but every time the plaque was mentioned, Simon still blushed with pleasure. He was that sort of man: a little pompous, a little foolish, full of bluster at the wrong moments; but to Virginia somehow charming.

'Gorgeous! Good morning!' he called from the shadows of his lair. On her way to the lift, Rosemarie heard him and ruffled her poodle ringlets; but Virginia knew, after all these years, that

78

the call was for her, purely to embarrass, and it did.

'Simon?'

'Give us the time of day, won't you? I haven't had a word, not a word! Have I offended?'

'It's been a hectic morning, in, out, in, out, the revolving door of temporary.' She could see her hands trembling so she clasped them firmly on the back of the visitor's chair. 'What about you? You haven't exactly made a point of visiting me.'

'You're in my dreams, Virginia, I see you day and night.' Simon winked.

'Simon, please!' She felt a little dizzy at the insinuation, but she was still harbouring irritation underneath and recovered in time to make a barbed point in return—not for the first time either. 'If I'm dancing through your dream life, Simon, do you know what I'm saying?'

'Racy, Virginia. A little racy even for me.'

She lowered her voice. 'I'm telling you to sack that boy next door before he tears this department apart. And I mean it.'

Simon stopped grinning. 'For a Christian, that's pretty un-Christian, Miss Simpson.'

'God hasn't come into the office before. This isn't about God, and you know it—that boy's a sinner, fine, so are you and so, for that matter, am I. But he's an evil influence.'

'He's very good at his job.'

'So would thousands of others be. He chats up Mandy. He's rude to my prospectives and—'

'Familiar, not rude. They like it. *Mandy* likes it.'

'And I've said this before, Simon, he's got something against me. He wants my job.'

'Of course he does, Virginia. More to the point, he wants *my* job. Be worried if he didn't. Brains enough, ambition, someday maybe he'll get it. You and I won't be kicking around this corridor forever, you know.'

'Well, I don't know about you and maybe you don't care about me, but I like to think my job is safe for a few more years at least. And he's doing his best to gnaw away at it. At me.'

'You know me. You know I care. It's just that . . . I've got to consider the future, what's best for the future. I hardly see Mandy in this chair.'

Virginia smoothed the pleats in her skirt and spoke very slowly. Part of her wanted to say 'Why not *me* in that chair?', just because she knew it had never occurred to him; it hadn't really consciously occurred to her before now, not even when she joked with Mandy about Martin. But she didn't. What she said was more difficult than that, more embarrassing. She hissed, in a rasping, tight voice, 'If you care, make him stop doing the newsletters. They're *mine*.'

'Goodness.'

She didn't look up. She looked at her fingers and her pleats and the pulled threads in the ancient olive carpet.

'You've always hated those damn newsletters. And the boy needs to learn. I thought—he thought—it was doing you a favour. This can't go on, you know. From today, those newsletters are officially his. I'll send round a memo. You're behaving like a child. I would never have expected it. Jesus, Virginia.'

She glanced at him. He was bobbing and swivelling slightly, visibly upset. Even amid her rage and nerves she felt the twinge of her attraction. He was perhaps not beautiful when angry, but he was quite sweet.

'You know I don't like it when you take the Lord's name in vain,' she said.

'That's more like it, V. But I mean it about the newsletters. It's beneath you. Not another word, OK?'

'Beneath me! Beneath me! Not another word! We'll see about that!' As she crossed the hall to her office, Virginia's internal monologue was in a fine lather, and she was convinced the day could not

80

get any worse. Then she heard her mother's voice—a warbling echo from a couple of doors down. A warbling, but authoritative echo.

When Virginia dashed out of the door in a morning panic, Melody Simpson consciously lowered her shoulders and sat very still at the table, listening. Her hearing was unaffected by age. She heard chattering sparrows and starlings in the trees along the block, mingling with the passage of cars and footsteps; she heard phrases of classical music from the flat upstairs; she heard Bella whistling in her feline sleep; and she heard beneath it all the faint, rhythmic hum of blood in her ears—the movements of her heart. It was only recently that she had started to listen in this way, until she felt she could catch the gurgling of inner workings right down to her toes. The sounds were reassuring; she knew she was alive.

During the war, her husband gone, Melody would stand in the doorway of her daughters' room and listen in this way, her face forward, her nose and eyes listening too, all recording the soft soughing of their infant breaths and the innocent, infrequent rustlings when they rolled or shifted. Then, despite Melody Simpson's early knowledge of loss—of her husband, of the future she had wanted—hers was a defiant listening, as though simply absorbing the sounds of her children's sleep could protect them forever, as though she alone, by doing this, kept them alive.

But now, listening for herself, she was much less confident: she did so because she feared that one morning she wouldn't hear anything. Her veins and arteries and lungs and bowels might simply cease their music, and were she not attentive, she might not even know it. Melody Simpson, who had not even been truly afraid when the surgeons hacked off one, and later, the other breast (she had known all along the tumours would be benign)—Melody Simpson was afraid of death.

She could find nothing perceptibly wrong with herself, no aches or illnesses, no loss of memory or coordination, but something had changed since the night a month or so before when she awoke unreasonably from a sound sleep, heard the bedside clock ticking in the blackness and thought just this: soon I will die. She felt it as certainly as she had felt her invincibility for so many years and there was no arguing with this knowledge, no point in talking about it to Virginia or to anyone else.

In the subsequent weeks, Mrs Simpson had resolved two things: not to do any more anything she did not want to do, and to go to the Isle of Skye before the summer was out. The former decision was behind the basket and the winch, behind her suggestion of a picnic (she *wanted* one, after all), and the latter, she knew, was driving Virginia crazy. But Melody Simpson was known for her strong will, and to Skye they would go. That's all there was to it.

She cleaned up the breakfast dishes and wiped the table with special care: such tasks had become quite exciting, now that she could so easily have eschewed them, as she had the shopping, on the grounds of Resolution Number One. Cleaning was now a choice rather than a duty, a secret pleasure. She sometimes joked to herself that if she had known it would be so simple to relieve the aura of burden around housework, she would have done so years ago.

Today she did not even mind the shopping, because it was for her picnic. She bought plump cherry tomatoes and scrubbed potatoes from the stall at the bottom of the hill; she bought a Viennese loaf from the baker, still hot and reeking deliciously of dough; she bought slices of baked ham and coarse, foreign smoked sausage from the surly Italian grocer; and she took at the last minute a small container of spiced, cracked black olives from the same man, insisting before she did so that he offer her one to taste. She spent the morning making a potato salad in garlic mayonnaise, a dish she and Virginia both loved. She packed the food in plastic boxes and placed it, along with the cutlery and two of her finest plates, in a large plastic bag from John Lewis.

After some thought she wore an old summer dress of flowered cotton, and a lilac cardigan with scalloped edges over her shoulders. She made certain that her foam bust was even and firmly secured. She combed and fussed over her hair until she was certain that the thinner moments in her scalp were spanned by sufficient curls. Like spun sugar, her hair did not move once it had been sculpted, but she wore a hairnet anyway, just in case.

It was not pure altruism that had Melody Simpson taking such care over lunch with her daughter: she had more complex motives than a delightful *déjeuner sur l'herbe*. Her plan was to let her needs be known to the University—that is, to the executive enclave of Directors of Personnel, Permanent & Temporary: she was going to make damn sure that she and Virginia got to Skye. To this end she even rouged her cheeks and splashed her wrists with toilet water. And as she set out to find a taxi, her best china clanking in her large plastic bag, Melody Simpson felt a full surge of her old confidence.

It was only a quarter to one when she greeted the large, bald guard at the entrance to Virginia's building. He, surprised by such good humour, accompanied her to the third floor and pointed a route through the warren of passages that would take her to Personnel.

Peering into cubicles as she wound around the building, Mrs Simpson's mind was twitching so fast that she almost bypassed the department—which looked the same as it had on her last visit five years before, only slightly more worn. The offices on the left—where Virginia's was, she knew, but not which one—were closed to the corridor, so she stepped into the first on the right and almost bumped into a freckled youth in tinted glasses.

'How can I help you?' he asked, unperturbed. 'I don't suppose you're looking for a job?'

'Who are you?'

'Martin Evans, at your service. Older than I look.'

'Martin, may I sit?'

He waved at the chair where Simon's interviewees waited to be seen. 'Rest your young self. Refresh your beauty.'

'Young?' Melody Simpson trilled with laughter. The lad was cocky, and she liked him. 'Aren't you a charmer! A recent addition to this dull corner?'

'Dull? Not dull here! A laugh a minute.'

'I think my daughter finds it dull.'

'You? A daughter? Who might she be?'

'That isn't quite right. She wouldn't think to find it tiresome. I find it tiresome for her. Virginia Simpson, and she needs a holiday.'

'Don't we all! You're Mrs Simpson, then?'

'That's been my name since before you were born. I don't know what *you* do. It's not in your power to dole out holidays, is it?'

'Not even jobs, yet, let alone holidays. But I'm working on it. Tell me what you're after.'

'Just a couple of weeks for the poor lamb. She's over-tired. A couple of weeks in a couple of weeks.'

'That's pretty short notice, Mrs Simpson. I gather she *wants* a holiday?'

'She's never known what's good for her. She wouldn't have ended up an old maid if she had. She wouldn't have ended up *here*. Her sister was always much more sensible, although even that's backfired. Divorce, you know. Very distressing.'

'Of course. Very.' His smile now was something Mrs Simpson didn't quite recognize, or approve of. Perhaps she didn't like him after all.

'Mother, you're early.' Virginia emerged from behind a filing cabinet. Mrs Simpson realized that there was a second door to the corridor she had not noticed when she came in.

'It's bad manners to eavesdrop, Virginia.'

'I'll be right with you. It's not one yet. Now, Martin, about the newsletters—'

'I've actually just—'

'About the newsletters, Simon and I have discussed it and we think it's best if you take them over officially. I don't really have time any more. He'll send round a memo this afternoon.'

'Oh good,' said Mrs Simpson, piqued by her daughter's brusqueness. 'Less work, more chance of a holiday. Go on, Martin, I'm sure you can do *all* of Virginia's work. You look capable enough.'

'No doubt, Mother.' Virginia's hands were making and un-making little fists. 'Let's go now. I can leave the rest till after lunch.'

Martin, whose eyes were not wholly clear behind their brownish glass, was grinning again. As they walked out, Mrs Simpson could have sworn he winked at her.

Virginia did not speak until they reached their picnic spot, a bench beneath a copper beech in the communal garden opposite. The lawn was dotted with other university employees, all of whom looked more cheerful about their lives than Virginia felt. She was immensely tired.

'What exactly are you trying to do, Mother, lose me my job?'

'Honestly. I'd swear that when you found God you lost your sense of humour, you crabby thing. It was a *joke*.'

'You don't know who you were talking to. You think it's funny, you don't do battle with him every day.'

'Martin seemed perfectly charming to me. If he weren't so young I'd suggest him as a prospect.'

Virginia glared. At her mother, at the plastic boxes, at the china. 'I'm not sure I'll stay for lunch.'

'I've made potato salad. And brought the best plates.'

'I'm surprised they didn't break.' Virginia was grudging, but when presented with a cherry tomato she popped it in her mouth.

'I thought I might take the bus to Marks after lunch,' said Mrs Simpson between bites. 'I'd like to buy a new dress.'

Virginia nodded, a small glob of garlic mayonnaise on her lip, her jaws champing in time with her nods.

'I thought,' Mrs Simpson went on, 'It would be useful for our holiday. For the trip to Skye.'

It was hard to tell whether Virginia had heard. She kept nodding and chewing for a moment and then settled into just chewing. She was scanning the lawn as if checking the horizon at sea, as if everything were blurred and far away. But she didn't say anything, and Mrs Simpson knew they would go after all.

Melody Simpson chose nylon against her better judgement. The saleswoman, a buxom girl with a lank pony-tail, insisted that the cut was flattering, and Mrs Simpson allowed herself to be convinced. The print was red and blue stripes on white—'Vertical,' said the girl in a Liverpudlian accent, 'Very nice. I wouldn't advise horizontal stripes, but vertical . . . Looks very nice indeed.'

And Mrs Simpson was so pleased to hear this, as well as quite taken by the matching red leatherette belt, that she bought it almost at once. She was halfway home when she realized that she had abandoned her John Lewis bag in the fitting-room at Marks & Spencer, and that inside the bag were the two china plates, now smeared and greasy but her very best plates nonetheless. It wasn't easy to force herself off the bus and across the road to the stop opposite, but she did, and so didn't get back to Chalk Farm until well after six.

It was a surprise to see Virginia already sitting at the kitchen table, with the *Evening Standard* in front of her and the late mail

86

unopened in her lap. Mrs Simpson was not by nature demonstrat-
ive, or even eminently sympathetic, but she could see that Virginia
was in some distress and she wanted to do the right thing.

'Lovely dress, I've got,' she said. 'You can have one just the
same if you're nice to me.'

Virginia smiled weakly. 'Show?'

'In a minute. In a minute. Such a fuss, all this wrapping. My
dear, but aren't you home early!'

Maybe it was because Mrs Simpson, usually so gruff, called
her daughter 'dear'; maybe it was because Virginia was so very
tired; or maybe it was just bound to happen. Virginia put her
head in her hands and burst into noisy tears.

'What on earth is wrong?'

Virginia shook her head. 'Everything. Everything's wrong.'

Mrs Simpson too behaved in uncharacteristc fashion: she
stood next to her daughter and pressed Virginia's trembling head
to her foam bosom. She stroked her daughter's hair as she hadn't
done for years, and worried about who might do so when she
herself was gone. 'There, there, dear, it can't be so bad. You can
tell me. Tell me everything.'

Virginia didn't want to, but at the same time, she did. She
struggled against an inner weight that wouldn't let her speak. It
had been so many years, after all, since she had confided in her
mother. 'Everything,' she said again, muffled against her mother's
cardigan. 'It's just . . . '

'You weren't attacked, Virginia? Or hurt? Were you?'

'No.' But the shuddering sobs worsened. 'It's everything. It's
last night and Angelica . . . and my Bible and *today*.'

'Today? We had a delicious lunch, didn't we? Should I not
have come? Did I spoil it?'

Virginia's torrent of tears gurgled on, unabated, louder.

'Is it today? It's this afternoon, isn't it? What's happened?
Something this afternoon—what is it? You must tell me, force

yourself.'

Virginia began to make a high, keening sound, like a medium in a trance. In between the pure moaning, Mrs Simpson heard her daughter say, like a faraway truth in a language not her own, 'They've sent . . . me, sent me . . . away.'

Guilt was on Mrs Simpson at once, heavy, clouding the room. 'Virginia, Virginia, don't tell me you've been sacked?'

She gave her daughter the words and Virginia used them. 'I've been sacked,' she wailed. And again, 'Sacked. I've been sacked.'

The full story, or as much of it as Virginia could bring herself to tell, was a long time coming. She had not, in fact, been sacked; her own words were more accurate: she had been sent away, for a month at least, six weeks, it wasn't clear.

When she came back from lunch, there was a note on her telephone in Simon's squat, messy handwriting. 'V,' it said, 'Come and see me when you're free.' She decided she wasn't. She got on with the requests for temporaries that had come in that morning, sorting them into types of skilled and unskilled work and then making small piles of possible candidates for each one, drawn from the sectioned file-cards in the boxes on her desk, each 'possible' pile containing at least one person who had worked successfully for the University before, and preferably one with a red star on their card that meant they had been highly thought of. But, distracted, she put a typist in with the security staff pile, and failed to find a tried worker for the gardening post, although she could conjure the faces of at least two temporary gardeners not already in use. Her inefficiency annoyed her, and when Simon poked his head around her door, she was jittery and ready for a break.

She had not thought anything of the summons, but Simon was stiff with her, and this heightened her already anxious mood. When he shut the doors to his office and offered her a seat, she felt her chest tighten and declined. This, she knew, was the formula for hiring and firing people. This, she thought at the same time, had something to do with Martin. Simon, too, would not sit: he paced the room and straightened all the pictures, one by one. He brushed his plaque for dust. He did not seem to know how to begin. She noticed that his bottom was wide in its loose covering and in her confused state she couldn't tell whether this was appealing or not.

'I've been thinking, since this morning—'

'Yes? What?' Her eyes popped open and shut. 'Is it something I've said?'

'Don't be so defensive, Virginia. I just wondered whether you had any holiday plans? You haven't mentioned it.' He took from his desk a chart that marked off all the holidays and sick days members of the department had taken. 'It's June now. You've only taken two days all year, you know. And one was for a root canal.'

Virginia shrugged. 'I've got a lot to take care of.'

'We all do, but we take holidays. Don't you want some time off?'

Something about this didn't ring true to Virginia. 'Why since this morning?'

'Sorry?'

'Why have you been thinking about it since this morning?'

'You seem tired.'

'Of course I'm tired. But it doesn't mean I want a holiday. You don't take a holiday just because you get out of bed on the wrong side, do you? There's work to be done!' Even as she finished she could hear her shrill voice. It echoed among the pictures. 'Besides,' she said more calmly, 'Selina is taking a lot of time very soon. Maybe I'll take some later on, August, or September.'

'You don't do Selina's job. It doesn't matter.'

'The summer's very busy for me. I can't leave everything on Mandy's shoulders.'

'You don't have to: Martin needs to learn. He can fill in for a couple of weeks. He'll do it fine.'

Little fluorescent bulbs exploded in her head. 'No,' she said, only it came out of her mouth as a shriek, and a long one at that. Later, to her mother, she said, 'I suppose I saw red.'

'Virginia—' Simon was coming towards her.

'I knew it. I knew he was behind this. It's his idea, and you— I thought we were friends! I thought we were colleagues.' She spat this out, her eyes screwed shut as she tried to regain composure, so far lost she couldn't imagine it. He put his arm on her back, on her shoulder.

'I won't go. Not for him, I won't go. You can't make me.' She could feel Simon's chest very close and she pummelled at it a little but he didn't move away.

'I think you need it,' he said, and she opened her eyes to see a mixture of curiosity and pity on his close, coarse face. And of course she cried: for the first time in the many years they had worked together, she cried in front of him, fell against him and cried into his damp neck, into his department store cologne smell, while he patted her awkwardly on the back. To Mrs Simpson she said only, 'I had a bit of a tantrum.'

And the funny thing was that amid all the fuss and the tension and the clammy body fluids, Virginia could see the absurdity of her fantasies, of ever having imagined this man crooning to her or disrobing. She almost started to laugh among her sobs; and for a second she didn't care that her whole life had gone wrong, that she had lost control at such an inopportune time. It was just plain funny.

The hilarity didn't last long. She didn't remember it as she told her story to Mrs Simpson—although she wouldn't have said had she recalled—and it was certainly not very amusing to be on indefinite leave on the grounds of nervous exhaustion. It was not amusing at all.

In the telling, however circumspect, of the afternoon's

goings-on, Virginia shed still more tears. It was like losing blood: she was reduced, trembling and small by the time Mrs Simpson more or less understood what had happened, her eyes swollen and bloodshot, her nose crimson and damp. But the rest of Virginia's face was pale—testimony, Mrs Simpson felt, to great trauma and shock.

After plying her daughter with Bovril, Mrs Simpson called the doctor, who came swiftly and provided an immediate sedative along with a prescription for some more. At the door she whispered to Mrs Simpson, 'We'll see how it goes. Might be a good idea for her to talk to someone. Therapy, you know. NHS covers it, although a lot of people don't know.'

'Thank you, Doctor, but I don't think she'll need to. My daughter gets her counselling straight from the source. She's probably praying as we speak.'

Virginia wasn't, in fact. She was lying in bed, where it seemed she had not been for ages, watching little transparent creatures swim back and forth across her closed eyelids. She felt free of the leaden weight of her limbs, inconvenienced only by the blockage in her nostrils, and sleepy, terribly sleepy. By the time Melody Simpson came in and kissed her daughter's brow, Virginia was almost smiling and very far away.

Which left Mrs Simpson to the dusk, to a tin of baked beans, and to the past that had led her and Virginia here. This was not as bad as it could have been; it was not as bad as the other two times, after the last of which Virginia had found God, and after the first of which she had come home for good.

Virginia had been pretty then, always better built than her sister, with delicate wrists and only a slightly too-long face. Emmy had already left, and Virginia was jealous. Melody Simpson could see her eldest tight-lipped at the mention of William Richmond's growing fortune, listening over Sunday lunch to stories of Emmy's climb through Sydney society.

For almost a year Sunday lunch was the only time Mrs Simpson saw Virginia. Even then they didn't get along; Virginia wasn't exactly rebellious, but when Emmy left she grew ambitious out of spite, and needled her mother in ways Mrs Simpson could not stand. Virginia was a secretary, taking evening classes, in control, never late, never a ladder in her stockings. But terribly shy, really, which only her mother knew—no wonder she hated her mother so—and which, at that time, was about all Mrs Simpson could have said with certainty about her daughter.

She never saw the flat Virginia lived in with two other girls; she was never invited and wasn't the sort to poke her nose in unwanted. She never met the man, and once it was all over, he was never mentioned again. But when her Ginny slumped on to the settee in three-day-dirty clothes, without stockings in March, without having called in sick to work, Mrs Simpson had known how to take care of her own. It was much worse than 'nervous exhaustion' then: the words for it left you blighted for life, were better left unsaid. Remembering that time, Melody Simpson thought again that one didn't live through such periods and grow to like people any better—she would always prefer Emmy as a person, selfish though she was—but that one learned something stronger, and better, than easy affections. And she poked at her baked beans in a fury as she thought how Virginia's flatmates had only been to visit her once.

It wasn't until she had finished her meal; not until she had washed the few dishes and hung up her new dress—which looked, now, with its red leatherette belt, like an announcement of her guilt for Virginia's state of mind; not until she was wiping down the table and tidying for bed that Mrs Simpson came across the pile of late mail.

There wasn't usually much in the noon delivery; a flyer or an insurance document, perhaps a reminder for Virginia from the greedy dentist. But this evening, among the worthless waste-paper, Mrs Simpson found a worn blue envelope of the cheapest quality, one half of one side covered with large, ornate stamps. These threw her slightly, and she turned it this way and that unopened, and examined the smudged postmark, before recognizing the generous, swooping slant of her younger daughter's hand. She was tempted to run into Virginia's room and shake her, to force her awake to the rare prize of a letter from Emmy, but she did not. Mrs Simpson took a sharp knife from the drawer, slit the top of the envelope, stealthy as a spy, and withdrew the flimsy sheets. She paused before unfolding them to fetch a bar of chocolate from the fridge, then settled down to the compounded indulgence of devouring sweets and words at once.

BALI

EMMY WAS WAKENED by the workmen shattering stones outside her room. When she peered through the slats of her door-shutters, she could see men silhouetted around and inside the hole that would be the swimming-pool. Behind them hovered the shadow of the gorge, then the sacred ridge, then the blood-orange disk of the sun, creeping up the sky. As she rubbed at the sleep in her eyes and at the film of sweat across her cheeks, she became aware of the stirrings above her in the house, and of the early-morning movements along the road outside.

After almost two weeks in this household, this was the moment in the day that she liked best: it was secret and serene. She almost felt like a conjuror, in her room against the hillside beneath the rest of the building, as if she could emerge into a world of her own imagining. By the time she was dressed, however, and faced with the prospect of opening her shutters on to the men and the pool, this supreme confidence had inevitably dissipated.

Staying here had just sort of happened. Max had pushed for it—they got on well—and somehow Emmy had been caught up in the strange Sparke dynamic. Not that Buddy was attentive: he hardly spoke to her except when she protested that she ought to leave. She felt a bit like an old servant on the sidelines, observing.

But Emmy didn't mind. She was fascinated, horrified, entranced by this life, and said to herself almost every evening that she would stay just a few days longer, just long enough to understand.

After the meal on the edge of the Monkey Forest all that time ago, it had been too late for the trip back to Kintamani, and Emmy had not been sorry to follow Buddy, Max and the two women back to the house. Arriving exhausted as night fell, she had not appreciated the beauty of the place, and only after a long rest for her twisted muscles, on a generous and welcoming bed, had she first seen the sacred sunrise.

From then on, things seemed to be beyond her control, despite her fantasies to the contrary. When, over a haphazard breakfast in the vast main room of the house, Max asked if she would stay another day or two, she thought just long enough to slip a spoonful of papaya into her mouth, and accepted, only to discover that K'tut had already been dispatched to return Gdé and young Wayan to Kintamani and to retrieve her bag from the dreary *losmen* there.

Her new accommodation was quite splendid. She had this room to herself, with its sprawling framed bed, carved armoire and cool stone floor, and even a little bathroom with a shower and erratic plumbing, all separate from the body of the house, so that her privacy (and theirs) was not infringed. Above her was the main room, which she reached via a pathway and some concrete steps. It was a large room, with sofas and armchairs and another, immense bed in one corner, everything covered in intricate batiks. Off this room, open to it, stretched a long, thatch-covered porch looking across the ridge; and at the other side of the house, a narrow kitchen. To reach Buddy's private quarters, one had to go outside again and climb a flight of steps. There, off an external corridor, were three more bedrooms with private facilities, one for Max, one for Buddy, and one for any of a variety of visitors— women, mostly.

The patterns of life in this place were at the same time orderly and random: orderly in terms of Buddy's life, and indifferent, hence random, in terms of everyone else's. It had its natural movements—the rustling of geckos in the thatch, the rotation of the days around the sun's progress, so that bedtime came with nightfall and the day began for all at five. And then the rest: Buddy did not take breakfast, so none was regularly provided. But he took his other meals like clockwork, and already at sunrise a group of Ubud girls and women had arrived and begun work. They prepared lunch and washed the floors daily; they beat the cushions and refilled the oil lamps; they created what semblance of normality there was, talking and laughing among themselves and blushing at the sight of young Max. They did not leave until the last dish was washed, the last mosquito coil set and smouldering, and then they set off down the rutted path by torchlight, still talking and joking in the night.

For Emmy, her stay had been calm. She and Max frequently set off together to see the temples or markets within easy reach. They had wandered together like mother and son, wading through rice paddies to visit villages unattainable by road, stopping for meals at *warungs*. She had gone with him to a tailor in Ubud, and had counselled him on which fabrics would suit shirts or jackets for himself, dresses for his mother. She had stopped comparing him to Pod, had stopped considering Pod so much at all, but in this way she felt she was coming to understand her daughter better.

She knew that Buddy considered her purely as a companion for Max, a toy as his own women were toys, and she suspected that this extraordinary father would be unperturbed, relieved even, if she and Max were to go to bed together. He obviously saw little other purpose for women, no matter what their age; and it wounded her pride. She struggled not to take his indifference as a challenge or a slight, but it was nonetheless a struggle.

And when she had, on occasion, found Buddy in the sitting-room alone, and had attempted conversation, she had felt her usually dormant temper bubbling to the surface. Hence her dread, in the mornings, at the few short steps to the main house.

Sometimes she was included in family events, taken in K'tut's bus to ceremonies or public gatherings, to Den Pasar for household trips. Buddy was planning a trip to Komodo, and spoke as if Emmy would go with them. And other times she enjoyed a sublime, serene solitude. She watched the bus pull off loaded with Sparkes and retinue, and she returned to read, or to walk along the pebbled riverside at the bottom of the gorge, or to swim in the spring-fed pool that belonged to the neighbouring hotel and that Buddy and his guests were welcome to use until their own pool was completed.

She enjoyed a certain status, staying with Buddy: there were chuckles and whispers, but all the locals asked if she was well, if she needed anything, if they could escort her anywhere. She was beginning to know some of them by name, particularly the men, because they wandered up to the house in the afternoon or early evening to recline on the bed in the sitting-room and watch Ubud's only colour television, complete with video recorder. The younger men came in groups, with gallon jugs of rice liquor, and grew raucous over Clint Eastwood videos. The older ones generally came alone, seeking conferences with Buddy about their rice harvest, their daughters' marriages, the feuding of local politics. When they watched television, it was stealthily, from the corners of their eyes, as they stood contemplating greater things.

Emmy was fascinated by these people who accepted Buddy's life as ordinary and who made niches for themselves inside it. And she was fascinated, above all, by the women. Sylvia and Sasha had moved on almost at once, and Max—who could hear everything—assured Emmy that nothing had come of their fledgling intimacy with Buddy. Since their departure, two others, New

Zealanders, had stayed one night and scuttled northwards, but none of them learned what Emmy knew, from Max and from her quiet observation.

There was Suchi, Buddy's official girlfriend and expectant mother of his child. She was young and physically frail, her belly as yet only gently swollen. K'tut would pick her up from her parents' house in the bus and bring her to Buddy in the evenings. She spoke no English, he hardly any Balinese or Indonesian, except the phrase 'shy as a cat'. They would be sitting over supper—Buddy, Max, Emmy, Suchi and any others—and he would tap lightly on Suchi's nose and recite his foreign phrase: 'shy as a cat'. Whereupon her face would crinkle, orchid-like, into an expression of delight, and she would cover her eyes with her hands. He would grin and pat her on the arm as if to praise her performance: a party-trick, used over and over again.

It wasn't clear to Emmy whether Suchi knew about the others. She was friendly with the women who cared for the house, and perhaps they had told her, but one of Buddy's favourites, Jenny, was among them, and Emmy could not tell where the women's loyalties lay.

Jenny, unlike Suchi, was sturdy and small, with a broad face and clever eyes. She spoke a fair amount of English—she had been to Den Pasar, to the university, she told Emmy, although she hadn't had the money to finish her studies. She was twenty-four. She functioned as the housekeeper, leader of the troupe of younger women. More than anything, she hoped that Buddy would arrange a visa for her so she could go to Australia, to study accounting and to work.

She never spoke of her liaison with her employer; she seemed to value discretion more than he did, and Emmy sometimes wondered whether strategy did not play a large part in Jenny's surrender to his charms. If anything, she seemed to be interested in Max, engaging him in conversation, asking him to correct her

English letters, standing close enough to smell his skin for longer than was necessary. It was only because of Max's firm reports that Emmy knew Jenny and Buddy were entangled at all, and it seemed a shame to her because she knew how Max felt about women his father had 'had', and because she could see that when Jenny stood at Max's elbow, he didn't really want to move away.

There were others, too. There was a brassy peroxided American living further up the road, who made brightly-coloured children's clothes for export. She accosted Max in town as though he were her son, but defiantly cut Buddy dead when he passed. There was a plain woman who ran the restaurant in the hotel next door, and who also suffered from being discarded: she responded by swinging her head and laughing sharply whenever Buddy came near.

And then, of course, there were the ones who came and went, tourists, tour guides, just women passing through, although there had been none since Emmy's arrival. She knew there were people who would think she was one such, despite her age. Whether this was somehow pleasing or purely a source for alarm she couldn't quite decide.

But on this day, eleven days into Emmy's stay with the Sparkes, two things were supposed to take place that might, Emmy felt, radically alter her fragile grasp on the household. When she had said as much to Max, he laughed and said, a little bitterly, 'Damn right they will. You'll have to stay another six months to figure it out.'

Figuring it out, Emmy was convinced, would mean being able to pass judgement, which in turn would mean knowing where she stood, what she believed. And only then would she be able to go home and know how to begin again. In spite of everything, she was half in love with this life, and she knew Max was too. They both needed to understand; their pleasure and their quiet horror needed explaining. She sometimes thought Max already knew

more than he pretended, but as with the women, it wasn't ultimately clear where his loyalties lay.

Two things, two events. Emmy remembered them both
before she even washed her face. She remembered them as she
peered out into the growing daylight. Today, first of all, little
Ruby was arriving from Thailand, all of three years old, to stay
with her father and half-brother. What nobody seemed to know
for certain, and what Max seemed most concerned about, was
whether Aimée, Ruby's mother, would be coming to stay as
well. She had been to the house before, in the time of the
American clothes exporter, and the visit had not been fortuitous.
K'tut had told Max this. He thought the strain of that time had
brought on his ulcer, a wound that still had him driving to a
doctor in Den Pasar every week. K'tut didn't want to go to meet
the plane, because if Aimée was on it, he didn't want to know.
Just thinking about it made him sweat, he said.

And the second thing was a party, the celebration of a
wedding. It would be a chance to see Buddy's real friends, who
were coming to celebrate the marriage of a foreigner from the
north of the island, whom Buddy fondly referred to as 'Kraut', to a
Balinese woman named Madé, whose family lived in a village near
Ubud. Emmy could not help her curiosity: she wanted to see what
these friends, foreign and native, were like, what it meant for a
man like Buddy to have friends, and she wanted to know whether
Buddy would continue to play the role of feudal lord amid his
minions, or whether a new aspect would reveal itself.

When she stepped outside, she could tell that the whole
house was already humming. The workmen did not pause, as on
other mornings, to greet and to appraise her. A young girl she
hadn't seen before was arranging frangipani flowers around the
carved gateway at the foot of the path that separated Buddy's
world from the hotel below and from the road. And the number
of flip-flops piled outside the sitting-room door indicated that

there were many more women at work than usual.

The large room had been turned upside down: the women were brushing and mopping, and more were calling to each other in the narrow kitchen. Rolls of mosquito netting had been brought in to encase the porch after dark, and were half-spread, like huge spider webs across one end of the room, where two women knelt to inspect the laced pattern for holes. Spiced smells and heat hung already on the air.

Only K'tut remained unaffected by the commotion; he sat cross-legged on the bed in a white shirt and sarong, smoking, intent upon a seventies film playing without sound on the television.

'Busy busy, isn't it?' ventured Emmy, perching beside him. 'Good film?'

'Max is still sleeping,' he said. 'Buddy's out.'

'In town? With Suchi?'

He shrugged.

'Are you worried about today?'

He looked up from the television and narrowed his eyes at her. 'I'm going to the doctor today. I'm always worrying about the doctor. I think he's a bad man. Very bad man.'

'I meant about Ruby coming. And Aimée.'

'Aimée?' He made a face. 'I'm going to the doctor. Then maybe I'm taking a holiday. Buddy don't know trouble when she's coming.'

'Well . . . no chance of breakfast today, I suppose?' Emmy thought K'tut looked at her disapprovingly.

'Ask Jenny,' he said, his gaze flitting back to the television screen.

When Emmy had hovered for a few moments and had not found any sign of Jenny's efficient movements, or any sounds of life from upstairs, she decided to walk to the western-style *warung* halfway into town, down by the bridge, to have a slice of chocolate mousse cake for breakfast. If K'tut's monosyllabic chill was any indication, this day, Emmy thought, might be less exciting and less revealing than she had hoped.

Max, semi-somnolent, scratched himself. This was the big day. He rolled over and tried to go back to sleep, but instead found himself listening, with his whole body, to the tiniest sounds. He heard the creak of his father's door, and then nothing.

It was the silence that was telling: if it had been Buddy, Max would have heard his jaunty, heavy tread, and perhaps a whistle or some muttering. When it was Suchi, there was a little noise, breathy cooings as the lovers parted at Buddy's door, speaking their empty lovers' language for public benefit. But silence meant it was Jenny, slipping out and down the road, just to wait and walk up again as though coming from home. Max didn't know why she bothered; everyone knew. And as Suchi got more pregnant and less inclined to love, the dawn was increasingly punctuated by what Max named Jenny's moment of silence.

Sometimes he imagined, as a joke, the morning when Emmy might emerge from that bedroom. He would hear a prim clearing of the throat, the swishing of her skirt on the stairs. It was hilarious because it was unthinkable, but even as he taunted himself with it, he knew it would be the worst betrayal. Worse, even, than Jenny's, in a way. The whole point of Emmy was that she wasn't part of it, and not being part of it, she was on his side. In her peculiar, conservative way, she was good enough fun, as well as proof to Buddy that Max ought to be taken seriously.

Max kicked the sheet and ploughed his head further into the pillow. Every night when he went to bed, an oval gecko dropping lay on the sheet. It was supposed to mean good luck, but this day ahead was proof that he had no luck. And Jenny's moment of silence only made it worse: most fathers don't fuck girls their sons have kissed, and then remind them of it every morning.

There was noise now, from everywhere. He heard Emmy's voice. He didn't hear his father moving, and decided Buddy must have gone out before Jenny. Max couldn't ever sustain his anger against him for very long. There were times when he loved his father, smoking dope with him or reminiscing about the relationship they had barely had. They laughed over Buddy's visits to Sydney, the trips to Luna Park or the zoo, when, in between daredevil rides or animal pens, Buddy and Chris (he had been Chris then, after all) dished the dirt to each other about Chris's stern mother, or about Buddy's mother even, a wide old woman who tried crabbily to control the lives of her son and grandchildren. They could laugh still, remembering remembering. They could talk about Chris's trips to the sheep station and his childhood fear of the kangaroos leaping in the distance.

Can you really hate someone who makes you laugh, someone who loves you unconditionally? But then, Max was not always sure that unconditional love could be cobbled together of those occasional afternoons where Buddy did his best to charm an eager son. And what of now: did Buddy feel any more for Max than he felt for Suchi, or Aimée, or K'tut? Then there was the rest, the secrets, the women. And back to Jenny.

Max tried, most of all, to feel nothing for his father, to distance Buddy and silence the worst rebellions in his mind. Emmy was a help because she stood so far outside, because she listened, because she didn't guess the half of it. At least, not before today.

The sun was showing its entire yellow orb, flooding the room with light. Max got up and threw on shorts and a singlet. The whole house felt clammy. He didn't look into the main room, or call for his father. He brushed through the gate, knocking the careful frangipanis, and set off down the hill towards town.

★

It was early for a *warung* catering to Western clientele to be open, and Emmy was the first customer. The owner, who also ran a gift shop full of carvings, jewellery and clothes, was still hanging out those more solid wares. She was obviously less than delighted to stop doing so for a solitary plump woman, even if she did recognize Emmy as one of the Sparke household. She manifested her displeasure in a feigned ignorance of the English language. But Emmy planted herself at one of the roadside tables in the sunshine and refused to move, and eventually she was served. She ordered coffee, pineapple juice and a slice of chocolate mousse cake (yesterday's).

The sun was warm, the coffee surprisingly good, and Emmy was suffused with contentment. She did not know why she thought, at such a wholly positive moment, of her mother and her sister, but once she had done so, she felt she ought to write them a letter. Usually, in Double Bay, she phoned every two or three weeks, on a Sunday. But the telephone in Bali, even for Buddy and his guests, was erratic and expensive. She asked the woman for some paper and a pen from the gift shop, and then composed the first letter she had written to her family for years.

Dear Mother and Virginia,
Sorry not to have called lately, but as I warned you, it's not so easy from here. The holiday is going well. I'm glad I left my return flight open. I feel I could stay until my visa expires. It really is paradise. I've met up with an Australian father and son who are accommodating me in Ubud. *Nothing romantic*, although Mother, you would doubtless have a good laugh about my host, a man about my age, and his escapades with girls hardly older than Portia. His son is, like Virginia I'm sure, disapproving. They have graciously invited me to stay for as long as I want to.

I did climb my mountain, although I very nearly

didn't make it. That was how I met the Sparkes. This island is a real adventure, in spite of the tourists. The people are spiritually alive in a way I can't explain, except to say that I'm envious. Everyone is at peace with and in awe of their island. Or they seem to be. As for the expatriate community, it's hard to say. I think Buddy Sparke probably loves this island for precisely that spiritual element, but he's not part of it. Sometimes I think he's bent on destroying it. He sets out to do admirable things, but he's like a bull in a china shop. His sexual exploits aside, I haven't yet decided whether he is a very good or a very wicked man. Probably I will discover he is both.

I don't know when I expect to go back to Sydney. Maybe I'll just set up house here.

While she was writing, Max strode past her table on his way into town, but she didn't look up, and he, seeing her, chose to pretend he hadn't. He did not yet know where he was going, and he rather thought he would like to be alone.

When someone came and cast a shadow across her page, Emmy expected it to be him. Or Buddy. In that moment before she looked up, she had an internal flutter of hope that it might be Buddy, a flutter she would not admit even to herself.

Before she had focused her eyes on this blot across the sun, she knew from the voice that it was neither Max nor Buddy.

'Fancy,' said Frank. 'Fancy meeting you here.' He was turning his crumpled panama in his hands. 'Mind if I sit down?' He took her silence for assent. 'Didn't think I'd see you again. Thought you were mountain climbing.' He sneered. 'Thought maybe you'd fall off.'

'How charming. The surprise is mutual. I thought *you* were taking the sun in Singaraja.'

'Did you? Climb? Fall off?'

Emmy closed her eyes. Maybe he would go away.

'Didn't make it?'

'Does it matter? What brings *you* here?'

'Is this your town, then? I have my reasons. Gets a bit boring, a beach, after a while.' He called over the owner and ordered a beer, eyeing the woman's bottom as she walked away. 'More going on in Ubud. Always is.'

'I see.'

'I knew you'd be here, you know. I knew it would be you.'

'Sorry?'

'Word travels. The oldest concubine to our lord and master, eh?'

Emmy's temples thundered. She hadn't known her face could hold so much blood.

'Be careful about robbing cradle robbers, my dear.' He winked. 'Some infants have sharp teeth.'

'I have no idea what you're talking about.'

The beer came, and Frank drank it, guzzling it down almost in one. Emmy decided against sputtering her innocence; such vermin didn't merit it. Insinuating, always insinuating. But she couldn't lower her colour. When he was done, he stood to go, and he was back on the road when he called, 'See you tonight, m'dear.' Only then did Emmy realize she would have to pay for his drink.

Max didn't storm through town, exactly, but his pace was far from leisurely. Further along the road, having bypassed Emmy, he averted his eyes to avoid one of Buddy's friends, the Chief of Police. When Nyoman, the tailor's daughter, danced out into the street and clasped his arm with her eight-year-old hands, it was harder to keep going. She wanted to talk. She wanted to grow up and be a doctor, she knew already, and she wanted to tell Max all about it. Now. He patted her head and kept walking, but more slowly, with Nyoman wriggling and snatching at his side. She babbled in perfect English, but Max wasn't listening. He wanted only to get far enough from his father's house to be free of its torments and secrets. If only for an hour.

Maybe he would travel around the island on his own. Maybe he would go back to Sydney early and forget about this whole thing. Why did he really need to know his father, when his father was so much trouble? Having parents, he thought, was easily as difficult as having children must be.

Nyoman did not go away. Max turned down the Monkey Forest Road with the little girl as she explained how she would save the lives of animals and people both, all over the world. She was still with him when he reached the dip in the land that marked the beginning of the forest.

The trees and vines sprang up suddenly and made an arch above the asphalt, a jungle tunnel. Nyoman held his hand now, firmly, and her voice dropped to a whisper, but Max did not stop. He was too busy hearing the dawn silence, Jenny's sly egress from Buddy's bed. He could have been walking with his eyes shut.

Max saw the monkeys all at the same time, the moment when he realized Nyoman's singsong had stopped altogether and been replaced by a chatter that was not birdsong. Monkeys of all sizes were everywhere, great-grandfathers, infants clinging to the necks of howling mothers, macho youths batting at each other. They dangled from the branches overhead, they squatted in the undergrowth, they ran out into the road. Each one was jabbering and squealing, and every black monkey's eye was on Max and Nyoman, each wise, sharp face following the humans' every move. Some had their long, furry arms extended, waggling their prehensile thumbs.

'This is a very bad place, Max,' said Nyoman. 'Why have you brought us here?'

'What do they want?' He didn't want Nyoman to know that

he was afraid too. 'Why do you think they're looking at us?'

'My mother says they want our souls. My mother says that they are naughty spirits.'

They were coming closer. The more adventurous monkeys were sidling right up to them, shrieking.

'We should have brought offerings,' said Nyoman. 'The tourists feed them peanuts. I'm frightened.' Her arms were around his waist.

'Don't be scared, kiddo. If they're just greedy, we'll get rid of them.'

He bent and scooped up a handful of dust and pebbles, which he flung at the most aggressive monkeys. Enraged, they simply howled louder and advanced, taking courage in their numbers, an army of maddened creatures more agile than Max could have suspected.

'Run!' Max yelled, trying to disentangle himself from the little girl at his side, slapping at her hands, 'Run!'

She did, back up the road, towards the break in the trees. He saw her running, and the monkeys loping angrily towards him, baring little white teeth and pushing with their strong, furry arms, and he hesitated. He thought if he could throw them something—his watch, maybe—they would stop. He wasn't sure he could get away.

And then it struck him: from deep in his stomach, he roared. Louder than their screaming, louder than anything, he roared so it ripped inside his throat. Bewildered now, the monkeys ceased movement and sound altogether.

Max turned to walk back out of the forest, impressed with himself. That, he thought, is how to deal with the lot of them. That is how I will deal with my father. I have won, he thought.

He heard Nyoman cry out from only a few yards away, and then he crumpled almost to the ground beneath the weight of a young buck like himself, a monkey who had seen his moment.

Max had forgotten about the monkeys in the trees. He had forgotten they were everywhere. He had imagined their strength but not the smell and the heat of them. He ran with the creature clawing at his back, and he cried, the tears hot down his cheeks. At the edge of the forest, the avenged monkey simply let go, slid off to rejoin his family; but not before he sank his sharp, white teeth into Max's neck, just below the ear, and left a bloodied but perfect little love bite.

Emmy arrived back at Buddy's close to lunch-time. She had been strolling up the riverside after her breakfast, past the women beating their washing on the rocks, and had discerned a path to the sacred ridge. Although the climb was arduous, Emmy was unafraid: it was brief, for one thing, its end in sight from the outset. Nor was the path dank and overgrown, as on the mountainside; rather, it was dusty with use, and wherever the ground was steepest there were the footholds of thousands to follow.

From the summit, the river looked smaller than from Buddy's house, an idle snake beset by tiny bright insects—the women with their clothes. The air was clear, the view prolonged and crystalline, and Emmy followed the ridge northwards further than she had expected to, enjoying its flat, superior position and the gentle trickle of sweat in the small of her back. She picked out the hotel opposite, and then the house, and then, much further on, a large colonial-style residence where she pictured Buddy's American ex reclining in languorous splendour. She imagined herself in such a setting, a fascinating recluse to whom all would pay court, visited by Pod and by Mother and yes, even by a penitent William. Perhaps, as she had first thought when he left her, she had simply become too familiar to him, and such a strong whiff of the exotic would lure him back?

And then what? She kicked some hairy tufts of grass and eyed the pillared, terraced structure across the gorge. Then, a return to her lost respectability. And a loss of the exotic. So what did she want? Emmy most wanted, as she walked along the ridge, to have been born into this world, to be a part of it rather than a white ghost passing through. She would happily have given up her solid sandshoes and her gold watch to have one of four names, to be one of the women knee-deep in the river below, pounding at sarongs and cheap T-shirts from Hong Kong, to feel the air thick with ancestors and the world dominated by an unquestionable hierarchy. But by the time she was climbing across the river rocks to return to Buddy's house, she knew she longed for this simplicity only because it seemed, to a ghost like herself, simple. And it would take as unreflective a soul as Buddy's to keep going in this place, without respect or curiosity or, well, reality. Life is only simple, she thought, for the observing tourist, and even then it's not the tourist's life that is simple.

The house was in chaos when she returned. Max was lying on the vast raised bed in front of the television, with three women buzzing around, mopping his brow and fanning him. The television was on, and the women's directions were delivered at a shrill pitch to transcend the racket. Jenny emerged pestling leaves in a small bowl, to make a poultice for the wounded boy. Buddy and K'tut conversed in hushed, frowning tones. Around all this, preparations for the party continued unabated. The spicy heat from the kitchen was stronger by far than at dawn, and the two women who had so methodically examined the mosquito netting were busy encasing the veranda with it.

'What,' Emmy asked Jenny, 'is going on?'

'It's Max.' Jenny was crushing furiously at the juicy leaves. She had been crying.

'What's happened?' But Jenny had moved on.

Emmy tried Buddy next. He was slightly more forthcoming, less panic-stricken. 'He's been bitten. By a mother-fucking monkey. Looks like he'll be going to town for some shots.'

'Rabies?'

'Yeah. Not a pretty notion. You would've thought he'd know better.'

K'tut looked mournful, and said, 'I will take him with me. We will go to the doctor together.'

'And the airport? What about the plane?'

'Seeing as you mention it, you could do us a favour,' Buddy said, looking full at her for the first time in days. He had a rim of sweat on his upper lip that made him seem imperfect, needy, and Emmy knew she would acquiesce.

'It's a question of time, you see. K'tut here has got to get to the doctor, and now Max too. And I've got to be here, no question, to oversee the party. So if you could pick up Ruby and well, if anyone's with her, like Aimée or someone? And then K'tut and Max'd swing by with the bus and bring you back. In plenty of time for the party, of course.'

'But I won't recognize them, will I?'

'Yeah, you will. Take my word for it. You'd really be helping us out.'

It was true, Emmy thought, that she hadn't been earning her keep. 'It's the least I can do. If it's a help.'

'Great. You'll be going right after lunch, right?'

K'tut lingered at Emmy's side after Buddy had drifted away. 'What is the expression? Better you than me, I think you say.'

Loading Max into the bus was not easy. This was not due to his wound itself—a nip which, had its provenance been other than it was, might have passed unremarked—but rather to the attendant fuss, whipped up, in particular, by Jenny: it entailed piling more cushions upon the already plump bed at the rear of the bus; installing Max, still prone, swathed in a batik sheet, with cushions strategically placed in the small of his back and at the nape of his neck; loading water, and juice (in case he felt faint), and a large rush fan. And of course, an individual was enlisted for the purpose of fanning, should the need arise. Nyoman, witness to Max's trauma, volunteered for this mission, and it was agreed that she should go, as she would, if necessary, be able to provide any details of the experience that Max, in his fevered condition, did not recall.

Max didn't seem too shaken to Emmy. He just seemed to be annoyed, playing the role of spoilt child more aggressively than usual. He hadn't liked the poultice, he didn't like being trussed up, he didn't want to go to the doctor, but Jesus it hurt, could everyone please just leave him alone?

Soon after they set off, Emmy made her way to the back of the bus. Nyoman, far from fanning Max with subservient devotion, as Jenny would have willed her to, had succumbed to her exhausted eight-year-old nature and gone to sleep, curled at his side amid the tumbled bolsters. Emmy whispered, so as not to waken the child. 'You all right?'

'Of course I'm bloody all right. You'd think I was topped, wouldn't ya, with all the bloody carrying on.'

'You were bitten by a potentially rabid ape, weren't you? I mean, there is some cause for concern?'

'I just didn't see the fucker. Took me by surprise.'

'They give me the willies, those monkeys. That forest is a nightmare. What were you doing there, anyway?'

'Are you my fucking mother?'

Emmy, who a fortnight before would have been horrified at such language, took this without flinching. 'Sorry I asked. Just thought you might like to talk about it. The argument, or whatever it was.'

'There wasn't any argument.' Max patted at the gauze on his neck and sat up against the pillows. 'If you want to know, it's the whole frigging thing. The set-up, the party—the guests, you'll see—the arrival of my "sister" '—he spat this word—'oh, and of course, my unofficial stepmother, who could easily be mistaken for my girlfriend. The whole thing. Him.'

'Are you angry with your father then?' Emmy felt like the counsellor she had been to talk to when William first left her: foolish, clumsy, inadequate.

Max leaned back. 'Not in principle. He's allowed. Mostly I hate my own stupidity. I can't go home now, not for ages. I could've gone tomorrow.'

'Sorry?'

'The rabies.' He bared his teeth. 'I might go mad. Foam at the mouth. Devour you all.'

'How will I recognize these people at the airport?' Emmy asked.

'You will. Ruby'll probably be the littlest on the plane. And she'll either be with her nanny, or with Aimée. And if it's Aimée, you'll know.'

'Is she very beautiful?'

'Nothing like. It's not that. You'll know.'

In order that K'tut might make his appointment on time, and to ensure that the doctor would fit in both his ulcerous and his rabid clients, the bus let Emmy off at the airport some time before the plane was due. She had nothing to read; she bought a Coke and sat on one of the plastic seats to wait. She recalled her arrival at the airport not so long before, dizzied by valium and strong drink, suddenly loosed at dusk into the tropical smells and the teeming bustle she had imagined from inside the air-conditioned comfort of the jet. There had been porters and taxi drivers, hawkers of all sorts, sinister to the bewildered person she had been, all trying, she had thought, to lure her into their vans or cars, drive her to remote corners of the darkened island and dismember her.

In the shaded afternoon silence, she found those irrational fears painful to recall, as she envisioned her puffing, flustered former self hauling her suitcase across the floor, brushing away offers of help like so many equatorial insects. How much of that arrival had been imagined? How full and clamorous could this hall have been? The image of her staggering self seemed murky, distant, unrelated to the calm, browned woman in linen shorts she had become, sitting in the shade with a Coke, watching a handful of airport employees loiter with as much professional poise as herself.

All her most pressing anxieties had receded also: since taking on the problems of Buddy's household, she found those of her own hard to remember. Emmy sat thinking of William, of her own place in Sydney society, of being divorced, of her alien daughter and Pod's still more alien boyfriend—it was almost inconceivable that so distant an existence could continue concurrently with the one in which she now found herself. That a world of turquoise swimming-pools, modern art and picture windows overlooking Sydney harbour, of coiffed, bejewelled women and well-manicured, suited men, could proceed beneath the same glowing sunrise and the same thick, black night as the world of K'tut, or Jenny, or even Buddy himself—it was hard to believe. That world of Emmy's entire adult life felt as distant as the blurred, childhood photographs in her mind's eye: herself and Virginia raising a secret command tent in the back garden of their south London terraced house, or Emmy's fistfights at school, when Virginia would purse her lips and inform the teacher that her sister was 'at it again'.

When Emmy had left Sydney, she hadn't considered staying away more than a month. Sitting in the airport lounge, she couldn't imagine going back, just as she had never considered returning to a London she wouldn't even know, and she wondered when the urge, the need, for her real life might overcome her. Until she had made certain things clear to herself, she knew the allure of the island would not allow her to leave.

When she had decided to climb Abang, Emmy had been looking for a change, a spiritual sign by which to guide her old

114

life. She had found many things, as yet undeciphered, that crowded around in the still, scented afternoons and the blackest nights. She felt but could not see them, and she longed for the filter that would make them visible, throw them into moral relief. Emmy, in this Sparke life, was simply waiting, watching, until her own outline might become clear.

The plane from Bangkok was the only one due to arrive that afternoon, and few people came to meet it. But Emmy had not realized that the flight from Bangkok was also the flight from Jakarta, Kuala Lumpur, Abu Dhabi and London. What landed was not a modest jet but a great silver fish, a Garuda 747, which spilled out hundreds of people of all ages and races and sizes on to the steaming tarmac.

Within moments, the sleepy airport was transformed: taxis and *bemos* lurched up to the doors; customs officers leapt into their plexiglass booths; the agents at the hotel and car counters stubbed out their cigarettes and stepped forward with professional eagerness. Noises erupted everywhere, whirrings and clatterings, the aggressive thud of immigration stamps, the whooshing of feet, suitcases and trolleys on the linoleum floor. And above all, the calling, growling and screeching of nervous tourists and polished salespeople, striking bargains and making deals for the ride to the beach resorts. Emmy was more discomfited by this activity than she liked, and was forced to concede that her inner transformation was less than complete, but more than that, she was aware that in this vast stream of people, she was likely to miss little Ruby altogether.

The sea of faces was overwhelming: British, unboiled and boiled, starting or continuing their vacations; leathered Australians stopping off for R&R on their way home; urban Javanese who had flown rather than driven to their holiday site; a few Balinese returning to their families; and a sprinkling of Thais and Malaysian Chinese, whose reasons Emmy could only guess at. It was among these last that she would hope to find the child, at the side of a woman, either recognizable or not. Emmy craned her neck. Looking for Ruby, she stood up and tried to peer between the crowd's knees. She was jostled and bumped as she stood.

Only when the flood thinned to a trickle did Emmy see, and know she had seen, the right faces. They were standing at a customs desk, or rather, Aimée was, with Ruby propped on her hip. Ruby was Eurasian—Emmy had forgotten that she would be—with dark, almond eyes and pale skin, the solid, purposeful air of Buddy and a tiny replica of his bulbed nose. She resembled a small, darker version of Max, her chubby child's body smothered by a pink frilled concoction that looked both inappropriate and expensive. As for her mother, Emmy thought, Max had been right. She just knew that the woman was Aimée, and could not entirely explain why.

The woman was very young—she looked no older than Pod. She was not particularly beautiful; not, certainly, in the way that Suchi was. Nor was she elaborately dressed: she wore jeans, a white T-shirt and sandals. She resembled a Sydney university student. But she moved and looked around her with a certain assurance—or was it determination?—that spoke of experience, perhaps of disappointment, and of a bitter will. She was the sort of woman who attracted attention, who elicited in others at once a vague unease and a desire to protect.

'Aimée?' Emmy asked, when at last the woman and child walked through to the waiting area.

'Yes?' The woman's gaze was harsh.

'I—my name is Emmy Richmond—I've been sent to meet you. By Buddy. There was something of a crisis, Max was bitten, and . . . May I help you carry something? This must be Ruby?'

'I see. Horace was not able to come himself.' She said this as a statement, and not a pleasing one. Her accent was finishing-school British.

'Well, as I'm sure you know, the party . . . and K'tut and

116

Max have gone to the doctor. Rabies shots, you see. They'll be along soon, I expect.'

Ruby tittered appreciatively and tugged at her mother's hair. But Aimée only said again, 'I see.'

'Would you like something to drink? Was the trip tiring?'

'The landing is difficult for Ruby. Her ears. Yes, a drink. Very nice.' She spoke to her daughter in Thai. When she did, her face changed, let go, became prettier. 'Ruby will have a grape Fanta. And I—a gin and tonic. Thank you.'

Emmy puzzled over the choice as she left them to settle in the sticky vinyl seats. It was so laughably wrong, like the little pink dress. But there was no laughter in this young woman.

'I should perhaps explain,' Emmy said on her return, 'that I'm not—my connection is—I'm just staying with the Sparkes. A coincidence, really.'

'A friend from Australia?'

'That's where I live. But no, we met climbing Abang, you see, and Max, you know, Buddy's, uh, son—he offered me a place to stay. I'm just visiting the island on my own.'

'Sacred Abang, of course. Horace is very keen on conquering that mountain, time and again. In Thailand, there are other things that have the same effect on him.' She sipped daintily at her gin and tonic and watched Ruby sucking at the Fanta. Ruby's lips and tongue were purpling, and Emmy knew it was only a matter of time till there was purple down the front of her dress as well. Ruby wore pink shoes. Her little socks were trimmed with lace.

'Your daughter's beautiful. A lovely little girl. And so well-behaved.'

Aimée seemed almost to laugh. Then she said, 'I would like her to grow up in Australia. Or in England. I would like that very much.'

'Would you? Surely in Thailand . . . '

'Bangkok is not a good place for children. I know—I myself

was one not so long ago.'

Emmy smiled a fake smile. She could not think of an answer to that. After a moment, she said, 'I had a lovely childhood in London. Of course, that *was* a long time ago. I suspect one city is much like another, nowadays.'

'I do not,' Aimée said.

Emmy felt annoyed. She had, after all, just been making conversation. She looked at her watch. The airport had sunk to its earlier sleepy state and she dreaded the wait for her vaccinated saviours. It was not easy to speak to this old young woman, who seemed unable to laugh, and who already made her feel an interloper. As if watching were not such an innocent activity after all.

When, at last, the bus arrived, there were only muted greetings for Aimée, although K'tut swung Ruby into the air and hugged her warmly.

'They love children, these people,' said Aimée, as if K'tut couldn't hear.

'You'd better get this show on the road, or we'll miss Buddy's precious party,' yelled Max from the rear of the bus. 'It's gonna be a beaut.'

When they arrived back in Ubud, it was dusk. The path to the house was lit with firesticks, and the main room had fallen into prepared quiet. There were no shoes at the door, and nobody emerged to greet the returned travellers. Those who had worked so hard all day had retreated to ready themselves, to bathe and scent their skin and to smoothe the creases in their most elegant clothes.

K'tut carried a sleeping Ruby and the luggage to the spare bedroom, upstairs. Aimée settled into a wicker armchair on the netted veranda and lit a long, drooping cigarette, and Max, stepping haltingly, as if in pain, climbed to lie a while on his bed. Emmy was about to go down to her room when Aimée spoke, without turning her head.

'I see Horace is not here either. I thought he might take some interest in his daughter.'

'He can't be far. Last minute details, I expect.'

'Or a woman, perhaps?'

'Oh, I wouldn't think so. Business, rather.' Emmy felt defensive on his behalf.

'Ah, yes. There will doubtless be a lot of business this evening. How forgetful of me.' So saying, Aimée stubbed out her cigarette on the pristine floor, ignoring the ashtray in front of her. As if she knew about Jenny and were making a point.

Max felt terrible. He felt worse than when the monkey bit him. The doctor hadn't inspired confidence—even K'tut thought him a very bad man. And the shots made him feel like someone had unpacked his insides on a table and stuffed them in again any old way.

It was hard to tell how much of this pain was in his head. When the doctor stuck the needle into him, Max had tried to think of good things, but Sydney and its range of good and bad were too distant for him to focus on; and when he thought of the best thing he thought, despite himself, of the taste of Jenny's mouth. He thought of having sex, which he hadn't ever done (although he pretended to all his friends and even to his father that he had), and which he imagined would be the best thing, superior to anything else. And when he thought of sex—just as the doctor jabbed at the soft flesh of his stomach—it was Jenny's face he saw, and the texture of her skin he felt beneath his fingertips. It was since then that he had felt terrible.

Max didn't know whether to lock his door and pull the shutters and lie absolutely still, or whether to give in and go to the party, as his father wanted him to. Buddy had left an envelope on Max's bed, which contained two substantial joints and a note which said, 'These should do the trick. I'm counting on you. See you at 7.'

In an attempt to make up his mind, he lit one of the joints and sat down cross-legged on the floor. He heard an unfamiliar tread on the stair—Aimée—and heard her pause outside his door. He inhaled and held the acrid smoke in his lungs until it trickled from his nostrils of its own accord. He shut his eyes and sat motionless, smoking, until he heard her steps continue down the corridor.

The first guests arrived before Buddy had returned. Suchi and her parents, who had come on foot, walked up the path promptly at seven. Emmy heard them and peered from behind her door to see who it was, but she did not then rush upstairs. She left them instead to Jenny's care. Jenny and at least a dozen helpers had come up the path while Emmy was dressing. They all wore sarongs of the most elaborate batiks, beneath lacy-bodiced blouses with fitted sleeves. Each woman had her hair sleekly knotted behind her head, and a flower at her ear. As they passed, Emmy heard the jangle of jewellery. These women were the hostesses—in the absence of the host—and they laid out platters and served drinks and settled their guests into comfortable chairs from which they could watch the last glimmerings in the evening sky and the night stars awakening.

Others came after Suchi and her parents, until a steady murmur of conversation wafted down to Emmy's room. But still she couldn't hear the broad twang of Buddy's accent. Someone—Emmy assumed it was Jenny—put on music, popular Indonesian singing with a steady beat. It struck Emmy somehow as an act of desperation. She decided that it was time to join the crowd. She dreaded, for Jenny and for Suchi, the appearance of Aimée without Buddy there: Aimée was a woman who would just *know* about Buddy's connection to these two. She thought of what Max had told her about Buddy saying that Eastern and Western women, in such matters, did not mix, and she thought that Aimée was just that, a dangerous mix of Eastern and Western, clearly seeing both ways of being and yet belonging to neither. Emmy thought she should be there.

Emmy wore the one good dress she had brought with her, made of white linen and cotton, with large blue cornflowers on it. It was sleeveless, revealing her ample but well-bronzed arms, and skilfully belted to minimize her hips and full bosom. She wore a long lapis necklace that brought out the blue of the flowers. Her hair swung neatly at her chin. She applied a little make-up and felt quite elegant, worthy of the most sophisticated Double Bay garden party.

But as soon as she walked into the gathering, she felt all wrong. Too old, for one thing, and at a great remove. She had dressed for the wrong life.

The room was filling up, and although there were guests of all ages, the women were all young, with the exception of Suchi's mother and one other Balinese woman in late middle age. They were dressed in sarongs and blouses similar to those that Jenny and the other girls wore, only finer still, spun in silk, threaded with gold or silver. The younger guests, both Balinese and Western, were clad in an array of styles, but all of them casual. Or trendier. Or something. Emmy wished she had worn her batik shift, sewn by the Ubud tailor. But it was too late for that.

The room was divided into knots of conversation, largely Westerners together and Balinese among themselves. Suchi's parents sat on the sofa and spoke to no one, alternately smiling at the room at large, and looking nervous. The guests of honour—Kraut and Madé—did not appear to have arrived. Nor were Max or K'tut or Aimée in evidence. Nobody looked around when Emmy came in; nobody seemed to be waiting for Buddy to show up, or even expecting him.

She was wondering whether a discreet retreat would be remarked upon, when Jenny, extricating herself from a conversation with a bloated Australian man in a Hawaiian print shirt, came up to greet her.

'Emmy, come to meet some guests.' Jenny took her arm. 'A glass of punch?'

The punch was made with fruit juices and rice liquor and it was strong and sweet.

'Where's Buddy?'

'I expect him back any time. He is perhaps with the groom. They have always business. The party is going well, yes?'

'Looks it. Aimée did come, you know.'

Jenny nodded, while smiling across the room at Suchi's parents. 'Of course she did. We knew she would. She will come downstairs soon. She hates me.'

'You? Why?'

'She says I steal her clothes. She said. Last time. I cleaned them for her and she says it was stealing. Did K'tut not tell you this? She is from Thailand. People from Thailand are often very wicked. Come, meet this nice couple.'

Jenny said all this while nodding and smiling at guests. Her expression was unchanged as she accosted a man and a woman who stood smoking. They were perhaps a decade younger than Emmy, both with long, lank hair tucked behind their ears. The man, Aaron, had a beaked nose and wore an expensive rumpled suit, with Birkenstocks poking out clumsily beneath it. The woman, Gaya, was tiny and draped in tinkling silver. Her batik halter mini-dress gaped to reveal small freckled breasts. No tan-line, Emmy noted.

They gave her the once-over and didn't seem too interested, but when Jenny introduced her as Buddy's house-guest, their expressions changed. They were Americans.

'Been with Buddy long, then?' Gaya asked.

'I've been here a couple of weeks. We met mountain climbing, and . . . I'm Max's guest, really, I suppose. He invited me. Do you both live here?'

'Wouldn't live anywhere else! Couldn't go back. We're trying to Westernize the kids enough so that they have a choice, but it's tough.' Aaron pointed out Raven and Azure, a scruffy little boy of eight or nine and a smaller, slightly more presentable girl. They were tussling in a corner over a hand-held computer game. They looked pretty Western to Emmy.

Gaya explained that Raven attended a progressive boarding-school in California, but that Azure, at six, didn't yet go to school. She helped them in the French restaurant they ran on Kuta Beach, handing sweets to customers along with their bills. Gaya seemed to think this was cute; Emmy thought of child labour laws.

She could see that Gaya and Aaron couldn't live anywhere else, and looking around the party she was aware that there were numerous exiles in a similar position, long-haired idealists, wrinkling and thickening, leftovers from the seventies.

'You wouldn't think it, but we're quite a tight community. We look out for each other. We hang out together. You know. It's hilarious, really, I mean, people come and can't go. We just love it so much. And of course you can't get a proper working visa, or own land or anything, so we're all a bit on the sly. Helping each other out, like I said.' Gaya laughed. 'Buddy's pretty new, but he's a *big* helper. He's really got this town under his thumb—he's in with all the right people.' She winked. 'It must come in handy for you, no?'

'I hadn't really thought about it.' Emmy looked around and saw all these white faces as a strong, taut vine, spreading and choking the island. A tight community indeed.

'Speak of the devil,' said Aaron.

Buddy was in the doorway, red-faced, grinning, his arm around a younger man with pointed ears who looked somehow familiar.

'Come on everyone, listen here a minute. Let's have a cheer for the man of the evening'—he pushed his companion forward and brought a Balinese woman from behind him—'and his lovely new wife.'

'Good on ya, Kraut!' called the fat man in the Hawaiian shirt.

'Gustav and Madé! Awright!' Aaron boomed, raising his glass.

The room filled with whistles and catcalls. 'To the bride and groom!' 'Hooray!' 'Cheers, mate!' 'Madé, you're fucking gorgeous!'

'Isn't she?' whispered Gaya. Madé was tall and supple. She looked like an Indonesian cover girl, with her long, black hair framing her face and swooping down her back, and her perfect, open features. She seemed pleased and embarrassed and she reached for Gustav's hand.

'Kiss!' someone shouted. 'Let's have a kiss!'

Gustav turned and planted a smacking embrace on Madé's lips. She flushed. A flashbulb went off.

'They're not much for kissing, the Balinese,' whispered Gaya. 'Not big on PDA.'

'Sorry?'

'Public displays of affection. You know.'

But Emmy wasn't really listening. She was looking at Gustav, Kraut, the German. She had placed him: a sinister adviser on a *bemo* outside Kintamani. A Westerner who lived there. It was like a conspiracy, these people who kept reappearing. The tightening vine. And behind them, on the doorstep, she caught a glimpse of Frank, veined and leering.

The crowd moved forward to enfold and congratulate. Or the Western crowd did: Emmy noticed that the Balinese, like herself, lingered on the edges, restrained. She spotted K'tut standing beside the Ubud Police Chief, by the door to the veranda, and she made her way over to him.

'You're not going to kiss the bride?' she said. He didn't answer.

After a moment, he replied: 'This party is for Kraut. She celebrates with her own people.'

Emmy looked at him, his serious, thin face. It was the first indication that not everyone approved of this match.

'Do you think it's a mistake?'

His gaze flickered back to the doorway. 'There is no attention for the elders,' he said. And it was true that an older Balinese couple, presumably Madé's parents, hovered by the entrance, unattended. They were not smiling.

K'tut spoke to the Police Chief in Balinese, and the two of them left Emmy's side for the company of this pair, with much nodding and courtesy and, Emmy could see, an exaggerated *politesse* on K'tut's part that he would never waste on Westerners.

When the loud toasts were over, the party went on, and Emmy stood for a time on the sidelines, watching, sipping her punch. She watched Buddy's American ex shake her peroxide curls at the neck of the Chief of Police; she watched Frank clap Aaron on the back and then spill his drink on the other man's expensive linen suit; she observed the knot of Ubud youths pouring straight *arak* into their punch glasses from a jug behind the television. Her eyes followed Jenny through the crowd, and she winced as she saw hands, Australian, American, men's hands, clap Jenny on the shoulder, catch Jenny for a hug, rest on Jenny's small behind, and Jenny smiled all the while because amused endurance was her only ticket to Sydney and accounting school. She watched Madé's parents join Suchi's on the sofa, where all four sat looking bewildered and addressing each other only occasionally; and she saw Suchi, looking frail and even pregnant, clinging with both arms to one of Buddy's while he laughed and drank amid a group of men and paid her presence no heed whatsoever.

Someone offered Emmy more punch and she took it, drinking

less cautiously now, accustomed to the burning in the back of her throat. She tried to imagine the pasts that had brought these people to this place, and found she couldn't at all. She wasn't capable of knowing the lives of the Balinese around her, and as for the others, who could say what choices or mistakes or desires had made them leave everything for this delicious, empty life 'on the sly', as Gaya put it? She could not even read them through her code of luck: they had made their own, it was true, but she didn't know whether it was good or bad. There was something amoral in the atmosphere, an absence of absolutes.

Wearied, she took another glass of punch and wandered on to the netted veranda. It was quieter there, and she could hear nature hissing and singing and croaking beneath the voices. She sat and sipped and ignored a young Balinese couple who, at the other end of the balcony, whispered and fumbled at each other.

They rejoined the party when dance music started—Jenny's doing again, Emmy thought—and then she was alone on the darkened fringe of the festivities. Until, that is, Buddy emerged at the far door, in conversation. With Kraut, Emmy realized, and with Frank. They spoke quickly and earnestly, and although the *arak* was making everything swim a little, Emmy listened.

' . . . about it tonight?' the German was saying. 'Here?'

'Just the basics. The dates.' Buddy said.

'Next month, I don't know more.'

'I've got to kick around here another month?' Frank whined.

'You can go to Bangkok sooner if you like. We can contact you there. As long as you don't get yourself arrested on drunk and disorderly, like last time. Aimée can bring you the cash later. She doesn't need to know. Kraut, just tell me, you're sure of the quality?'

Drugs, Emmy thought. You're paranoid, she thought.

'You've seen the Polaroids yourself. A lot of temple carvings this time. And one—'

'OK, fine. Are you sure they've got to go across by Chiang Mai? I would've thought—'

Kraut broke in: 'It's still the safest. Better pay off the scouts in—'

There was a sudden clatter and a mop of black curls pressed up against Buddy's knee. He whooped and slung the small cloud of pink frills into the air above his head. 'Hey beautiful! How's my baby? How's my Ruby?'

He twirled her and she chuckled, and Aimée stepped outside to join them. She wore a luminous white chiffon dress and seemed to move in a pool of quiet. A pool, Emmy thought, of hostile quiet. In the moment of her coming, Frank and Kraut managed to make themselves scarce.

'Aimée, gorgeous!'—Buddy's cheer struck Emmy as forced— 'How's the mother of my daughter, eh?' With Ruby still clasped against one hip, Buddy threw an arm around Aimée's neck and slurped at it.

'Busy as usual?'

'C'mon Aimée, show us a little affection?'

He was twice her age, easily. It was unseemly. Emmy longed to leave but feared that she would be noticed if she did so, caught eavesdropping. Her head spun a little more, and her throat tickled furiously from the dregs of the punch. If she was going to cough anyway, Emmy figured, she might as well go back inside.

Many people, particularly the Balinese, had left. Suchi, for example, had apparently gone and taken her parents with her. The powerful *arak* had taken effect, and those remaining were speaking or dancing intently, above all intimately, like members of the tight community they were. Emmy saw Frank and saw him see her, and she cast around for any group to join to avoid him. A child molester and a drug runner, she thought. It boggled the mind.

Max and Jenny leaned by the front door. Emmy was on the verge of approaching them when she saw that their fingers were interlaced, their feet shuffling into mutually satisfying crevices, their murmurings barely audible. She stood next to them, they next to the door, so she passed beside them and went out.

It was, perhaps, best. Elsewhere, Emmy had always held to her policy of leaving the party before there was no party left. This was part of her code, but she felt, nonetheless, that in this place, at this time, her code led only to anticlimax. There must have been something she had missed? She stood on the doorstep and struggled with an itch of anticipation that she hadn't felt so strongly since adolescence: there were truths and adventures in the room behind her. Perhaps there was even evil.

But Emmy's adult self was destined to triumph. She followed this tingling flurry with the thought that, among other things, the room contained Frank. Responsible Emmy reached for the railing and started down the steps.

'Emmy?' It was an unfamiliar voice. Or rather, a voice unfamiliar in the pronunciation of her name. 'Are you off already? Let me walk you to your room?'

Buddy joined her on the grass. Emmy said nothing, but her heart jolted into complicated palpitations. He had seen her, she supposed, seeing him.

'I've been wanting to talk to you,' he went on. 'All night. If only to tell you how great you look. Best-looking woman at the party.'

'*Really*, Buddy—'

'I'm not trying to chat you up. Believe me, if I wanted to do that, I've had plenty of time. It's just—in the run of things, we've hardly spoken. And I don't want you to think I'm an ungracious bastard.'

'Not at all. Not at all.'

They had started walking, and strolled over to the low stone barrier beyond the pool site, to the point where the land dropped sharply and the view, in the daytime, was best. Now it was merely an array of amorphous dark forms that seemed to Emmy to swell and contract with her irregular breathing.

'I suppose I really wanted to say thank you, especially for being such a friend to Max. A surrogate mum, almost.'

Emmy frowned.

'I mean, in the nicest possible way. Him and me, getting acquainted, it's been a bit of a rough ride. And I know I don't set the easiest example for a kid.'

'I think this is a wonderful experience for Max. I really do.'

'No need to lie. But he's a good bloke.' Buddy took her arm. 'You would've thought we'd have met before,' he said. His voice sounded peculiar. 'Australia isn't so big. Maybe when Max goes home, you'll look after him?'

'He has a mother, doesn't he?'

'She's not your class. Don't think I don't know it.'

This struck Emmy simultaneously as vulgar and strangely exciting, and she wasn't at all surprised when his thick face suddenly blocked her view of the night, and his lips landed somewhere between her cheek and her mouth. She didn't resist, but he didn't pursue the embrace. Rather, he took her arm again and walked her back towards her door. There, with the discretion and grace befitting, Emmy thought, a far more sophisticated host than he, he bade her a swift goodnight and departed.

Neither Buddy nor Emmy saw the fluttering white chiffon on the veranda, but Aimée had watched them, closely, until they had disappeared together beneath the veranda's overhang beneath her feet.

Max couldn't believe it. This was like a nightmare. He was stoned but not that stoned. He and Jenny: only minutes ago he had been tracing the outline of her shoulder, her neck, her jaw—and it had been fantastic, as if there wasn't anyone in the room besides them.

She had looked pretty happy too. Or so he had thought. His stomach had been hurting, but he had hardly felt it; what had been bothering him far more was the need to pee. And when it couldn't be ignored any longer, he had gone.

In the loo, the combination of his bladder and the aftermath of his shots had assailed him and, while peeing, he had almost puked. But he had finished and washed his face. He could guarantee that his malaise had lasted no more than a minute.

But now she was gone. There were still people in the room, even some dancing, but she wasn't one of them. He looked on the veranda, where Ruby lay sleeping on a rattan sofa, and Aimée, impassive, chain-smoked beside her. But Jenny wasn't there.

It occurred to him that she might have chosen to prepare herself, in his room, so he went up. But no lights were on, and nothing stirred but the gecko in the thatch. He went out to his small terrace, to see whether he could see her, wandering, perhaps, in the garden by the pool, or on the path towards the road.

And then he heard her childlike giggle. It came again, from next door, muffled by the half-open shutters of his father's room and by the billowing curtains. But it was Jenny, no doubt about it.

Max took off his clothes, lay on the bed, and tried to cry. Short of tearing the house down, it seemed the only appropriate response. No tears would come, but as his eyes remained resolutely dry, great whorls of pain spiralled outwards from the bite on his neck.

He felt as though he was on fire. He knew it was the doctor's fault. He got up to vomit, and his toes seemed to strike shards of glass with each step. Vomiting eased the pain a little, and brought tears to his eyes, but Max still felt as though he were being stabbed inside and out. Even his soul, he thought, was being stabbed.

He lay there and felt terrible and wondered whether he would throw up again, until he started to sweat and fell asleep— two things, both at once pleasant and unpleasant, that occurred at exactly the same time.

Emmy listened to the fading sounds of the disbanding guests, as she lay in bed and pressed her toes against the crisp sheet. She didn't know what to make of anything any more. Buddy's breath, so briefly against her cheek, had been warm, sweet and alcoholic, reminiscent of rum. She could still feel and smell it.

She conjured his stocky, athletic form in her mind's eye and compared it with the lean, patrician physique of her ex-husband. William had never been sexy. She imagined Buddy meeting Pod, and she smiled. It would be absurd if, after all the tension over Pietro, Emmy were to bring home someone equally unsuitable.

But this was nonsense. An amicable kiss did not constitute a romance. Nothing of the kind. The man hadn't bothered to notice her, Emmy knew, until she was somehow useful. He abused trust and affection; he chased girls, not women; he was possibly a law-breaker, a drug-dealer, even. And Emmy was not, she reassured herself, a fool. Absolutely not. But still, but yes, she had to ask herself whether, if the opportunity were to arise . . . And no, she didn't want to, couldn't, answer.

LONDON

AS ANGELICA REACHED for the mixing bowl in which she intended to make the salad, she could feel it splitting, slightly, along its large crack. Twice repaired, it was really two halves of a bowl held together by Superglue and some obscure law of physics. An obscure and obviously defective law of physics. But Angelica had neither time nor another bowl; Nikhil was coming for supper, in a matter of minutes, and the salad wasn't made, the salmon mousse hadn't been decorated, while she herself was still in her slip, with her hair pinned up in a ramshackle, inelegant way. And Angelica wanted things to go well.

Were she to pursue her duty rather than her pleasure, she ought to be visiting Virginia on this evening. It was Saturday, and Virginia's mother had called yesterday to say that 'Virginia was feeling very poorly and might be for some time'. Unfortunately, she'd called when Angelica was extremely busy at work, and while Angelica had heard, and hadn't forgotten, she had been unable to garner the details of Virginia's illness, which, in a funny way, made it seem unreal. And of course she *had* invited Nikhil on Thursday, before she had known that there was anything the matter with Virginia, and there was a certain degree of duty—neighbourly, friendly—being discharged in this engagement as well.

Angelica, as she smattered her face with powder using a large, feathery brush, decided to consider who needed her more, this being where her Christian duty obviously lay. Virginia, if ill, was most likely asleep; if not, then she was being tended by her mother—granted, an imperfect companion, but certainly her friend was not alone. Angelica knew that Virginia would be secretly hoping for a visit from her Angel, but were she to abandon Nikhil, he would sit amid textbooks in his little flat, alone and possibly unloved in a country far from home. Dismayed at the thought, Angelica squeezed rather feverishly at the pump spray of her perfume, and succeeded in enveloping both herself and her clothing in a daunting volume of scent. At which juncture, of course, there was a knock at the door.

Nikhil came into the centre of her sitting-room and blinked in the early evening light. She saw him eye the table set for two, and blink more furiously still.

'Drink? What would you like?' she twittered. 'I've got both gin and scotch hidden away here—although you mustn't tell Virginia. She's practically signed the pledge!' She paused, attempting to gauge Nikhil's discomfort. 'How about a glass of this delightful-looking Soave you've brought? Yummy!'

'I don't actually drink alcohol,' he said.

'Never mind then—you and everyone else I know.'

He settled on a mixture of orange juice and mineral water, which he held on his knee, looking dark and faintly miserable in the embrace of a voluptuous peach armchair.

'I'll be right with you,' Angelica called from the kitchen. She hadn't expected such nerves. She resolved to generate patter. Perhaps she would be visiting Virginia after all.

'I hope you don't mind,' she called, 'that I didn't ask anyone else. I mean, you might have preferred it?'

His protest, from the depths of the chair, was feeble.

'It's just that I only ever see you with a cast of thousands— our neighbourhood God Squad! And I thought, after all those helpings of cake and all the times you've listened to us chattering away, that it'd be nice for me to get to know you a little. To hear what interests you, you know? Really nice.'

There was silence from the sitting-room and then Nikhil said, 'You've been speaking about me to Virginia Simpson?'

This brought Angelica to the kitchen door, from which she fixed his dark eyes with her large blue ones. 'What on earth makes you say that? How very peculiar! Of course not.'

'But she came to see me.'

'She stopped off, I know, before the meeting on Wednesday, because I wasn't home yet. I suppose, subconsciously, it may have made me think, but—'

'So this is not a campaign to convert me?'

Angelica, indelicate though it was, guffawed. 'To convert you? Whatever to? To our God Squad?'

He nodded.

'Certainly not.' There was a level on which she found Nikhil's suggestion offensive, although this was in itself troubling, as prose-lytizing was part of her Christian mission. 'Look at it this way,' she said after a generous swallow of her gin and tonic, 'the best adver-tisement for what we're on about is our meeting itself.' He made a face, which made her laugh. 'OK, maybe not the *best* advert. But you *come*, after all, which is more than most. And you're not even a Christian! So you see, if you're willing to do our recruitment for us, why would we work overtime? If I wanted a potential Christ-ian around for supper, trust me, I know plenty of them. I have other friends, you know. Unlike some of our number.'

'Surely the company of the ungodly must put you at con-stant risk?' Nikhil asked. He didn't seem to be joking.

'It's not as though I've taken closed orders, honestly, just because I live through my faith and am happy to admit it.'

'What does it mean, then, for you to do so?'

'Goodness, you are serious. Be careful, or I'll mistake you for a potential after all!'

'I'd like to know.'

'Oh, Nikhil. I don't much feel like talking about it.' This was not the turn Angelica had hoped the conversation would take. She had even given herself licence to forget all that this evening. She had decided to sin a little, if it seemed appropriate. And then, of course, to repent. But this could hardly be admitted. 'It's not easy to talk about,' she said. 'It's very personal, I think. Let's just say that I had some bad experiences, and it was God who showed me a way out. I mean, I really believe that song you're taught as children, "God is Love", you don't know it, I suppose? Well, I guess it just means that God's love is there for me if I allow it to be, and it's the only thing that makes life meaningful. The only thing I've found, anyway.'

'And the church, your church?'

'What about it? They're the people who believe what I believe, and we celebrate together. In a way that's truly alive. Our faith is very strong. Is that so strange?'

'But the teachings?'

'You'll have to come and see, Nikhil. You'll have to come to church and see. It's the only way to explain. God is there, like an energy, this incredible force in the room. And He can work miracles. He does.'

'And His judgements?'

'I just don't think my feelings can be put into words. Not properly. Anyway, you hear all this from the group, all the time. Surely it's my turn to ask questions?'

Nikhil gestured acquiescence.

'For example, why do you want to know?'

'Isn't it about who you are?'

'Oh honestly, it's part of who I am, but so is whether I eat oysters or whether my parents divorced when I was a child.'

'I see.'

'They did, in case you care. But I wanted to ask *you* questions. About India. About what it's like?'

Nikhil was not as shy as she had thought, and proved eager to talk about his home. He conjured up smells and tastes and the little noises of people living their lives, but against this backdrop he set the outline of a life that sounded remarkably unexotic, that sounded, in some respects, quite akin to an adolescence in north London. Oh, of course, in many ways he made clear how different it was, and when he spoke about his sister, her upbringing sounded more constrained than Angelica's. But she didn't sound such a different person to Angelica; she sounded like someone Angelica could be friends with, with whom she could indulge the wild streak that had to be hidden at all costs from people like Virginia Simpson. When Nikhil told her about Rupica's elopement, Angelica felt deeply satisfied.

'That's exactly,' she said, 'what I would've done.'

Nikhil recoiled in surprise, and a glob of salmon mousse fell from his fork to his trousers.

'Why?' he asked. 'Maybe then you can tell me why?'

'Lust for adventure, I suppose. For the new, for what's unknown and exciting.'

'These alone are not reasons, not for this decision. It has something to do with her understanding of God, with the appeal of Christianity.'

'Well, maybe,' Angelica said, hoping the room's pink light would mask her embarrassment. 'Maybe it's a whole lot of things at once. Maybe she found him exciting, and she found his beliefs exciting, because loving a person and loving God—or the gods_ —it's all bound up together, isn't it? Like, it's like, loving him gave her access to a new way of loving *everything*. So that then she had two ways, her own and his.'

'Hmph,' Nikhil said, to his mousse.

'Well, it's just a thought. It's just how I would feel, I mean, say, if I fell in love with a Hindu, say, with someone like you—'

He looked up and quickly down again. Angelica had over-stepped, she felt. She'd embarrassed both of them. She stood up and started to clear, aware that Nikhil was looking her in the bosom because he couldn't bring himself to look her in the face.

'I'd love to meet her. She sounds terrific. Tell me again, where is she living?'

'Scotland. The Isle of Skye. I have an address. I haven't written.'

'Skye's gorgeous. And summer is *the* time to go. Right around now, it's daylight till midnight. It's spectacular. Have you thought of it?'

'I have a lot of work. And she and I, we have not spoken since then.'

'I'm sure you don't have *that* much work. And there's no time like the present for healing rifts. You know, in the Jewish faith they have a day set aside in the calendar for making amends. For patching up broken relationships. It's a brilliant idea.'

'Yom Kippur is in the autumn. And I am not Jewish.' Nikhil was getting prickly.

'I could go with you. I could be your guide. I *love* Skye. We used to go there on holiday when I was a child. I'd take you to all my favourite places. We always stayed in a wonderful old hunting lodge called the Tarbish Hotel, where I used to fish in the river with my father. And there are amazing mountains—the landscape is incredible! I could show you so much—we'd have such fun! I'm on holiday this coming week, in fact.'

Angelica had overstepped again, this time perhaps too far.

'You will forgive me,' Nikhil said, with a stiffness and solemnity whose origin was not clear, 'If I protest that we hardly know each other.'

She ground the coffee in a rage. Rage at herself and her stupidity. Because now it was perfectly clear—it was the only thing she *could* see clearly—that she would be visiting Virginia this evening after all.

By Saturday afternoon, Virginia was ready to get out of bed. The events of a few days before seemed to have receded to a fuzzy past that might have been weeks or even months ago. She knew she had been sleeping a lot, and she knew that there were reasons why she wanted only to keep on sleeping, but she wasn't quite sure what they were, and her irritating tree-trunk of a mother wouldn't say.

'You're just a little worn out, Ginny,' Mrs Simpson kept repeating, as she tucked the sheets around Virginia's chin and tried to keep her from rising. 'You've been overwrought. And the doctor has left these for you to take.' Whereupon she would pop a smooth, plasticky tablet on Virginia's horrified tongue and ply her with water.

By late Saturday afternoon, it simply seemed imperative that Virginia get up. When her mother came in yet again and started fiddling with the sheets, Virginia slid up from her prone position—as slippery as a fish, she thought, as she did so—and swung her feet to the floor. Nothing Mrs Simpson could say could stop Virginia running a bath and laying out her clothes and announcing that when she was dressed she was going to see the vicar.

To that, Mrs Simpson merely threw up her hands and muttered something incomprehensible about where angels fear to tread, which Virginia hardly noticed because she was eagerly sliding her bony self—once again, she made note, with an ichthyoid ease—into bathwater which proved far too hot. By the time she was dressed, she felt much less like venturing out. Wooziness had overcome her while she buckled her sandals. But Mrs Simpson had only to ask whether she thought her outing absolutely wise and necessary for Virginia to become obdurate.

The church was silent and desolate. To the passer-by, on a weekday, it might almost have appeared a redundant church, with its overgrown shrubberies, its faded, graffiti-smeared sign and the abundance of pigeon droppings on its doorstep. It might almost have been described as forlorn, were it not that Virginia knew Sunday morning would bring life, fervour and spirit anew.

St Luke's was a dilapidated country-style church with hideous hexagonal glass extensions—modern, shabby, with tatty brown curtains—one at each end of the original building. One addition, the one most visible from the street, was for the Sunday school, and offered up scabby beanbag chairs and primitive crayon renditions of Christ among his disciples to the observant pedestrian. The extension where the choir rehearsed, and where morning coffee was held after the service, might have given a more presentable view to the world, but it was screened from the road by the bulk of the church itself.

Treading the overgrown path to the grimed church doors required all of Virginia's concentration. She watched her white sandals plant step after step, and she paused on the threshold to regain her composure. One wanted, after all, to be utterly oneself when entering the house of the Lord. She wasn't sure whether the Reverend would be in the church or at home in his vicarage, a grim modern edifice of similar architecture to the extensions, but she thought to seek him first in the place of worship, thereby allowing herself the luxury of a prayer before an empty altar. Saturday was not a time when she generally made this pilgrimage, unless, of course, it was her turn with the flowers. But when, in the past, she had popped in for counsel or reflection, she had often found the Reverend Thompson busy in the vestry, sorting books, or making order after a wedding. Upon occasion she had found him simply praying, kneeling in a pew like a common parishioner, with his eyes upon the altar and his thoughts, Virginia always assumed, on the glory of the infinite.

A late shaft of sunlight filtered in one of the higher windows, casting shadows in the corners of the church. But otherwise, Virginia felt this was a calm and untroubled place. A weight and a confusion were lifted from her, and she slipped on to one of the hard benches as if into the arms of a lover. She rested her forehead on the back of the pew in front, and she opened her dialogue with her Maker.

'What is it,' she asked aloud, after a brief, silent prayer, 'that You are testing me for? There are changes all around me, and maybe changes in me too, and it is Your will, I know. But I don't see Your plan. Not, of course, that I *need* to, or that I would ever *presume*, but suddenly the direction doesn't seem clear any more. Everything's turned upside down. This hasn't happened since I came to You, and I have to say I'm a little annoyed. Well, bewildered, I suppose, is a better way of putting it. I know only that these are signs—'

She interrupted her muttering because she thought she heard a sound. A soft thud—perhaps a pigeon against the glass, or noise from the road outside. But she *never* prayed aloud if anyone was near, and could not continue until she had established her solitude with certainty. She knew there was nobody with her in the nave, but she tiptoed up to check the chancel. It did not *feel* to her as though the Reverend was there: his was an open presence, despite his nervousness. And there was no sign of disruption near the altar. She was about to return to her pew—the same she took on Sundays, fourth from the front, on the right-hand side—when her ear caught a breathy whispering, like the movement of the wind. Only more rhythmic. More human.

It came, Virginia surmised, from the vestry, the door to which stood at the rear left of the chancel, slightly ajar. It didn't occur to her not to pursue it, not once she heard it. She didn't think of her own safety; the sanctity of the church was uppermost in her mind. She envisaged a gang of vandalizing youths; a hungry, homeless tramp with his snout in the communion wine; even the image of a bloodied Reverend, attacked by thugs and abandoned, rose unprompted to her mind. The walls and contours of the church, which had only ever stood safe and reassuring, were now made strange by the concurrent haziness and peculiar focus of her movements.

Stealth was not Virginia's forte, and usually she had little occasion to deploy it. But in this instance she moved without hesitation and without a sound to the crack in the vestry door. She could see nothing but the whitewashed wall of the corridor, but ascertained that the sighing—accompanied by creaking and vigorous slithering sounds—was indeed emanating from this point. The door didn't creak when she slid it open; she was quiveringly attuned, and heard nothing. She inched along the little corridor and peered through the actual vestry door—not through its opening, where she might have been seen, but through the sliver of light between door and frame, between one hinge and the next.

First she saw the black-clad, slight shoulder of the Reverend; and his upright presence so reassured her that she almost disclosed herself. It was as if that slice of his left side put all the earth to rights again, and removed the surreal filter from her eyes. She hung back only because he was obviously not alone. Counselling, perhaps?

She saw an arm on his black back, the fingers splayed, and moving. Embracing a bereaved parishioner, then? The irregular, rapid breaths were thus explained. Satisfied, Virginia looked away, then heard a moan which drew her eye back to the light. She examined the hand again, and as she followed its caresses—they were caresses—recognized that it was a male hand. And that the movements, and the sounds, were those of a particular sort of comfort. And with one eye pressed up close to the chink of the doorway, Virginia Simpson saw, undeniably and definitely and irretrievably, her world turned upside down forever: she saw the

141

Reverend Thompson—whose passion had always been all for God, confined to the pulpit, just as it should be—making earthly and physical love to Philip Taylor. Or was it Stephen Mills? The one with the glasses, anyhow.

The silence with which she greeted this revelation was absolute. Despite the shrill whistling inside her head, Virginia didn't allow a scream, or even a sharp intake of breath, to escape her. Because if this vision was a horror unimagined, how much more so would be any actual encounter, any exchange of words, any acknowledgement?

By the time she paused among the pigeon droppings on the steps outside, after scurrying undetected through the body of the church, she could almost attribute her sighting of Evil to the sedatives pressed upon her by her mother. It just didn't seem real. Already, the moment was frozen into discrete frames: the contour of the chink before her eye; the arm; the fingers splayed across God's sombre vestments; the turn; the flicker of a tongue. The sounds.

That was that. She couldn't go home. The other time, the other day, had been easier: this time she couldn't even cry. After all, what was there to mourn? The passing of a few trumped-up ideas, not of a livelihood. That's what her mother would say. She walked down her street, though. She even looked up and saw the precious basket perched upon the window-ledge, unused now for a couple of days. Virginia dropped her eyes, in case her mother happened to be looking, and walked on, to the end of the road. To the park. To the top of the hump that was Primrose Hill.

It was early yet, fully light, and the park was still crowded. Women—girls, most of them—encouraged and embraced their stumbling, bandy-legged infants, some alongside their loose-limbed men. A group of teenage boys spun a frisbee among themselves. Some dogs circulated: lolloping, slobbering labradors, a Jack Russell, a mongrel, a squat bull terrier firmly chained to his frail mistress's arm. Occasional couples, immobile, or almost, lounged entwined beneath trees in what had been, when the sun was higher, the shade. But it felt, and on closer inspection, looked, as though everywhere the first efforts towards departure were being made.

Virginia, just short of the crest of the hill, crumpled on to the grass. She was tired. She didn't know what to think. She didn't know whether to think. The fingers. The tongue. The sounds. She watched the people around her leaving, saw a girl run back for her pullover, caught the beat of pounding music from a passing car. But mostly she saw before her the almost convulsive caresses of the fingertips, and heard the murky, mucky rustlings of the vicar making love.

Melody Simpson expected it to be Virginia. She so expected it to be Virginia that she cursed her aloud as she made her way to the door. Which then necessitated apology, when the caller proved to be Angelica.

'Won't you come in, Angelica? How *have* you been?' Her own voice struck her as so painfully artificial that she almost commented on the fact.

She turned off the television before looking her visitor in the face. Not that she had anything against Angelica, but the young woman was plump. Plump, flushed and squishy. A physical type Mrs Simpson found distasteful; her Emmy bore her bulk with a compact sophistication, like a German car. A different proposition altogether. 'I know Virginia was eager to see you,' she said, 'but she's not here just now. I rather thought she'd gone to visit you.'

Angelica flushed pinker and shook her leonine blonde mane. 'Oh dear. Oh crumbs,' she breathed. 'I hope we didn't cross each other without realizing it. I knew I should've come earlier.'

'She's been gone a couple of hours now, so I doubt it. Unless you've been wandering the streets for that long?' Mrs Simpson tacked on a chuckle, as near as she could manage to good-natured. To her dismay, Angelica sat.

'It's not like her, is it? Where would she have gone, if not to my house?'

Melody Simpson shrugged. 'She's a bit dopey, you know, with the stuff the doctor prescribed. I suppose she could be wandering the streets. I don't know.'

'It's hardly something to be amused about! I feel terribly guilty.'

'You? Why?'

Angelica fidgeted, but then looked Mrs Simpson clear in the eye and said, as if reciting confession, 'I knew Virginia needed me, and I was seeing a chap in my building, for dinner, and I thought I wouldn't come round till afterwards. I put myself first, and it was very wrong, and now look.'

'At least you were seeing someone. Very healthy. Although it can't have gone too well, or you wouldn't have come round at all, eh?'

'I frightened him a bit, I think. Shall I make us some tea?'

'I'm not so feeble as I look. Sit still and I'll take care of it.'

Angelica could not sit still, and she followed Mrs Simpson to the kitchen, where she stood vigorously stroking Bella, who lay on the kitchen table. Great tufts of Bella's fur floated around in the wake of Angelica's hand. One clump, Mrs Simpson noted, wafted into the sugar bowl.

'Shouldn't we do something?' Angelica asked. 'It's getting dark.'

'Such as?'

'Call the Reverend, or Frieda, or someone. Find out where Ginny's got to.'

Mrs Simpson didn't answer.

'You did say, if I understood, that her illness was some kind of a breakdown, didn't you? For heaven's sake, she could have jumped off the railway bridge.'

This shook Mrs Simpson slightly, but she was determined to be firm. 'Angelica, I am no longer my daughter's keeper. She is almost twice your age. We have reached the point where she is free to dance with the dustman, inject herself with heroin or fly to the moon and I will not intervene.'

Angelica wrinkled her nose. She knew how highly strung Virginia could be. She remembered her tears only a couple of nights before. Angelica hated Mrs Simpson.

'That said,' Mrs Simpson continued, jabbing at the air with her teaspoon, 'she *is* suffering from a form of nervous exhaustion. She pushes herself too hard and she needs a proper holiday. Now that she's on leave from the office, I've been trying to persuade her that a trip to Skye would be just the ticket.'

'Skye's awfully far away.' Angelica was still determined to go to Skye with Nikhil, and she wasn't sure how she felt about Virginia and her mother going at roughly the same time.

'I would drive, of course.'

Angelica hardly heard this. She was thinking that there was no reason why they would *need* to see each other, that they probably wouldn't go at the same time. She was thinking that it might really be the best thing for Virginia, and that her friend was in need and should be prayed for and supported, and that she herself was falling into wickedness to consider her own pleasure first. God's will, and all that. Look where her selfishness had already led: it was night, and Virginia was lost, possibly in danger.

'I know you have her ear,' Mrs Simpson was saying, 'And I would be so very grateful if you could say to her.'

'Say to her what?'

'That you think it's a good idea. I'd take care of everything. It would be a *proper* rest.'

'Of course. Of course I will. I agree, there's nothing quite like the Scottish air . . . But don't you think we ought to do something? Now, I mean?'

Mrs Simpson's resolve was wavering. It was, after all, getting late. 'What could we do?' she asked doubtfully. 'If she's with friends, we'll look downright foolish, and if she's lost, it's difficult to know where to begin.'

'Another hour. Perhaps we should give her another hour? Then it will be decidedly late.'

They settled in the sitting-room, the television on, with the windows open to the street—in order, Mrs Simpson did not say, to hear the sirens of any passing ambulances or police cars—and Angelica with Bella on her lap. They watched a police drama in silence, each transposing what they saw on the screen to a private catalogue of imagined gore concerning Virginia. Angelica continued to stroke Bella, vigorously, eventually sweatily, as a means of calming her nerves.

The hour of reckoning came and went, and both knew it and said nothing. They kept their eyes firmly on the television. Mrs Simpson broke out in little beads of sweat. After a time she said, 'It's a very warm night.'

'I'm sure she's just at someone's house,' said Angelica, although she now had butterflies. 'Don't worry, I'll stay.'

'Did I say I was worried? Did I?'

It was well past eleven when they heard the key in the lock. Mrs Simpson made a whistling noise and thrust herself out of her chair as if jolted by an electrical current. 'Virginia?' she called. 'Virginia Simpson, is that you?'

'Hello, Mother,' said Virginia. Mrs Simpson was surprised by the softness of her daughter's voice. Virginia was obviously tired, but she looked like a girl. A soft, loose smile played about her lips. She stood there, plucking at her skirt. Damnation, thought Mrs Simpson as she reached up and stroked her daughter's pale cheek: damnation, she's lost it.

But aloud she growled, 'Where the devil have you been, you ghastly woman? We've been worried sick.'

'We?'

'Angelica's here. She's practically skinned the poor cat in her worry. If Bella's bald, you wicked thing, you've only yourself to blame.'

'Pardon?'

'Oh bother, just come in.' Mrs Simpson pushed her daughter along the corridor to the sitting-room. Her hand encountered mud and stalks of damp grass clumped into Virginia's clothing. Melody Simpson knew she would never ask: she had not asked last time and could not now.

'Darling, you look exhausted! Sit down and I'll get you some tea.'

'Angel, how kind.' Virginia's voice was listless but not dejected.

Angelica bustled about with the kettle and water, called out, 'Where were you? Where on earth were you?'

'I went for a walk.'

'At this hour?'

'I fell asleep in the park.'

'You didn't!' Angelica paused dramatically and made a pop-eyed face. 'That's very dangerous! The park—at night!'

'I'm sure there are plenty of tramps who do it all the time,' said Virginia.

'My daughter is hardly a tramp,' said Mrs Simpson, suddenly defeated by it all.

'I'm very tired,' said Virginia. 'I think I'll go to bed.' She wandered out of the room, and the two women heard her bedroom door shut with an indifferent little click.

'Should we do something? Call a doctor? Do you think?'

'She's home now,' said Mrs Simpson. 'It must be time for you to get home too. I could call you a taxi.'

'I really—I mean, she's not *well*,' spluttered Angelica.

'I know her. She'll be all right. A trip to Scotland, that's the ticket. And right now I think we could all be doing with some sleep.'

The next day, Virginia Simpson missed the morning service at St Luke's for the first time since Angelica had known her. Not that she was surprised, given Virginia's state, but the experience was very different without Virginia to gossip or exchange comments with. Reverend Thompson's sermon seemed flabby and forced, and the sight of Mrs Hammond nodding and sucking her dentures further down the pew was, on this day, more repulsive than affectionately familiar. It just wasn't very *fun*. ('That's all you young people think about these days,' Frieda Watson frequently complained. 'Fun, fun, fun.' Spitting it out as though it was the devil's own work.) Angelica was restless in her seat and folded the Order of Service into a dozen abortive shapes. And when it was over, she fled, in a way she had never done before, after only one brief exchange—with Philip, who asked after Virginia and blinked obsequiously behind his specs.

She didn't go to visit her friend, although she had intended to. She couldn't face Mrs Simpson, and couldn't see Virginia without first seeing her mother. The sun was shining, but a brisk wind blew all the litter round in festive whirligigs. Things, thought Angelica, as she made her way home, were not going well. Things, she thought as she climbed to her door, had not been so bad for some time. She was on the verge of deeply depressing herself when she ran into Nikhil in the stairwell.

He was cowering on the landing between his floor and hers, apparently uncertain of whether he was coming or going, and he waved a folded piece of foolscap at her. 'You are supposed to be in church,' he said. 'Not here.'

'It's over. I came home. Is that all right with you?'

As if remembering himself, he snapped into a more dignified posture. 'Of course. By all means. I was . . . bringing you a note.'

'Oh, yummy,' said Angelica, reaching for the fluttering page, 'I *love* notes. What does it say?'

But he snatched it back.

'You were *going* to leave it?'

'It says I'm sorry.'

'How peculiar.'

'I'm sorry for yesterday evening.'

Angelica's stomach jumped slightly.

'Because I was prying into your privacy. Because I fear I offended you. Because of course I come to the meetings because you are there. And because I have been thinking, you are right, I must make amends with Rupica. And so I would be honoured to go in your company to Skye. Honoured and respectful.' He sped through his speech and down the stairs without once looking at Angelica, calling up, at the last, 'I must go. I am late.'

To Angelica, he looked tremendously handsome as he spun around the banister on the landing below and retreated, blurred limbs and a crop of black hair, to the bottom of the house. He had been right, of course; they hardly knew each other. But that was the delight and therein lay the triumph, and Angelica's dark hours receded as fast as they had come. After a solid, grinning pause, she marched on to her front door humming 'Now Thank We All Our God'.

Whatever her other faults, Melody Simpson did not waste time. Not when it was important, anyhow. First thing Monday morning, she put on her Marks & Spencer dress and red leatherette belt and took a taxi to the car rental office. A bit rusty behind the wheel, she had a few narrow misses on the way home, but she and the royal blue Ford Fiesta parked outside the flat without incident. She even hooted the horn, in a jaunty rather than an offensive manner, to try to lure her daughter to the window, but Virginia did not appear. Mrs Simpson then stopped by Mrs Reece's house to arrange to leave Bella, and to ensure that their downstairs neighbour's plants would continue to be watered. Only then did she go back up to the flat, where Virginia was sitting with one of her mother's paperback novels, visibly failing to turn the pages.

The thing was that aside from a few little signs—the novel, her apparent indifference to the fact that she had missed church, her amiable and unresistant reaction to their imminent departure for Skye—Virginia seemed perfectly normal. More than that, she seemed rather nicer than normal.

It was also true that since Virginia had thrust her life into crisis, Melody Simpson had been relieved of the peculiar preoccupation that had plagued her all spring: she hadn't been listening to her heart. Not in the same way. She was too busy. Not, of course, that this rendered her any less certain that her end was nigh, and she had not lost sight of the purpose behind the trip to Skye, but considering the circumstances Mrs Simpson thought things were proceeding much better than they had been.

She thought of Emmy, away in her extraordinary exotic place, doubtless much better off than when attending to that boring husband. The girls could never see it, either of them, when something good slapped them across the face. In their different ways—although they would hate to be compared—they were both afraid of change. Like their father had been. And look where that had landed him: dead as a dodo, rest his soul. If he had one. If anyone did.

Melody Simpson remembered her two daughters as children, playing with one of his model aeroplanes, never disposed of after his death. It was chubby-kneed little Emmy who guided it in for

150

its crash landing, unwilling to throw it to the wind and let it fall where it might. And after the plane's choreographed nose-dive into the pinks, it was Virginia who insisted on digging a shallow grave beneath the camellia bush in order to bury a peg doll she pretended had been the pilot. To top it off, she had held some vile, earnest little ceremony. A morbid child. Melody Simpson remembered the late summer day exactly. She had hung up the washing and was reclining in a deck-chair, still in her pinafore, trying to read a novel. How acutely her frolicking daughters had annoyed her! Their loud play had distracted her, all the more so because it was punctuated by 'Mummy, look!'s and 'ooh, Mummy!'s. Strange how such prickling irritation could feel, when minutely recalled, like a moment of pure and intense maternal love.

Her own spare little case packed and locked, Melody Simpson went to check on Virginia's progress. To her dismay, Virginia hadn't even begun to prepare, and was perched on the edge of her bed wearing an unlikely expression that looked two-thirds of the way to laughter or tears and probably, thought Mrs Simpson, signified the cusp of some tiresome hysteria.

'For God's sake, wipe that foolish look off your face,' she snapped. She derived a certain satisfaction from the fact that Virginia obeyed. Virginia even smiled politely.

'Sorry Mum. I was off in the clouds.'

'Will it take you long to get ready? It's getting on, and if we're to get away this afternoon—'

'Well, actually, that's one of the things I was thinking about. I know you're in a hurry, but—'

'But what?'

'There are a number of things I really ought to do before we go. I've got to tell the church. I was rude to Angelica the other night and I must go round and apologize. And I have clothes at the cleaners.'

If Melody Simpson had waited all this time to be certain of the trip, she supposed she could wait another few hours to depart. 'I don't know,' she said. 'We pay for the car by the day. And it costs. You didn't even come to the window to see it. Sporty little thing.'

'I'll pay for the car. I always pay.'

'Fair enough. But *you* don't drive. And as I've got to drive the whole way myself, surely *I* should dictate when we go?'

'Mother, please.' Virginia was suddenly firm, her old short-tempered self. 'Don't make me lose my temper.' She stood, and seemed her usual height and her usual age—no longer strangely small and young.

'Fine, fine. Bullied by my own daughter. Have it your way,' hissed Mrs Simpson gleefully.

Just sitting, on this Monday morning, Virginia could sense the vague breezes ruffling the hairs on her arms. Every object in the flat seemed precisely placed, and appeared to have a fine tracing of light around it, giving it depth. The world seemed substantial, Virginia thought. It seemed matter-of-fact. Which was just as well because she was tired of being tired, and tired of being con-fused. Skye, as her mother insisted, might be just the ticket: by the time she came back, Virginia thought, life might look more like itself. The abstract—relationships, work, religion—might regain the substance of the concrete. If they didn't, of course—she reflected with a sigh, and then stopped. She was tired of thinking, and she had a new dictum, adopted as she had lain on the wet grass hiding from the ubiquitous night, trying not to hear or see anything. The new dictum was: no more lies. And she would follow it if it killed her.

She had told her mother that she would go by the church, but Virginia did no such thing. Not yet. She made her way directly to Angelica's house, and when she got no answer from Angelica's bell, she rang Nikhil's without thinking twice.

Nikhil was alone, and stiffer than ever. As he showed her in, he said, with a slight bow, 'I must thank you.'

'Whatever for?'

'Your help.'

'Help? I've been ill.'

'I'm so sorry.' He looked at her as if seeking the location of her ailment.

'No need. A purgative illness. It clears the decks.'

He said nothing.

'I won't keep you. I won't stay. I wondered if you knew where I might find Angelica?'

'She's having the car serviced.'

'Of course.'

'So she's told you? I am so glad.'

Virginia raised an eyebrow in as convincing as possible an imitation of the way she might have raised an eyebrow the week before. 'Told me?'

'About our trip.'

'My trip?'

'Are you coming too?'

'Surely I should ask, are you? Is this something Mother and Angel have cooked up?'

'I was not aware. Angelica and I are to take a trip.'

'I see.'

'It's not the way you think. It's a trip with a mission.'

'I see.'

'We're going to find Rupica.'

Virginia almost asked who Rupica was, and then remembered. The sister. The prodigal. 'So you're going to Scotland?'

He nodded. He was very young. His face was gawkily disproportionate, at once sweet and ugly.

'Tomorrow?'

'Just for a few days.'

Virginia smiled an exhausted smile. Perhaps she was less ready for the world than she had thought. 'How very pleasant. Maybe—Mother and I are going the same way. I'm not sure—I don't know what you—but perhaps we could all have supper, if we do wind up in the same place.'

'Of course.'

'Scotland *is* big. You don't know where?'

'The Isle of Skye. Near somewhere called Portree, I think.'

It was Virginia's turn to say 'Of course.' Of course. 'Well then, maybe we will? Do tell Angelica I dropped by. If she has a moment, before you go, she could phone; or if not, well, tell her I'll see her in a while. And to drive carefully.'

'I will.'

Virginia felt Nikhil was as eager to see the back of her as she was to leave, although he ran after her moments later—to return her Bible, about which she had completely forgotten. She had thought, the other night, that she had fallen to a safe place, but still the ground beneath her shifted. And the movement caused her almost physical pain.

She didn't go home. Nor did she go to the church. She went instead to the park, to the summit of Primrose Hill, and she surveyed the city.

She was surprised to see the landscape unchanged, all of its monuments still planted in much the same configuration as before. Perhaps the quality of light was slightly altered, but not significantly. She shivered despite the sun, disappointed. It was the trial of Job, to have seen signs and yet not to know their meaning. Not yet. Circling, bound for Heathrow, a plane cut the haze to the south, catching the light with its silvery wing and creating a swift, brilliant flash. What was a sign, anyway? As Virginia watched the plane slide away, out of sight, she said aloud, to the kite-flying children and the galloping dogs and to the Divine if he was listening, 'Well, there we are.'

THE ISLE OF SKYE

WHEN SHE GOT out of the car on the port in Portree, Virginia Simpson was drenched and miserable. The rainclouds had rolled back into the long evening and were visible far out to sea, but the earth they had left in their wake was a vast puddle. The drive had been awful.

Or rather, the second day had been awful. The first, Tuesday, had been relatively calm: Mrs Simpson and Virginia had set off early beneath a golden sky and had covered the miles to Edinburgh in comfortable silence: Mrs Simpson had not gloated over her victory, and Virginia had chosen not to see the trip as a capitulation to her mother.

They had arrived in Edinburgh in time to stroll amid its sombre magnificence, and had dined in a lively Italian restaurant where fellow customers sang with the waiters and danced around the tables. For Virginia, this experience was alien and discomfiting (she had never moved in rowdy circles in her youth and found the clutch of powdered secretaries at the adjacent table deeply suspect), but Mrs Simpson tapped her fingers busily in time to the music and jigged her head back and forth with pleasure. Ginny thought that had her mother been alone, she might actually have pushed out her chair and joined the fray. Back at their bed and breakfast, Mrs Simpson had slipped out of her teeth and into despondency, whereas Virginia had only then been able to relax.

But Wednesday had not gone well. They had quarrelled at breakfast, and the tension that hung between them for much of their journey was matched only by the darkness of the day. It had poured, but Mrs Simpson had driven fiendishly nonetheless, swishing along the narrow Highlands roads in a LeMans-like fury, honking at sloe-eyed sheep and pulling out sharply alongside caravans and tractors when the road ahead was not at all clear. And all the way it had poured.

Most miserable of all, the Ford Fiesta had proven defective: on the passenger side, the window would not rise to meet the doorframe; despite all efforts, a half-inch was left to the whistling wind, a situation which, in sunshine, had cooled the car slightly, but which, over the course of the stormy day, provided passage for more spitting raindrops, it seemed, than the rest of the car kept out. Virginia tried to stuff the gap with a plastic bag, but found the bulk of it trailing across her face or flapping at the top of her head. And the raindrops, seeming to relish the challenge, merely wormed and wriggled their way along the plastic to drip the more effectively on to her lap, her neck or, most unpleasantly, her scalp.

Virginia stood by the sea rail, plucked at her skirt and blouse and pitied herself while her mother went to park the car. Glistening wet still, the port was shabbily beautiful, and limp and weary though she was, Virginia could dwell on that beauty. The row of multi-coloured houses clustered up against the sea wall; the fishing boats, strewn with nets and traps and other odds and ends, jostled against each other; and at the end of the pier, where the wet asphalt shone iridescent with traces of petrol, two rusty pumps abutted a trim, tidy phone box that looked as though it had been dropped there, by mistake, that very morning.

Melody Simpson parked the Fiesta in front of the phone box.

Virginia watched as her mother opened the boot of the car and hauled out their two cases. She knew she ought to make her way over and offer assistance, but she didn't move. She saw her mother staggering as she tried to keep from placing either case on the wet ground.

'Don't just stand there like a bloody lump,' hissed Mrs Simpson as she tottered past to the bed and breakfast door. 'Go and lock up the car.'

'I haven't got the key,' Virginia protested. But she ambled to the pier end, found the key in the lock and did as her mother had asked.

She noticed as she walked the hundred yards that what looked like dockside warehouses, in the row that ran perpendicular to the row of houses (and looked eminently less appealing than they) were not warehouses at all. One housed an evangelical bookshop; one, pink, looked like a brothel; and yet another, which had the same smeared windows and mottled paintwash as its neighbours, emitted smoke and sound from its half-open door: the sound of taped music, and of men's voices. Although there was no sign to advertise the fact, it was a pub, and a lively one at that. And it was only six in the evening.

It occurred to Virginia that it might not be a bad idea to go there for a drink—with her mother, of course. She knew it was not the sort of establishment they were accustomed to, but from a quick look around the harbour, it appeared to be all there was nearby.

The room Virginia and her mother were to share looked straight out across the water at the spit of land opposite. Although not a large room, it was comfortably furnished and it had a television. The carpet was a soothing powder blue, thick pile, and the headboards on the two neat single beds were covered with matching Dralon. On the window-ledge sat a porcelain donkey pulling a cart full of yellowy-brown dried flowers, and a china figurine of a girl in a full-length dress, clutching a poodle. Mrs Simpson made fun of these touches, but they were comforting to Virginia. They reminded her of the knick-knacks she had collected in her childhood, when such things seemed to have an innate significance that somehow saved them from being ugly or in poor taste. She liked to think that their hostess still held on to that innocence: that for her these items were talismans of some kind, and that she could not see that the dried flowers were crumbling to dust, or that the paint of the poodle's eyes had flaked off.

Virginia stood at the window and fingered the ornaments, looking out at the sheet metal of the sea beyond the port and at the mountainous grey land in the distance.

Mrs Simpson, who lay on one of the beds with her shoes off and her spindly ankles crossed (for although she was by no means a slim old woman, she had ankles and calves like matchsticks), said, 'Too bad there's no sun. It'll be light almost all night, you know. Marvellous!'

Virginia watched the sea ripple; it looked like corrugated iron. She did not see that light in and of itself was a virtue, but refrained from saying so because she knew her mother was excited. 'Where exactly were your people from?' she asked instead.

'Oh, a tiny village, a way, still, from here. I took you and Emmy once when you were small, but you probably don't remember.'

'I remember.' Virginia remembered the train ride, as far as Fort William. And she remembered rain, and cold, and running across a field that stung her shins. She remembered her mother holding her sister's hand, and herself standing alone in the roar of the wind. She couldn't picture a village, or land, or sea, or people. 'But there aren't any relatives, are there? Not close enough to speak of?'

Mrs Simpson shifted uncomfortably. 'Not that I was ever in touch with. Mother had a sister, but they lost contact early on. I never met her. She didn't marry.'

'Did your mother bring you back here, then, when *you* were young?'

'No, never.'

Virginia reflected that it was odd that her mother should have clung so to her own mother's birthplace, when there had clearly never been any obvious connection. But aloud, she said, 'What should we do about supper? I don't really feel like sitting around doing nothing.'

'No, true, thinking never did anybody any good.' Mrs Simpson swivelled, with some effort, and put her feet to the floor. 'My back aches,' she said, 'from sitting all that time in the car. I'm not up to going far, to tell the truth.'

'There's a pub along the pier,' said Virginia. 'They might have something.'

'Full of sailors and navvies, on a port.'

'It's worth a look. I don't know that there's much else around.'

'I remember having a delicious meal—when we came that time—where was it now?'

'That was forty years ago.'

'It was more than that.'

Virginia wanted to take her mother's arm on the stairs, because from behind Mrs Simpson looked so bent and frail. It crossed her mind that the disruptions of the past week were nothing compared to the rupture that her mother's death would be. Sometimes, it was true, she felt only a most un-Christian hatred for her parent, but with her faith wavering, it suddenly seemed that this was the relationship that defined Virginia's reality, that Mrs Simpson had been the only solid ground in all the years since Virginia had come home to her. And now she was so small.

Mrs Simpson stumbled slightly on the penultimate step, and clung to the banister with both hands.

'Mother!' Virginia cried, trying to embrace her and set her aright, finding in this mishap an outlet for her high emotion.

'Damnation, Ginny!' said Mrs Simpson, regaining her balance and slapping at her daughter, 'Look what you've done to my bust!'

It was true that on one side the prosthesis had slipped, but Ginny didn't see that it could have been her fault and she said as much. She tried to set the foam to rights, but Mrs Simpson slapped her away again, grumbling. 'You're just making it worse. Absolutely useless. Always have been.'

The pub was now hushed. Its dim lights were still on, and the tinny music still dribbled out into the evening air, but the customers had vanished. A lone fisherman in an oilcloth jacket sat astride a stool, with three pints lined up in front of him on the bar. Mrs Simpson took a seat by the door and scowled at the room around her.

'It doesn't look to me as though there's any supper to be had here,' she said. 'So I suppose I'll settle for a whisky and water.' She tucked her ankles underneath her chair and straightened her back.

Even in the dim light, Virginia could see the dark pockets beneath her mother's eyes, the complicated tracery of lined skin and exhaustion.

'They must be able to get us something,' Virginia said.

''Fraid not,' the surly landlord informed her as he poured their drinks. 'You won't find anything to eat around here.'

'Nothing?'

'There's the White Lion on the hill, it's about fifteen minutes' walk, but they'll only be serving another half hour and you'd be lucky to make it, with your companion slow on her feet. Cost you, too, the White Lion.'

'Nothing else? At all?'

'There's the chippie,' said the landlord. He didn't look convinced. There was a gurgling sound as the fisherman drained one of his three pints.

161

'I'm sure that would suit us very well. Where's that?'

'Just up from the pier here, towards the square. 'Tisn't the finest, but it'll do.'

'There's a fish and chip shop, Mother,' said Virginia, carefully placing their drinks on the cardboard coasters provided. 'That'll be OK, won't it?'

'Absolutely OK.' Mrs Simpson didn't look at Virginia. Her overly-bright eyes were taking in the smeared whitewash walls, the sticky plank floor, the fisherman's broad backside. She brought her drink to her lips without looking at it, like a blind person, and took a very little sip. 'It's odd to be here,' she said. 'I didn't really believe we'd make it.'

'Do you suppose it's changed a lot?'

'Since when?'

Virginia was silent. Since when, indeed? Her mother had clearly hardly ever been to this place in all her seventy-nine years, and her idea of it was practically fictional. One visit, forty-two years before, with two small children in tow, did not constitute any kind of real knowledge. 'Is it what you expected, then?'

'It's more or less what I remembered,' said Mrs Simpson. 'I don't think it's changed too much.'

'Remembered from when?'

Mrs Simpson sipped thoughtfully at her drink. 'Tomorrow, I'll take you across to Alt-na-Ross. Perhaps we could take a picnic if the weather's fine.'

'Are you planning to ask about your relatives?'

'Yours too,' snapped Mrs Simpson. 'I hadn't really thought about it.'

Virginia considered losing her temper: what was the point of this trip, after all? But instead she merely nodded and traced the word 'stupid' in the sweat of her cider glass, invisible to anyone but herself. 'Are you hungry then?'

'Yes. Although, fish and chips . . . '

'There's no choice.'

'No.'

They sat in silence, but for the sounds of the fisherman swilling and clinking, and the muffled rendition of a popular song coming from a distant speaker. When a telephone rang, it made both Simpsons start.

'Kenneth Campbell?' asked the landlord loudly, as though calling through a crowd. 'It's for Kenneth Campbell.'

The fisherman grunted and slid off his stool. He stood at the end of the bar and muttered into the receiver for some time, and while he did so, Virginia took her mother's elbow and helped her to her feet. 'Thank you,' she called to the landlord. 'We're off for supper now.' She was disappointed. She had thought the pub would be an adventure.

'Up to the corner, turn left,' said the landlord. 'It's the only place with any lights on.'

'Where *is* everybody?' asked Virginia.

'They've all gone home. Everybody's home now.'

'Not me,' said Kenneth Campbell, back on his stool, tapping at his two empty pint glasses and preparing to make inroads into the third. 'Fill 'em up.'

Outside, the light was as it had been, although it was getting late. It was pale grey, neither bright nor ominous, a light that did not indicate any time of day at all, as though a brief moment had been held and stretched, indefinitely.

'Midsummer light,' said Mrs Simpson. 'Remarkable.'

'I find it a bit sinister myself. I like day to be day and night to be night. The air is the colour of the sea. It's wrong.'

'Whatever happened to the Scot in your soul, Virginia?'

'I wasn't aware of his presence. And his absence has not exactly been a cause for concern all these years.'

'Maybe not for you. But I'm convinced that if you had been more Scottish you would have been happier in life.'

'I see.'

Mrs Simpson's ramblings were making Virginia herself feel very stable indeed, and more than a little annoyed with her mother.

'I've had quite a happy time, despite everything, and I feel I owe it to my Scottish nature,' Mrs Simpson went on. 'I have always considered my deepest impulses to be Scottish.'

'Do I take it, then, that you've spent your life in exile?'

'Not at all. It's something you take with you. I think Emmy has it. And look how far she's gone. I always thought you took after your father. He, of course, dear man, was not remotely Scottish.'

'No. Of course not.'

The chip shop did not look particularly salubrious. It had a fluorescent light, and a grinning fish in a top hat painted on the window in blue paint. Neither the floor nor the counter nor the pinafore of the waitress was very clean. There was nowhere to sit down. And the girl's forearms were covered with burns from the spattered fat, as well as some scabby places she had quite obviously been picking at when they came in. She wore a little badge that said MARY on it.

'Good evening, Mary,' said Mrs Simpson. 'What might you have to offer us this evening?'

'I'm not Mary. Mary's off tonight. I'm Alice.' She fingered her badge. 'It's Mary's uniform, that's all.'

'So, Alice, what do you recommend?'

'T'all tastes the same, really, once it's fried. It's the batter, you see. We use the same batter for all of them.'

'I think I'll have scampi,' said Virginia, seeing it on the board.

'The scampi are frozen. They come from London. But they taste just the same. It'd take a while to do 'em.'

'What's done, then?'

Alice pointed with a pair of tongs at a little pile of assorted

164

food, huddled under the heat lamp. 'Sausage, one portion. Cod, three portions. Hake, one portion extra large. One chicken and mushroom pie. And we have chips.' She put down the tongs and started to pick at a scab on her elbow. 'Most people come for chips of an evening. So we don't fry up too much else. Wastage,' she explained, nodding.

'Cod for me,' said Mrs Simpson. 'And chips. And a Coca-Cola.'

'And the same.'

The girl slapped the lot on to two cardboard plates and salted and vinegared vigorously without asking. Then she rolled the plates into two cumbersome newsprint packages, through which the grease instantly started to seep.

'Is there anywhere we can go to eat this?' Virginia asked as she paid.

The girl looked blank. 'Outside somewhere, I reckon.'

'It's a bit damp, outside.'

The girl shrugged. 'You can ask at the pub on the pier if he'll let you eat in there. But he's no charmer, MacAllister. There's always the breakwater. But she'—a nod at Mrs Simpson—'might not be comfortable. Because of the gulls, you know.'

As the two women perched themselves on the breakwater, a flock of gulls did indeed swoop in from around the bay to scream and jeer at their feet. Some landed on the far side of the wall, in the water, where they bobbed up and down menacingly. They were very loud.

'Well,' said Virginia, unravelling her newsprint. 'Here we are.'

Mrs Simpson did not look up from her soggy mess of food. 'I won't grace that with a reply,' she said. 'There is no need to be sarcastic. I'm sure we'll do better tomorrow.'

'I wasn't being sarcastic.'

'Just shush. And eat, before these damn birds move in and pluck our eyes out.'

Both women were piling chips into their mouths with an air of quiet desolation when Kenneth Campbell emerged from the pub, pint in hand, and made his way over to where they sat.

'Evening, ladies,' he called before he reached them. 'Not so fine for eating out, is it?'

'No,' said Mrs Simpson. 'It's not.'

'Never mind. The weather's always rotten around here. Absolutely terrible. Mind if I join you?' He sat as he asked.

'I suppose not, Mr Campbell.'

'How d'you know—'

'In the pub. The phone call.'

'Right. He's a right creep, that MacAllister.'

'You're not Scottish,' said Virginia.

'Well, I am and I ain't, as they say. Grew up in Northumberland, as a matter of fact.'

'Are you tracing your roots? We're tracing our roots,' said Virginia.

'No way. Wouldn't want to find 'em. No. I run a fishing boat out of the Sound, here. Scallops.'

'How interesting.'

'I've been here a couple of years. That's two years too long if you ask me.' He balanced his drink on the wall and took a greasy handkerchief from his pocket. He proceeded to wipe his face with it. He was a wiry man of about forty-five, and his hair was oily and colourless, but his face, Virginia remarked, was not unattractive. He had the reddening of drink in his skin, but his eyes were clear.

'What's wrong with Skye?' asked Mrs Simpson, who had been eyeing him with disdain since he arrived. 'You should count yourself lucky to make a living in such a spectacular place.'

'Maybe I should. Good scallops, at any rate. But the people! And the weather! And even the landscape isn't a patch on Northumberland. Can I buy you ladies a drink?'

166

'We're eating our supper,' said Mrs Simpson sharply, as if that in itself were an answer.

'I'll bring 'em out to you.'

'How kind,' said Virginia. 'A cider for me—sweet. A half. And a whisky for Mother, with water.'

'What has come over you?' asked Mrs Simpson, as soon as Kenneth Campbell entered the pub. 'Must we consort with such people? He's not even Scottish! And I'm quite sure he's no Christian, if you're interested.'

'I was only meeting good manners with good manners, Mother. Something I thought you believed in.'

'You surprise me. You really do.'

Virginia had surprised herself, rather. But she was tired of waiting, she thought. She wasn't quite sure what she meant by this, but it seemed a good explanation.

Kenneth Campbell was gone for some minutes—long enough, Virginia suspected, for him to have a pint or two before rejoining them. And sure enough, when he re-emerged, he was more obviously weaving than before. He seemed to be splashing the three drinks he carried into each other as well as on to the ground and on to his coat.

'He's drunk, Virginia. How could you?'

'I'm not blind. It's a question of courtesy. We'll only stay a couple of minutes, and then we can go back to our room.'

'For the ladies!' He cheered as he plunked the drinks unsteadily on the wall. 'To your health.'

'I'm cold, Virginia. I'm going to catch cold.'

'In a minute, Mother.'

'Now that's a nice name, Virginia. A fancy name for a fancy lady,' said the fisherman, leaning towards her.

'It's just a name,' she said. 'I don't suppose, Mr Campbell, that you believe in God?'

'Hey?'

'Are you a Christian, Mr Campbell?'

'I'm not a Yid, if that's what you mean. Or an Arab. By God, no. Are you?'

'Oh Virginia, *really*,' interjected Mrs Simpson, 'this is ridiculous. I'm not a Christian and I can see that he's not either. It doesn't take a genius. And so what? Are you coming? Because if not, I'll go up to the room on my own.'

'That's a fine plan,' exclaimed Kenneth Campbell. 'Because I'd like to show you my boat.'

'That's very kind I'm sure,' said Mrs Simpson, now on her feet. She barely reached Kenneth Campbell's shoulder, and he was not a big man. 'We can discuss it in the morning.'

'Oh, I didn't mean *you*,' he said. 'I meant Virginia here. You're welcome to see the boat in the morning, if you like, but if you don't mind, I'll take the little lady tonight.'

This was too much even for Virginia's new self. 'It's a lovely thought for another time,' she said in her firmest office voice, as if sacking a temporary appointment for the gravest of misdemeanours, 'but just now we're both very tired and I think we'll retire for the evening.'

'It's a beautiful boat. Truly. Only a few miles up the road. C'mon.' He grabbed at her arm.

Virginia let out a little cry as she broke free. 'No! No thank you. Thank you for the drinks, it was very kind of you, but *no*.'

She and her mother hurried along the pier as fast as Mrs Simpson's legs would allow, leaving Kenneth Campbell with the remains of his drink and with both of theirs, untouched.

'What on earth, Virginia? What on earth? Haven't got the sense you were born with.' Mrs Simpson was mumbling furiously.

But Virginia, although shaken, felt strangely pleased. Kenneth Campbell had grabbed her arm, and she had broken free. Mrs Simpson had told her not to speak to him, and she had anyway. Although in one way it had all gone terribly wrong, in another it had proved something. She was proud of herself, and when she looked out of the bedroom window at the bent silhouette of Kenneth Campbell (the light, now, was dimming somewhat), she realized that she liked him for his part in the scene. He had played it just right.

Virginia's triumph didn't last long. Melody Simpson, irate, had decided that she was not speaking to her daughter, and let this be known by bangings and crashings and, ultimately, great shaking of her bedcovers—all of which announced to Virginia the impregnability of her mother's wrath and at the same time demanded her full attention. In this fury of noisy silence, Mrs Simpson snapped off the lamp, and both women courted sleep in the endless half-light, while Kenneth Campbell called out to the sky and threw three glasses one by one into the bay.

The weather on Skye changed very quickly indeed. When Melody Simpson awoke and saw the sun sparkling on the water, she felt a rush of pleasure: her mission would be so beautifully dispatched! It was a mission that seemed to be coalescing of its own accord: it was not born of any conscious reflection on Melody's part. All it required was her certainty: she had long been convinced of the power of her will to direct the course of events, to control reality. What she saw in her mind's eye were two beams of light, destined to cross: that of the necessary trip to Skye, and that of the impending but unknown moment of her death. Her mission was to locate their crossing, and Alt-na-Ross, her unthinking but unshakeable conviction assured her, was the place.

Beneath so clear a sky, the ancestral route and her place in it could only be thrown into the most perfect relief. Melody felt eager and, so far as her daughter was concerned, conciliatory.

But by the time they were poking at their rubbery fried eggs (served with a misplaced effort at sophistication by a pimpled youth in a blue waiter's jacket), Melody, Virginia and a gangly, drab Dutch couple with whom they shared the table were watching fat drops of rain against the picture window, and the bay had so blurred that it all but disappeared from view.

'It is very difficult, the rain in Scotland,' said the Dutch-woman, in a third, wilted attempt to make conversation.

'Does it rain a lot in Holland?' asked Virginia.

'Oh yes, quite a bit,' said the woman.

'Not so very much,' said the man.

'Not as much as here?' asked Virginia, with a thin laugh.

Mrs Simpson could not bring herself to look at their break-fast companions. They deflated her further. Virginia was having the same effect.

'I think my feet have swollen,' she said. 'My shoes are too tight.'

'Maybe you'd like a lie-down, after breakfast?' said Virginia, in that public, maternal tone which indicates, to non-family members, that such complaints are a recurring nuisance which must be humoured.

'No need to patronize. I shan't be napping, thank you.'

The Dutch couple, who were returning to the mainland and driving up to Inverness, excused themselves, and Virginia pushed back her chair as if to get up.

'Where might you be going then?'

'We've got to go *somewhere*. I thought I'd brush my teeth before we go.'

'Go where?'

'This is a bed and breakfast, Mother. It is not an hotel. Whether we like it or not, whether it is pouring or sleeting or snowing outside, we are not invited to stay here for the day. It's not *done*.'

Mrs Simpson knew that this was so, but decided to keep up her fight. 'According to *whom* is it not done? We've paid for our room, haven't we?'

'Mother, don't make a scene.'

Mrs Simpson looked around the little room. The pimpled youth was hovering forlornly by the door, hoping they would go away. 'I just don't see your point,' she said. 'We are paying good money, and quite a bit of it, for that little box with a sea view. And if I choose to lounge around it all day in my underwear, then surely that's my choice?'

'Mother, please. It doesn't even have a chair. There's nowhere even to sit.' Virginia was overwrought, Mrs Simpson realized suddenly. Caught up in her own schemes and disappointments, she had quite forgotten her daughter's precarious state. Although a bit of bullying never did anyone any harm. It made clear the fact that she, Melody Simpson, did not consider her daughter an emotional invalid, a strategy which ought to give the woman some pluck, but never seemed to. 'You are overwrought. But I suppose,' she conceded, 'that I would not want to be cooped up in that horrid little room without even a chair.'

A quarter of an hour later they relinquished their room to a very fat chambermaid ('Chambermadam, more like,' scoffed Mrs Simpson) and made their way, beneath a borrowed umbrella, to the Ford Fiesta, the passenger seat of which was completely sodden.

'I think I'll have to sit in the back,' said Virginia, after pressing at the cushion and watching the water rise up out of it, around her fingers. 'It's too wet.'

They sat in silence for a time, wondering what to do. After a while Virginia coughed. 'Well,' she said. 'This view of the pier is fine, but—'

'Fine but what?'

'We have to go somewhere.'

'Yes.'

'Maybe there are some Celtic churches we could visit. I know there are some very old places of worship on these islands.'

'Isn't that what your young friend is coming to do?'

'Angelica? Oh no, she's helping a young Indian fellow who lives downstairs from her to find his sister.'

'Wouldn't India be a better place to start?'

'She eloped to Scotland. To Skye.'

'Well I never. I suppose they were married in one of these ancient places of worship you refer to?'

'I've no idea.'

'Churches are gloomy. Count me out. I'll tell you what: if we can't sit in *our* hotel, let's find another hotel to sit in.'

'Sorry?'

'Let's find a smart hotel where we can have lunch, and where we can sit in the lounge for a siesta.'

'It may not rain all day.'

'But I'm not dragging you out to Alt-na-Ross until the weather has improved. Not at least until tomorrow. We need to do something.'

'We didn't bring a guide.'

'We can ask. Now let's go before I get a crick in my neck from turning to talk to you. I'm most cheered at the prospect of a delicious lunch. Most cheered.'

Virginia was less than cheered. She didn't see that there were any answers to be found in plush Scottish Tourist Board recommended hotels. She, like her mother, felt miserably cut adrift on this pier, at the end of the earth with nowhere to go. But unlike her mother, thought Virginia, she saw this as a chance to let go, to leap into the unknown—a quest which she fully expected would be, like the day, cold and wet and miserable. Virginia, because she was unafraid of what was 'right', was unafraid of misery. She always had been, which was why, perhaps, misery had so often found her. This willingness to be miserable was a quality she prided herself on, the quality in herself she considered most saintly.

'Fine, Mother,' she said nonetheless. 'Let's find a comfortable place for lunch. But you absolutely must let me sit in the front seat, to navigate.'

So saying, she slipped out of the car and back in again, squelching her bony buttocks firmly into the cushioned swamp, while Mrs Simpson looked on, appalled. But there were elements of righteousness, thought the triumphant Virginia, that nobody could take away from her.

The man at the petrol station recommended a hotel a few miles west of Portree. 'Fine food,' he said. 'Local specialities. Signposted off the main road just past the junction.'

'I bet it's run by his mother,' said Mrs Simpson. 'Or by his sister, or something.'

'We can't go there yet,' said Virginia. 'It's not even eleven o'clock.'

'You're so full of what we can't do. It's most irritating.' The car was sitting at the petrol station and the windows were steamed up. 'What would you suggest then?'

'I don't know. I don't know.'

'Then *I* would suggest we take morning coffee at this hotel. Then, if they have a television lounge, we can watch television. If not, we can read. Then we can have lunch. Then we can see.'

'And if we don't like the hotel?'

'Then we're not chained to it, are we? Honestly, my dear, you are so lacking in initiative it makes me want to weep.'

'What's that supposed to mean? What has that to do with anything?'

'Oh come off it, Ginny, you've never had enough initiative to fill up a *day* on your own. You've slipped into dreary routines, into a dreary job, into the arms of this suburban God of yours, alongside crackpots and wimps and excitable housewives. And you've just stayed there. And now your sun is past its midpoint, and where are you? Driving around Skye with your mother, for God's sake, and unable to fill up a bloody morning. What have you *done* with yourself? It's positively tragic.' Mrs Simpson's voice had risen throughout this speech. She couldn't help it. Her irritation had, after all, proved too strong for her.

Virginia sat rigid, her back straight as a pole. She pulled her hands from beneath her, where they had served, like two planks, to raise her posterior slightly from the puddle. She set them in her lap, where they quivered, raw and creased, like two alien newborns. She wore no rings.

'I'm not sure I need to answer that,' she said in a voice like a record playing with dust on the needle. 'All it makes clear is how very little idea you have of who I am. Do you not think—did it never occur to you—that all these places I seem to have slipped into so easily, that they might be choices? That perhaps I asked, perhaps I wondered what the point was? And He said'—she looked at her mother with a glare Mrs Simpson could only have described as hateful—'and He said my purpose was to persevere.'

'Oh Virginia—'

'Don't you think it's difficult to be where I am?'

'My dear, I'm so sorry. I've upset you—I—'

'And possibly now even that isn't clear to me. Things happen, Mother.' Virginia spat this out. 'Things happen and everything moves and it could be that right now I just don't have any idea where He is.'

Mrs Simpson, gravely alarmed but above all embarrassed, tried to make light of this. 'Maybe He's at the Tarbish Hotel?' she said, with her best approximation of a rinkly-tinkly laugh.

To her surprise, Virginia slumped in her seat as if punched, and said quietly, 'Yes, maybe. Fine. Let's go.'

The Tarbish Hotel was a hunting and fishing lodge by a river, a mile or so down a once-paved road. The Simpsons had been bouncing and juddering along the track, both silently convinced that a nightmarish ruin awaited them at the end, when the car rounded a bend and they saw a stately Victorian edifice with long rectangular windows and a sweeping drive, set among brilliant close-cropped lawns bordered with flowers. Everything glistened in the wet and, unlike elsewhere, seemed to be more colourful and definite because of it. All around there was the muted, constant roar of the river, swollen by the rain, raging over rocks and threatening its pebbled banks.

Mrs Simpson pulled up under the portico and parked. There were a few other cars, all in the car-park to the side of the hotel, but her comment was, 'I'm not going to be bothered with that.'

The lobby, vast and panelled, was deserted—something the Simpsons were coming to expect of this island—and its walls were decorated with old black-and-white photographs of the lodge: men in plus-fours and caps, with guns under their arms; anglers nestled proudly up to huge slimy fish; and a whole series depicting the river in flood, or close to it, showing the fury of which it was capable.

'Your father would have loved this,' said Mrs Simpson. 'It would have suited his gentlemanly dreams. It looks a fine hotel.'

'I've no doubt the prices are fine, too,' said Virginia, following her mother into a grand but reassuringly dowdy drawing-room, filled with clusters of overstuffed chintz armchairs. There were piles of magazines on all the tables and, on a small chest by the French windows, a stack of boxed games.

Mrs Simpson settled into a chair with a view of the gardens and rested her arms firmly on the armrests.

'Should we let someone know we're here?'

'Stop hovering, Ginny. They'll find us in good time, and meanwhile we can enjoy the adventure. Such a grand house, all to ourselves! If I were quicker on my pins, I'd go upstairs and have a look at the rooms. Why don't *you* go, and report back to me? It might cheer you up.'

'Certainly not. I'm going to find someone to get us some tea.'

'Have a spirit of fun, child!'

'I do. I do. I do have a spirit of fun. Do you want Earl Grey or Assam or China?'

Mrs Simpson waved a regal hand by way of reply and continued to smile at the gardens. She was pretending, Virginia thought, that they belonged to her.

Virginia tiptoed to the other end of the lounge and into the dining-room. There, the tables were elaborately set with crystal and silver—two glasses per person—and a fire flickered in the hearth, sending out a warm, peat smell. Aside from the fire's occasional expostulations, there was no sound. A door presented itself as, most probably, the kitchen door, behind which there had to be someone, preparing for the lunch to come, but Virginia didn't want to open it to find out. She crossed back through the sitting-room, past her rapturous mother, to the Great Hall. She felt like Beatrix Potter's Hunca Munca, a mouse let loose in a dolls' house. Although she could never have admitted it to her mother, she felt playful and almost happy.

The bar next to the reception area was empty too, and loud, because it gave on to the river and the water sounded as though it were practically in the room. Virginia could see a little footbridge over the torrents and, on the far side, the forlorn flags of a golf course. She noticed that there was ice, unmelted, in the ice-bucket on the bar. It, like the fire, awaited the invisible guests. She ran her hand across the seat of her skirt: she was drying. She half-hoped, like her mother, that they would remain undetected for some time. She even considered climbing the stairs to wander the passages above, but as she came back into the hall she heard her mother talking.

'—and biscuits please. Something sweet. Shortbread? Perfect.'

Virginia rejoined Mrs Simpson in time to see the neat black-and-white back of a uniformed maid clipping back to the dining-room.

'Your prowlings succeeded in raising somebody. Pity. But I ordered us up some tea.'

'It will be expensive, you know.'

'We don't do it every day, after all. And lunch is twenty-one pounds.'

'For two?'

'For each.'

'Mother, we can't possibly—'

'I'll take it out of your inheritance. It makes me happy. I'm not long for this world, after all.'

'Nonsense—'

'Fact. Now fetch us the Monopoly board and let's play a game.'

For Virginia, the arrival of their tea and shortbread and the spread of the game board signalled an end to the moment of adventure: she would willingly have gone back to the wet car and resumed their island peregrinations. But Mrs Simpson was having a ball, and kept whispering things like 'lovely' and 'wonderful', unprompted. At one point she looked up and said gleefully, 'I can't think of a better way to spend one's last day, can you?'

'We're here for a *week*, Mother. A *week*. And it's only just begun.'

'Of course.' But she was biting her tongue in a secretive manner that did not please Virginia at all.

They had been playing for the better part of an hour when they heard a car pulling up outside. They did not see it go past, and from where they were sitting its occupants were invisible, but they heard the clamour of arriving guests—doors banging and the reception bell being rung.

'Poke your nose around the door and tell me what they look like,' said Mrs Simpson.

'I'll do no such thing.'

'I suppose they'll have to come down to lunch.'

Ten minutes later, another vehicle came down the drive. This time Virginia looked out in time to see a small red car with snowy heads inside flit past. Minutes later, a stout matron of around seventy led her wizened spouse to a sofa not far from where the Simpsons sat. She nodded a chilly greeting and eyed the Monopoly with disdain.

Virginia looked back at her mother, who raised an eyebrow and winked. It was funny, and Virginia could only keep from tittering by turning her attention to the game—a game which Mrs Simpson, ever astute in money matters (although her acumen had never brought her wealth), was winning.

After that, the clientele arrived thick and fast: a trio of foreigners, clearly, were outsiders like the Simpsons, stopping off for lunch; then came a clutch of local women, prosperous, middle-aged, the Women's Institute type; and an American couple, of about Virginia's age, with their teenage son—hotel residents.

The patriarch was American-sized, a massive man with a vast expanse of pink shirt and an incongruous grey goatee; his wife, of an average size, looked minute next to him, her permanent wave close-knit against her head; and their son, plump and sullen, peered out through his glasses and alternately stroked his head or palpated his fleshy breasts through his garish check shirt.

'What a crew!' giggled Mrs Simpson, leaning forward to throw the dice. 'How do they *get* so fat?'

'It could be a thyroid problem.'

'It could be too many four-course meals.'

They both turned to stare at the fat man, who at once struck up conversation with the genteel Englishwoman and her invalid spouse.

Their attention was thus distracted when a high-pitched voice cried out, 'Virginia Simpson! Ginny, what on earth are you doing *here*?'

Angelica, a vision in pink and white, rushed over and tried to throw her arms around the seated Virginia, in what proved a cumbersome gesture.

'Are you staying here? This is too funny!' Angelica pulled back and her skirt hem scattered Mrs Simpson's Mayfair hotels.

'No,' said Virginia.

'We couldn't possibly afford it,' said Mrs Simpson.

'Oh, Mrs Simpson, I'm sorry, hello.' Angelica held out her hand for shaking, but Melody did not take it. She just nodded.

'Are *you* staying here then?'

'Well, I, I mean we, just arrived.' Angelica waved over at the door, where Nikhil stood looking odd in a tweed jacket and tie. 'We're, you know, in search of Nikhil's sister.'

Mrs Simpson turned her head, craning her neck. 'So you're the Indian boy? Come over here. I've heard a great deal about you.'

'How do you do?' he said. For him, Mrs Simpson extended an arm, which Nikhil pumped rather gingerly.

The foursome was not an immediately comfortable one. Mrs Simpson, whose dislike of Angelica seemed suddenly to have flowered, was at her most imperious; Nikhil, perched upright on the edge of his chair, said nothing; and Virginia felt confused, both because her Scottish dream-world had evaporated with the return of such familiar faces, and because Nikhil, she felt instinctively, held some key to her quest, but she wasn't at all sure what it was.

'How can you afford to stay here?' Mrs Simpson was asking.

'It's, um, only for a couple of nights . . . it's not so expensive.'

Mrs Simpson looked at Nikhil, and back at Angelica. 'For two rooms? . . . or one?'

'They do a good rate on dinner, bed and breakfast. It's—it's what I knew, really. I came here with my parents as a child.'

'I wonder what they would think of it now. Of you coming

179

here now, I mean,' said Mrs Simpson.

'I always think it's nice to go back to childhood places,' said Virginia, from her rather crumpled position at the back of her armchair. 'Don't you, Nikhil?'

'Nonsense,' said Mrs Simpson, for whom the day's unexpected delights had been thoroughly spoiled, and who was determined to make everyone pay for the fact. 'That's tripe. You've never looked back in your life. You don't even *remember* coming here when *you* were young.'

'I think it is wonderful as a new experience,' said Nikhil. 'This is my first visit, and even with the weather I find it very beautiful.'

'Yes,' Angelica put in, clearly relieved to be back on safer ground. 'Nikhil was dumbstruck by Glencoe.'

'I can imagine that my sister would find the open spaces and the wildness very—appealing.'

'It's melancholy, though,' said Virginia.

'I suppose. But my sister would not remark upon this. She has a very strong spirit and it is important to her always to feel free.'

'Yes. But you think you're getting away from it all by coming up here and "it" just follows right behind you,' said Mrs Simpson.

'I think lunch is being served now,' said Virginia. Distant clinking sounds and voices emerged from the dining-room.

'Does your deal include lunch?' asked Mrs Simpson. 'We came for a treat, ourselves. Because of the weather.'

'We thought we'd eat in, for the same reason.'

'Well, we can all have lunch together,' said Virginia with as bright a tone as she could muster. 'What an unexpected pleasure.'

Everyone looked faintly downcast at the prospect but knew there was no other option.

There were so many questions Virginia wanted to ask Angelica, but could not; and so many she knew she would want to ask Nikhil, if only she could think clearly. Much as she did not want to share her mother's ill-temper, she felt it would have been preferable not to encounter Angelica and Nikhil in this way: all opportunities were at once present and thwarted; only the banal was safe.

In fact, Nikhil proved adept at smoothing things over. He recounted again the loss of his sister, and Mrs Simpson was wholly absorbed by the story, not least because she considered herself, however inaccurately, an expert on Skye.

'Well she won't be hard to trace now you're here,' she said knowledgeably. 'Indian girls named Rupica—what a pretty name—don't grow on trees in these parts. And all the islanders, the locals that is, keep up on who's where. It's a very—how would I put it? Close-knit community. They help each other out.'

'The question is,' said Nikhil, buttering a roll with great daintiness (his fingers, Virginia noted, were long and slender), 'whether they will be willing to help an outsider like myself. I do not know where to begin: the address I have is a post office box in Portree.'

'But they're outsiders themselves, most of them,' said Mrs Simpson, blithely contradicting herself. 'I mean, take that Kenneth Campbell fellow on the docks last night. In some ways, he was as local as you get. But where was he from again?'

'Northumberland.'

'Named Kenneth Campbell?' said Angelica. 'How curious.'

'But that's my point exactly. They're part of it and they're not, at the same time. The lot of them.'

'I don't know, Mother, presumably there are those who were born here, who consider themselves "insiders" through and through?'

Mrs Simpson shrugged. 'Inside, outside, so what? I think they'll help you. They know what it's like to be bludgeoned and given the run-around, the Scots. They'll sympathize with you. I'm sure he's no Scot, this fellow Rupica's run off with.'

'Not a Scot and not a Christian. So what is he?'

'Maybe he doesn't exist,' said Angelica. 'Maybe he's a blank space.'

'Maybe he's a sign,' said Virginia, thinking this a very profound comment. 'Mother and I will do anything we can to help. Won't we?'

'I think we should start by ordering a bottle of wine,' said Mrs Simpson.

'With *lunch*?'

'Why not? A big one, because we're four.'

'I don't drink alcohol,' said Nikhil.

'Mother, *never* in the middle of the day,' said Virginia. 'It will put us all to sleep.'

'Well, I wouldn't say no,' said Angelica brightly. 'What a fun idea.'

Mrs Simpson looked Angelica up and down with a narrowed eye. And then she smiled, and Virginia realized that lunch would be all right after all.

Neither Melody nor Virginia Simpson found it easy to return to their bed and breakfast on the waterfront, particularly because they were leaving Angelica and Nikhil behind. For Mrs Simpson, this was shaming: 'Where does that girl get her money?' she asked at intervals, to which Virginia could only shrug and say, 'She's always had it. I don't know.'

Their room looked smaller and dingier after their outing, and the view of the port struck Virginia as a shabby, narrow view, littered with greasy bits of paper and petrol drums, gulls circling overhead. She sat on the end of her bed and looked out in silence.

'I'll just have a little lie-down, I think,' said her mother. 'And then maybe some television.'

It was only a matter of minutes before Mrs Simpson was

asleep. Her chin went slack, leaving her mouth slightly open. The whole area rippled as the air came in and out, like a sail heading into the wind. When she breathed out, Mrs Simpson made little 'pooh' noises.

Virginia tried to read her Bible, but the light in the room was very dim, and the print of the Bible was very small, and attempting to read proved a divine trial of itself, so she decided to go out.

The pub was not empty, like the evening before. Virginia was intimidated and almost turned back, but there was really nowhere else to be: the breakwater was wet, the sky still ominous, and, short of sitting in the car, she could see no alternative. She went in with her Bible clutched close against her chest.

The room was filled with large men. The smell, of beer and smoke and wet and sweat, was overpowering but not unpleasant. All the men were looking at her—she could feel it. Like a teenager in a mini-skirt, she felt at once terrified and delighted by the stir she caused. Mostly terrified.

She stepped up to the bar. 'Half a pint of cider, please.' Her voice came out with an unexpected assurance, which in turn gave her the courage to look at the sailors and fishermen. 'Good afternoon to all of you,' she said, politely but without smiling. She could see that their faces were neither angry nor lascivious—nor anything really. Large though they were, they had the open, expressionless faces of sheep, or cows.

She clasped her slippery cider glass with both hands, tucking the Bible under her arm, and made for the table nearest the window and furthest from the men. It was light there, and when she spread her Bible on the sticky table, she could see God's words distinctly. Sweaty, a bit shaky, she lowered her head to read, taking tiny sips of her cider.

She found it hard to concentrate, in part because of the hubbub and in part because she felt as though she were waiting for something. She kept looking up, between Godly sentences and earthly sips, to monitor the pub around her. She felt agitated, it was true, but somehow impressed with herself as well.

Melody Simpson was alone in the blue bedroom when she opened her eyes. Her elder daughter had, it appeared, gone off on her own. Shown some initiative. It was something of a relief, because there was work to be done.

Melody rummaged in her handbag for her glasses and a pen. She also looked for paper but found she had none. The bed and breakfast was not the sort of establishment that provided such items, and an unscrupulous dive into Virginia's suitcase did not turn up any there either. Eventually she tore out the endpapers and the title page of the mystery novel that served as her bedtime reading, and, using the volume to rest upon, she propped herself against her headboard and began to write.

Dear Emmy,
Thank you for your letter. I hope you don't settle on that peculiar island because I don't have your address there. Perhaps Portia will forward your mail.

I do not often write, as you know. I don't have the temperament for it. But there are things that now need to be said, and this is the only way. When I am gone, you must think more often of your sister. You and she are not alike except that unfortunately you are both proud. You have not always been good to each other; perhaps this is my fault. I wanted you to get on, but you were born with a thick skin and Virginia with no skin at all.

You may think you are a more interesting person than she is, and this may be so; but her efforts are just as important. She has taken good care of me. She has had to build a life with very little and that, too, is a noble thing. Her first sorrow, and every sorrow after, have stayed with her in the present; she does not find it easy to make a past, without which it is impossible to make a future. I hope you understand what I mean.

We are such a little family and have been so long apart. I urged you to seize your life with William when the chance came because I, like you, believe in freedom. And I urge you, now that your marriage is over, to find your self and what makes you happy. So it may seem strange that today I write to say that family is the only thing there is. But it is true: blood is the one tie that binds. I cannot say this to Virginia because although she lives her life as though this were the case, she does not think she believes it. Her God gets in the way.

But if when I am gone I have a will, or a wish, it is for the reconciliation of my daughters. You, who believe in a past and a future, will understand that the one is necessary for the other. Virginia is your past, and can give meaning to your future. I have in my life wanted everything for your happiness and for hers—

Here Melody Simpson began to run out of space. She also found herself unsure of how to end her letter. After a while, she wrote: 'And your friendship would be my greatest happiness.'

This seemed to her a little selfish, but she thought that Emmy, of all people, would not pass judgement on that count.

She put the pages down and rested for a minute, and then took them up and wrote, very small, at the bottom of the last sheet, 'Your new friends sound fun. But dangerous.' Then she folded the rough papers into a small, thick square, and tucked them into the zip compartment of her handbag.

Pleased and calm, she opened her mystery novel and settled

down to wait for Virginia, her thoughts on what they might have for her last supper.

The following morning when Angelica woke up, she still felt guilty. She lay sprawled beneath the eiderdown of her broad four-poster bed and listened to the rain slapping at the windows. Her guilt stemmed precisely from the sense of ease that she felt lying there, with an acreage of space stretching about her.

She had asked for two rooms, communicating if possible, and to her surprise, she and Nikhil had been provided with those in which she and her parents had stayed, many years ago, on the last holiday before the divorce. This time, however, it was she who had the luxury of the huge room with its elegant antique furnishings and its two deep windows; Nikhil had insisted on taking the tiny cell adjacent, no more than a cupboard really, clearly intended for a valet or a lady's maid, with a sink next to the window and a narrow bed that doubled as a divan in the daytime, as it was the only place to sit. Of course, it had been pleasantly decorated— there was a ruched blind in blue moiré that lent the tiny room an effect of incongruous grandeur—but it was, really, a safe hiding-place for a small girl whose parents were arguing, rather than a proper hotel room for a paying adult.

When Nikhil had insisted on taking the room, Angelica had suggested that they move to other, uncommunicating rooms, but he had rejected the idea out of hand. Ostensibly this was because he felt more comfortable in small spaces, but in reality she wondered whether he had refused because she was footing the bill or because he, like herself, felt they were teetering on the brink of something—something made manifest by the communicating door. Something that might, were they to move to wholly separate quarters, retreat irrevocably to the realm of the impossible. That, at least, was what she hoped he was thinking.

186

But when, eventually and in haste, they met for breakfast, it was clear that romance was far from Nikhil's thoughts. He was preoccupied, brusque even, indifferent to Angelica's efforts with her appearance. She did her best to hide her disappointment. Over kippers (for her) and scrambled eggs and toast (for him), she tried to prise out the source of his distress. 'Are you worried that she won't be pleased to see you?' she asked. 'Have a taste, these are delicious! Or that you won't be pleased to see her?'

'No, no. That's not it.'

'But there is *something*. Do you think you won't like the look of him?'

'I don't know.'

'Did you tell your parents you were coming? Do you think they disapprove?'

'Please stop asking so many questions.' Nikhil pushed the egg around on his plate.

Angelica sat back and dabbed at her chin with a napkin. 'Well,' she said, 'can I at least ask where we're supposed to start looking?'

'At the post office in Portree, I suppose.'

The woman at the post office on the square in the centre of town—or *Oifis a' Phuist*, as it was marked in bold Royal Mail lettering—was only moderately helpful. 'Aye, that's a box number here, indeed. But who they belong to, it's confidential you see.' She was unsmiling, a woman of Virginia's age with a pale sprinkling of freckles.

'I *know* who it belongs to,' said Nikhil. 'I just want to know where they live.'

'Are you from the police or something?'

'It belongs to my sister. My sister and her husband.'

'If she's your sister, how is it you don't know where she lives?'

'If she didn't want me to know, why would she give me her postal address?'

'I suppose. Just a minute. Charlie!' she shrieked over her shoulder. 'I'll let my husband take care of you. There's people waiting, right enough.'

There were two women queueing behind Nikhil and Angelica. They, like the postmistress, were unsmiling.

'How can I help you?' asked Charlie, a small man with a profusion of wrinkles. Nikhil proceeded patiently to recount his exchange with Charlie's wife. 'Aye, I know who you mean. Aren't many Indian girls on the island. A pretty lass. And the man with her, long hair and a beard. A sort of hippy type. Never imagined they were actually married. He's not the sort we islanders like too much, you know. Not that he's ever been anything but polite, mind. Your sister too. And such a pretty lass.'

'He's a religious man.'

'I see. Not *our* sort of religion, I don't think. Looks a bit like Jesus, of course, with the hair. Is he your sort of religion, then? A swami or a guru or whatever they're called over there?'

'He's a Christian, I believe. Do you know where they live?'

'Oh, we don't need to know that, you know, for a box. People can just rent a box.'

Angelica could see that Nikhil's patience was wearing thin. He was drumming with his fingernails on the counter. 'Have you got *any* idea where they live?'

'Out of town, I know that much. Because they only came in once a week for their mail.'

'Came?'

'They haven't been for—it'd be over a month, now. Not that you'd know—they don't get a lot of post. Never have.'

'Can you please tell me where they live?' Nikhil was now agitated.

'You might want to try Mrs MacKinnon in the newsagent's over the road. She was more friendly with them, I think. But me, I don't know where they live.'

Nikhil was very upset as they left the post office. 'Maybe this man is very wicked. Maybe he has killed her.'

'Don't be ridiculous,' said Angelica. 'Maybe they've started having mail delivered to their house. Maybe they've just moved.'

This was not the right thing to say. Nikhil's composure all fell away and he looked at her despairingly. 'What will my parents say? Here I am, on the same continent, and I have lost her.'

'But I thought they'd disowned her?'

'It would never occur to them that I would *lose* her. Britain is so small and Scotland is so empty. Not like Delhi, or Bombay. You can't just *lose* somebody. In India, we would find her.'

'You'll find her here, too. Don't worry.' Standing in the drizzle, in the square, she put an arm on his and he didn't remove it. 'God is on our side,' she said, and kissed his cheek.

Mrs MacKinnon was a bit more helpful. A bit. 'They drove a sort of lorry, you know,' she said. 'Open at the back, and their provisions'd get wet in the rain. People didn't like how he looked, but he was the kindest man. He'd help anybody. He was older than he looked, and she's young, and that always gets people talking, of course. Your sister, is it? A lovely-looking girl. Of course there are more Indian people up here than there once were,' she smiled, 'but that's not saying much. So we all noticed her. He'd been here for some time before, maybe a year or two. Maybe only a year? And then he went away for a while and came back with her.'

'But where did they live?'

'Out of town, I know that. North, maybe. North, I think. He studied nature, that's what he did, birds and things. Wildlife. He had binoculars. She must have been a painter or a sketcher or something, because she always bought those sorts of things.'

'I know what she does, Mrs MacKinnon. She's my sister. I just need to know how to find her.'

Mrs MacKinnon put her hands on her hips and looked at

Angelica and then at Nikhil and then at Angelica again. 'Thing is,' she said, 'I don't know where they lived. North, I think. Just drive north and start asking. Not far, maybe just a few miles. But not on the main road, because I remember him saying that the last stretch was rough on their lorry. I'd bet it's somewhere by the water, for the birds.'

Melody Simpson was not surprised to be wakened by rain. She had resolved the night before, in bed, in the half light, that rain or no rain they would go to the ancestral home today. There was no point losing one's temper over a little water, but she did wonder how her forebears had stuck it out. For the first time she understood why her own mother had never wanted to come back.

'Do you think it rained less, a hundred years ago?' she asked Virginia, who sat at the end of her bed, already fully dressed, reading her bloody Bible.

'Good morning, Mother. I don't know. Did your mother never say?'

'She didn't talk too much, my mother. Not like yours.'

Her daughter hardly cracked a smile.

'What's eating you, then?'

'I'm fine. I suppose the weather just gets to me a bit.'

'Don't let's let it.' Mrs Simpson pulled herself up in bed, her flannel nightie falling straight down her front where her prostheses were not. 'I thought we could go out to Alt-na-Ross today, regardless.'

'You don't want to see if the others need any help?'

'They came for their business, we came for ours. Surely they weren't expecting us to hare around after that girl, were they?'

'No. I just thought it would be kind.'

Mrs Simpson wanted very much not to get annoyed. The working of her plan, if plan it was, depended a great deal on Virginia. Whatever was destined to happen at Alt-na-Ross, and she didn't presume to guess, she might need someone. Even the swiftest and most true of endings needed a witness. When the two beams crossed—the place and the purpose—there had to be a flash of light. Of this she was certain. Although she thought for the first time that Virginia might, in fact, be the plan's undoing. 'You can help them, if you like. I'm happy to go alone. You wouldn't need to worry about me—it's not far, just across to the west side of the island.'

'Of course I'll go with you. Don't be silly. I thought that was the point. But I might give Angelica a ring to see if we can do anything for them while we're over there.'

Mrs Simpson had made the decision that today she wanted to do nothing for anybody but herself. It was, after all, her last day: she could feel it. She thought that she could feel beneath her breastbone that her heart was already beating less vigorously, although it was difficult to be certain when Virginia kept talking over the sound. Still, along with not doing anything for anyone else, she was determined to stay amiable.

'It's a shame Emmy couldn't be here, don't you think?' she said.

'Why?'

'She might have liked it. She has a sentimental streak. She and I have always got on.'

'Whereas you and I haven't?'

'That's not what I'm saying.' Melody Simpson, although loath to show affection, felt it important on this day to set a few things straight. 'You and I have been important to each other in ways that Emmy simply has not. We both know that. And I suppose in some measure Emmy has grown unnecessary to our lives—in a day to day way, of course.'

'Indeed,' said Virginia sourly. 'We've hardly seen her in thirty years.'

'Not *that* long. Now don't be disagreeable. I've always felt that you must stop blaming who you are and who you are not on your sister. You would be much the same person had she never been born. It's nature. And once I am gone, it's you who will have to write to her. And it *will* happen. You must see, dear, that she is the only certain thing. Family is all that's certain. Now, where was I? Yes, I was just going to say that Emmy's absence, generally rather than today, has made our lives bigger rather than smaller, and you should remember that.'

'Because she sends us postcards from Australia? For heaven's sake, what has she ever done for us? What connection could there be?'

'Stop it. And I just think it's a shame that on an important day like today she can't be with us. She would agree.'

'She's run so far and she ran so fast to get away that I can't think she'd be too interested in seeing where we came from. Where is she now, again?'

'Indonesia, I think.'

'Precisely.'

Melody Simpson decided to drop the subject. She couldn't make Virginia understand, and she didn't like to consider that Virginia might be right: that Emmy might be indifferent to her mother's last day. Although were that so, it would only show how similar mother and daughter were. You don't grieve over the inevitable. And Emmy was still her favourite child.

'I'd better get dressed,' she said aloud, 'so we can get down to that nasty breakfast.'

Melody Simpson wore her new Marks & Spencer dress and a navy cardigan. She combed and fluffed her snowy hair. She took her time. She powdered her face and scented her wrists. She wanted to look her best. It would have been difficult to express what she felt, the fizzing of excitement in her stomach, her utter certainty of the rightness of her gesture. But behind the surge of positive emotion, she could sense doubts lurking—little things. Things, perhaps, like the future of the cat: Virginia had never cared much for Bella. And things like what this was, that awaited her, and how this all would end. Such little things, though, that Melody Simpson was not going to listen to herself. The time had come for action. She was not a believer in reflection: it crippled people, weakened them. She relied on simple certainties, and of this mission, of this day, she was absolutely certain.

Over breakfast—shared, this morning, with two effete young men from Aberdeen who seemed to have a most peculiar effect on Virginia—Mrs Simpson suggested a visit to Dunvegan Castle on the way to Alt-na-Ross. 'To put it in perspective,' she said, 'where our people come from. The MacLeods have always run things here. It's worth seeing.'

Distracted, Virginia agreed. She was at once trying to ignore their two table-mates and to listen to their conversation. Their exchanges, about the probability of sunshine and the suspension of their car, were unrevealing, dull even. Mrs Simpson chose not to let Virginia's distance bother her. She decided they would go first to the Castle—that way, she reasoned, it would be quite late in the day by the time they reached Alt-na-Ross, which was better. She wanted to end with the day, not before it.

Tired of being a martyr, Virginia sat in the dry back seat of the Fiesta. Her mother was in good spirits; it was Melody Simpson's day, and Virginia was anxious to help her enjoy it. She forebore to mention the weather.

She was thinking about the two young men at breakfast who had, by the intimacy, the ordinariness of their chatter, intrigued her. It seemed to Virginia an extraordinary thing and made her think of the Reverend, of his own meek, ordinary self, of the fire of his sermons and the unexpected, horrifying fire of his passion:

perhaps such intimacy was as ordinary as the weather in its way. Which did not excuse the lies. Or alter God's teachings. Sitting in the back of the car, watching the misty grey-green and endless water passing outside, it was above all the lies that enraged Virginia, and made her dig her fingernails into her palms.

She endured their trip to the Castle, and even enjoyed their walk around its damp but well-tended gardens, two ageing women amid a hundred or more the same, most in brightly coloured anoraks, blobs of pink and mauve and teal in the grey. Eventually, fortified by lunch in Dunvegan's tourist cafeteria, she put aside her anxieties and attempted to share in her mother's enthusiasm.

When Melody Simpson stopped the car and pointed, saying 'There! There!', it took Virginia a moment to see what she was talking about. It was still some way in the distance, a speck almost, ahead and below them, practically at the water's edge.

They proceeded along the narrow, winding road, clinging to the hillside, and from her window Virginia watched the house appear and disappear with the bends, growing bigger. Then they came to the place where they could go no further, where the house was far beneath them, a vast, stony ruin on a tiny, stony promontory, invaded by the grey wind and attacked by the buffeting waves below.

'It's been abandoned, of course,' said Mrs Simpson.

'You can see why. Miles from the nearest village, on a road that goes nowhere—'

'Only a couple of miles. Off the road, actually. And it must go somewhere, this road, or they wouldn't have built it.'

'No town on the map.'

'*Some* habitation.' Mrs Simpson opened her door to the

shrieking winds. 'Shall we go and have a look?'

'Aren't we looking perfectly well?'

'I've come *all* this way . . . '

There was a track, or what had once been a track, that went off to their left and meandered uncertainly down to the house. But first, they came to a gate, peeled by the weather but still firmly standing. On it hung a red sign, fairly new, that warned: KEEP OUT. PRIVATE PROPERTY. TRESPASSERS WILL BE PROSECUTED.

'So it's not as abandoned as all that,' said Virginia.

'Impressive, though, isn't it?'

'Was, maybe. Bleak and miserable.'

'Do you remember it now? Coming here?'

'It's like a house from my nightmares,' said Virginia. 'Perhaps I do remember it. It had people in it, though, then.'

'Yes, do you remember? We went all the way down there and there was a horrid woman who wouldn't let us in. I tried to explain that it was where my mother was from, and she would have none of it. She shooed at you children as though you were seagulls. So I never saw the inside. Now is the time.'

When Mrs Simpson said, 'Now is the time,' she felt a tingling in her hands and feet. Things were starting to seem unreal now; it was coming together. The afternoon, grey as it was, was getting on (although it would lead only into a monotonously grey and interminable evening), and she did want Virginia, who couldn't drive, to be able to make it back to Portree in time for supper. She wanted to get this over with swiftly.

'Don't be ridiculous,' said Virginia. 'That path is far too steep and slippery for you to manage.'

'Well, I'm going. Stay here if you like. Wait in the car. But I have to see.' She whisked a plastic rainhat from her purse and tied it under her chin—'It breaks the wind'—and wound her scarf more tightly around her neck. Virginia stood by, arms crossed, shivering.

'Last chance, my dear. Want to say goodbye to your old mother?'

'I can't let you negotiate that hill alone. But this is the last time I indulge one of your crazy fantasies. I mean it.'

'It's the last time I'll ask. Don't spoil it.'

The way was longer than it had looked from above, and the flat, marshy distance to be covered was as great as the slope they descended. As they drew nearer, they could see that the house was even more imposing than Virginia had thought. Three storeys of darkness glared at them through the windows, and half the roof was gone.

'I wonder how long it's been empty,' said Mrs Simpson, almost slyly, her plastic bonnet flapping at her ears. 'I wonder what happened to the people who lived here.'

'They probably jumped at the chance to get away. I'm frozen. Are you sure you want to go all the way?'

'Go back to the car, then.'

Virginia clutched tighter at her mother's arm. 'Let's make it quick, shall we? Then we can get tea back at the village. I'm sure I saw a pub.'

When they came to the place where the front garden had been, the house looked more forlorn than frightening. Like a fat old man with no teeth, thought Virginia. It still had a front door, in spite of everything, and the door had an unrusted padlock on it. There was also another KEEP OUT sign.

'They may not be here, but it certainly belongs to someone. Maybe they're planning to renovate,' said Virginia, taking her arm back and wrapping it around herself for warmth. 'I'm afraid this is as far as we get.'

Mrs Simpson was trembling. 'I want to go in.'

'But can't you see—'

'Of course I can see! But I haven't come all this way for nothing—'

196

'What *are* you looking for, exactly?'

Mrs Simpson snorted. She, who never shed a tear, felt very close to it. Her certainty was evaporating with the wind. She stamped her foot. 'Damn,' she said. 'Damn and blast.'

'We might as well go back.'

'Go then, damn it. Stop whining and go.' She was trying to think. She hated her daughter as much as she had ever hated anyone. Melody Simpson had expected—what? what had she expected? A sign of some sort? A divine manifestation? She was furious with herself. Furious with the padlock. She went up and rattled the door, but it held firm. Whatever she had been so certain about must be inside. 'Where's your bloody God when you need him, then? That's what I'd like to know.'

'Working in mysterious ways, I suppose.' Virginia was cold and growing bored. It was a house; it was interesting to have seen it; but she wanted to be warm and dry and, like all the wise relatives, like her grandmother, away from this miserable end of the earth. The sea and the wind were loud; she realized she was having to shout to be heard. 'If you're so keen to see the inside, why don't we quickly have a look around the outside and try and see in the windows. And then let's go back to the car. OK?'

Virginia set off around the side of the house. For the most part, the windows were too high for her to see into, and she was taller than her mother. But on the far side, where the pathway between the house and the rocks was narrow as a footstep, she came to a place where she could stand on a flat rock and look into what had clearly been the kitchen.

The room was large, gloomy and barren, and in its depths lurked the darker gloom of open doorways to further rooms. There were sagging cabinets; there was, perhaps, an Aga in the corner; or perhaps it was just a shadow. The sea, here, was impossibly loud.

'Mum!' Virginia shrieked, and then went back around the

corner to find her mother, who was looking out towards Greenland, at nothing. 'Mum, come around here. You can see the kitchen. You'll see you aren't missing anything.'

She perched her mother on the flat rock—'Steady,' she said, and 'See?', as if to a child at a fair. 'It's the kitchen.'

Mrs Simpson had an idea. 'Ginny dear'—she managed a wheedling tone above the din—'I'll just stand here a moment and see all I can see, and would you go along and just check if there are any others we can see into? And then come back and help me down, and I will have seen enough. Then, I promise, we can go and get some tea.'

Melody Simpson could see: it was there, the truth was waiting. In the dark of the house she could glimpse a light, as if a candle were glowing in the hallway, waiting to guide her. As soon as Virginia was gone, Melody knew what she would do: she would climb in through the kitchen window. Never mind that she was old and feeble, she would find the strength because she had to. She hadn't foreseen the call for such effort in her last journey, but she would find it. She would have to, in her flimsy arms and legs, and the cushion of her body would help.

Melody Simpson stretched her arms out towards the windowsill, and allowed herself to fall forwards. With a thump against her foam prostheses, she found herself forming a triangle with the wall and the ground below, her feet on tiptoe on the rock. She looked down at the narrow footpath and up at the wall. The window was higher than she had thought, but at least her hands were there. Now it remained only to haul herself up, by her arms. She would do it because she had to. She had lived all this time because she had to, and in seeing the light she had known it was time for the next thing. She didn't have time, would not allow herself time, to think: Virginia would be back around the corner within moments. She let her legs go and tried to pull with her hands.

In the split second before she fell, as she felt her palms scraping back across the ledge, Melody Simpson cursed herself for being a fool. She cursed her certainty.

It was not far to fall—less than a foot. But she could not co-ordinate the straightening of her limbs as she fell. All her little strength abandoned her, and as she landed in the narrow, sandy crevice between the house and the rock, she heard a disagreeable snapping sound in her right ankle and felt a great, sickening wave of pain. She looked at her hands, and her palms were grated and dotted with gravel and blood. This was not at all what she had intended. Not at all. It was no peaceful ending, no justification of anything. She started to cry.

Virginia, who had found a slope on the fourth face of the house from which she could see into the former sitting-room, discovered her mother in a crying, crumpled heap, with her plastic rainbonnet still firmly tied beneath her chin.

'Mother, my goodness, what's happened?'

'What do you think? What does it look like? I fell. Foolish old woman that I am. Damn it.'

'You should've *waited*. Oh, dear, let me help you up.' Virginia started to pull and push and pummel at her mother.

'It's not going to be so easy. Something has broken.'

'How do you know? Oh no, how do you know?'

'Because I heard it, you ninny. Because I can bloody well feel it.'

Together they managed to get round to the front of the house, where Virginia sat her mother propped against the offending door. But it was a painful and slow process of leaning and pulling and hopping, and involved the agonizing use of Melody's Simpson's grated hands, while her right foot dangled at a useless and peculiar angle and her ankle, also oddly angled, throbbed and swelled.

When they were at rest, Virginia looked her mother square in the eye. 'What on earth were you doing? And what on earth are we to do now?' She herself was exhausted from the effort of moving Mrs Simpson—pencil-limbed but bodily substantial—this little way. And the car, she could see, was like a tiny blue blip at the top of the hill. She didn't know how to drive it anyway.

'This is not at all what I intended,' said Melody Simpson. She sighed, jagged with the pain. 'I don't know what we do now. I just don't know. I wish I could explain—I had a feeling—it's not what I intended, but I suppose I'll have to stay here. Outside the house. Just here.' Maybe that was the ugly, undignified truth of how it would have to be. 'You go on, Virginia. It's cold. You'd better go. But remember that I've always loved you dearly. And that Bella needs to be picked up when you get home.'

'Stop this. I won't have it. There isn't time.'

Virginia took off her coat and put it round her mother's shoulders. 'I'll hurry. I promise. I think it's best,' she added, trying to cover her panic with authority, 'if you don't go to sleep. Because of the cold. Stay awake. And move your good foot around, for circulation. Will you be all right?'

Mrs Simpson nodded vaguely. 'It's how it has to be,' she said. 'I just misunderstood.'

Without pausing to reply, Virginia set off at as close to a run as she could manage.

Angelica could tell that Nikhil was discouraged by the vagueness of the shop assistants. 'It'll be all right, love, we'll find her,' she said in her breathiest, most maternal voice, putting an arm across his shoulders.

He shrugged; whether in pure disbelief or with the added motive of avoiding her touch, she was unsure. She kept her hands to herself after that. They were standing by the car in the main square of Portree, the wet misery thick and palpable around them.

'What do you want to do now?' she asked, jangling the car keys. 'We can head up this coast, like the woman suggested. Ask around, you know?'

Nikhil turned to look at her and she could see it was a struggle for him to remain civil. It occurred to her that if they had slept together, it would have hastened intimacy and honesty, and he would at this moment have exploded, which would have been fine. As it was, he twisted his mouth into the icy sliver of a smile and said, 'I don't know what is best. There is no need for you to be part of this wild goose chase. Perhaps I could borrow the car?'

'Don't be silly. It's an adventure. I *want* to help. Now hop in.'

They drove out of town to the northern turn-off, and turned. After a while Angelica put on a tape of Graham Kendrick's evangelical rock songs. Kendrick was only halfway into his first tune when Nikhil asked if they might shut him off. Angelica felt a little annoyed. She was cheered by Graham Kendrick and she had wanted Nikhil to be cheered too.

After passing the Old Man of Storr, the first human site they came across, a couple of miles on, was an isolated croft above the road, looking out towards the sea. Angelica stopped the car.

'Do you want to go alone, or shall we both go?'

'Sorry?' Nikhil was scowling.

'Well, we've got to find out if they've seen them. Maybe they even live here. You never know.'

'Are we going to do this at every house we see? All day? And all tomorrow? And all for nothing?'

'There aren't that many houses, Nikhil. Have you got a better idea?'

He shrugged again.

'Do you want to give up, then?'

'Of course not.' He was fidgeting with the glove compartment. 'I just don't think we'll find them. They may be dead.'

'How likely is that?' Angelica felt much older than this squirming boy.

In the end they went together up the hill, but it was Angelica who knocked and spoke to the woman who came to the door. No, the woman had never seen any black girls around here. Maybe she'd heard about them—were they hippies, aye?—in which case it would be north of here. She didn't know how far. She didn't know for certain whether she knew anything about them.

The morning stretched into afternoon, and everywhere they found the same thing: uncertainty at best, ranging to complete ignorance. One woman peered from behind her curtain and then refused to open the door. Their progress was slow. It was three before they came across a small shop that sold stamps, milk, bread and chocolate, and locally-knit pullovers for the few passing tourists.

Angelica, who was feeling peckish and somewhat fed up, decided she would buy some sweets and not bother with the rest. Besides, the girl behind the counter, rolling a wad of gum on her tongue, did not look like a promising interview candidate.

Angelica's fingers roamed the small display of chocolate, deftly selecting a variety to last the afternoon. Nikhil pulled a plastic bottle of Coke from a shelf near the door.

'You friends of that other couple, then?' asked the girl, cud-chewing between words.

'Which other couple?'

'The long-haired bloke, the one that looks like Jesus. And the Indian lass.'

'You know them?'

'Nobody else has bought so many sweets in one go, but you and them. Sugar mad. And like—' she nodded at Nikhil, 'You being a compatriot and all.'

'Do they come often?' asked Nikhil, brightening for the first time.

'Depends what you mean by often.'

'*How* often?'

'They haven't been for at least a couple of weeks, if that's what you mean.'

Nikhil's features settled back into a frown.

'You don't know where they live, by any chance?'

'Can't say I do. But I'd say they aren't coming in because they aren't there any more, are they?'

'How do you know?'

'Well, the boat, eh? I guess they finished working on her, and went.'

'What boat?'

'Are you *certain* you know them? Because I don't see as you could know them even a wee bit and not know of the boat. I mean, I only know them a tiny wee bit, and I—'

'What about the boat?' Angelica insisted.

'Well they live on it, don't they? And they were going to see the birds when it was ready. Birds and other things. I'm not a bird-watcher, am I?' And with that her talkative bout was at an end. 'Is that all? That's one pound eighty-nine,' she said, and turned back to the comic she had been reading when they came in.

'Lovely pullovers,' ventured Angelica, in a sweeter tone, hoping to lure the unprepossessing oracle back into speech. They were hanging on hangers on a wire across the window, and there was a plum-coloured mohair jacket that she genuinely did like. 'Did you make them?'

The girl looked up and then back down. 'My mum does. If you want one you'll have to come by tomorrow, because she won't be back this afternoon.'

'Can you tell us which way they used to live? Which direction from here?' Nikhil wore that expression again, the almost-exploding one, but Angelica thought the outcome might well be tears.

The girl looked up, only halfway this time. 'By the water,' she said. 'It's obvious, isn't it?'

Back in the car, they spread the map across their laps and

shared some chocolate. There were only three needle-fine roads leading off the one they were on towards the water, two of them further north and one they had already passed.

'Do we go back or forward?' Angelica wondered. 'It would be a shame to go back and be wrong. We should've asked if there are any more shops north of here, to know whether they would have bothered . . . she wasn't very helpful, though. None of them are, are they? But she knew them—that's something.'

'In a place like this, it's more something when they *don't*, don't you think?'

'What do you mean?'

'Possibly they all know something, something more than they say. Only she's the first one to let it slip.'

'Like some sort of conspiracy? Don't be absurd. Why?'

'Because I am black. I don't know. Because she is. Because I'm not a Christian. Because I don't *belong*. What do I know about why? I just feel it.'

'You're letting the devil get to you. We'll find them. You can't blame a few simple country people for not going out of their way for us. How would they know anything? Why would they bother to conspire?'

Nikhil shrugged. 'You know their minds,' he said. 'You know the "Christian" mind of this man who looks like Jesus. You tell me.'

Angelica was silent for a moment, crunching on the last of her chocolate. 'I'll make you a deal,' she said. 'Or at least a proposition. I would say that we will only find your sister with God's help. That's what I think.'

'Your God, or my gods?'

'I'm pretty sure of my God, Nikhil. As you know. So my question, or my deal, or whatever you want to call it, is this: if we find them, will you become a Christian?'

Nikhil's hairline did a little jog as his brow rose and fell. 'This is the divine you are discussing,' he said, 'not some football team.'

'But if my God can prove to you that He exists—if He works miracles for you—shouldn't you reward Him with your faith? Only He can save your immortal soul. And He's the only one who can restore your sister to you. Come on—'

'You promised me there wouldn't be any of this. I won't go on if there is.'

'I didn't *mean* for there to be.'

As they sat and looked at the map on their knees, Nikhil said, 'I think we go forward. And we will discuss your God if and when we find them.'

It wasn't easy. They went forward to the farthest road—hardly a road, really, and the rain had started again, so it was muddy into the bargain—and they followed it to its natural end, just past a trio of abandoned crofts, where it became a path that crept off among the rocks. No place for a boat, they concurred. No signs of life apart from a screaming sea bird or two. They retreated.

The second route, only slightly to the south, appeared more promising at first: a few low white houses dotted the road on either side, and the tarmac ended in a small bay where it seemed conceivable that a vessel might anchor securely, or even be lifted out of the water for repairs. But no: inquiries yielded nothing, not even a sighting.

The last road was the best maintained of the three, although it appeared no more densely populated than the second. It was also the shortest, which was just as well, because it was coming up to six o'clock and both Angelica and Nikhil were weary. When they came to the end of the way, there on the slate-coloured water before them rolled a newly painted, lived-in-looking boat. A fishing boat, perhaps, originally. There was a light on in the cabin. And parked up against a hillock, at the turning-point where the road stopped, was a slightly rusted, open-backed lorry, a tarpaulin carelessly strung over its back to keep off the worst of the rain. A lorry just like the one Mrs MacKinnon had spoken about.

'They've come back,' breathed Nikhil. 'I don't believe it. It's incredible. You may be right about your God, or else it's fate— this is fantastic—they've come back!'

'I knew it,' said Angelica, softly, through her teeth. She leaned over and kissed Nikhil full on the mouth (banging her elbow on the steering wheel as she did so, but not minding). He didn't seem alarmed; he kissed her back. It was a triumphant kiss: a kiss, thought Angelica, endorsed by God.

When they paused in their embrace, Nikhil took her hand. 'Would you like to meet my sister?' he said, gravely and sweetly, as if asking her to marry him. The day's petulance was completely erased. She forgot it.

'I would like nothing more.'

He kissed the smooth back of her hand.

The man who came to answer their call did not remotely resemble Jesus. That was the first thing that crossed Angelica's mind but then, she thought, Jesus is all things to all people; why should he not bear different guises in different people's hearts? It did not occur to her that this man might be anyone other than Rupica's husband. And for Nikhil, instructed through his attendance at prayer group meetings and through Angelica's Sistine Chapel book in the appearance of many of the saints, but only, really, in the sight of Jesus as an infant on Mary's blue-cloth knee, Kenneth Campbell looked the image of Angelica's Saviour—a Saviour he would, for that one brief instant before he discovered that Kenneth Campbell fished for scallops for a living and only *wished* for female company ('Don't I just? Eh? Eh?'), have claimed as his own.

But it only took a brief exchange for him to realize that Kenneth Campbell was who he was—not Godly, not married, and only barely sober.

'Come in, come in,' he welcomed them. 'Come and have a drink. It's the season of the English, up here. I've been meeting a lot of you, the past few days, come up to join me. Some friendlier than others, mind.'

He would not take no for an answer: they were inside, each with a whisky in hand ('But I don't drink,' said Nikhil. 'Crap,' said Campbell), before they knew it. The cabin was small, low-ceilinged, but clean.

'What can I do for you then? Or is this simply a touristic visit?'

'It doesn't matter,' said Nikhil. 'We were mistaken. We thought this boat belonged—well, we thought—'

'She's your sister, is she? Did she go without telling you then?'

'You know them?'

'You look alike, you and she. Sure, I know them well. My neighbours in the cold, wet months. Not that it's warm and dry now, mind, but colder and wetter then. Not that it stopped them working.'

'No, of course not,' said Angelica for no reason.

'They were fixing a boat, yes?' Nikhil actually put his whisky to his lips and almost drank, but clearly the smell put him off.

'A fine little boat. Well, no, she wasn't fine. But they made her fine. He's a nice enough fellow, but peculiar—she, though, she's a dream. Beautiful lass.'

'Are they happy?' asked Angelica. She was curious. Nikhil looked annoyed.

Campbell made a funny, flighty gesture with his fingers. 'There are things,' he said, 'between men and women, that cannot be known. And that's what *I* believe. That's what I believe *in*.'

'Mr Campbell—' Nikhil was struggling to keep the conversation away from belief and, more specifically, on his sister—'When did they go? And where? And when will they come back?'

'Back? Now there's a good question. They've been gone a

few weeks now, I'd say, although I'm not much for dates. I don't know as they're coming back.'

'My sister hasn't gone to sail off the edge of the earth, has she? They've got to come back. Surely? What do you mean?'

'There's no call to get upset. It's not your sister's doing, is it? It's her man. It's the birds, isn't it?'

'Please explain,' said Angelica. She had been shredding a tissue during this conversation that went nowhere.

'Are you deaf, damn it? They've gone for the birds—out to Kilda for the birds. They'll be there till September at least, that's when their permission lasts until. Or his, rather. But he wants to stay the winter and prove that they can do it. They've got their own boat, after all, and there won't be anybody going to check.'

'What's Kilda? I don't understand. Can we hire a boat and go? Will you take us?'

St Kilda, Kenneth Campbell explained, pointing a fisherman's finger at the grey horizon, was as far out as the Outer Hebrides went. 'Last stop before Newfoundland,' he said, and winked at Angelica. '*You're* British, at the least. *You* know about St Kilda?'

It was a nature reserve, full of birds, said Campbell. Hence the voyage: puffins, fulmars, egrets, migrating, nesting, milling about in their thousands. It had been, until 1930, inhabited by an extraordinary, backward people who had never seen a tree, who had hardly invented the wheel, a tiny group of people inbred for generations; but now, there was only a small army base there. Nothing else. In the winter, no boats could land, not for months. Back in the twenties, all but starving in the winter, the people had begged to join the mainland. No protection, no security: this was why there was no permission for the winter even now, or possibly now more than ever. It simply wasn't safe.

'But why—what about Rupica? Why would they want to stay the winter? It's the decision of a madman!'

'To you or me, aye, that's the only word for it. But he's got

208

the fire of faith, doesn't he? He's a bloody Christian, isn't he?'

Angelica made a little coughing sound. '*I* am a Christian,' she said. Kenneth Campbell ignored her.

'And I'll tell you something, man, there's something of arrogance there, for all the humility he pretends. Sometimes I think he thinks he *is* God, you know. It's the *certainty* I can't abide.'

'What about my sister? Is she a Christian?'

'Damned if I know. Above all, the lass is in love with the fella. That was plain a mile off. So you could say she has faith of a kind.'

Angelica and Nikhil didn't stay long after that: there didn't seem much point. And besides, Campbell, drunk as he was getting, wanted to drive into Portree (in the lorry, a gift from the departed pair: 'Would they have given it to me for good if they were planning to come back? No they would not.'). But no, he could not take them to St Kilda, it was far—hours and hours, day and night—and would be dangerous. And even then there was no guarantee of landing. Besides which there was no *permission* for landing. Permission came from London, from some ministry in Whitehall, and didn't it take months—he'd heard all about it, from start to finish. To try to get there, even to try, he said, they would need to bribe a crooked fisherman with a big boat, with a great deal of money. And they would need time. And still, no guarantees. 'So you see,' he finished with a smile, 'so you see, it *is* more or less as if they'd sailed off the edge of this flat earth. Or as if they'd died and gone to heaven. There isn't any way to get to them. None at all.'

There was a weight like death in the car when they returned to it: the weight of their triumphant kiss, jubilantly weightless only an hour earlier. They sat there, staring out at the gloom, while Kenneth Campbell passed in front of them like an actor in a film, shrugging into his coat. He climbed into the lorry and tussled briefly with its engine before pulling away, amid a clatter

209

unseemly in the mournful seaside silence.

Angelica looked at Nikhil, at his pinched mouth and fine profile. She was trying to pray for some understanding, but she found that her mind could not utter the simplest formulations of prayer.

'It is late. We should get back,' said Nikhil.

Angelica couldn't tell what he was thinking and didn't know him well enough to ask. In any event, he would probably have lied. She wanted, then, to say something about the kiss. But what was there to say?

'If you like,' she said instead, 'we could ask Virginia and her mother to join us for supper. It might, you know, take our minds off things?'

Nikhil raised his shoulders almost imperceptibly to signal his indifference, and bit at his lower lip in an endeavour to communicate something Angelica didn't understand; or perhaps in an effort not to communicate at all.

When Melody Simpson woke up and saw the white-white of the hospital room around her, she did not think for one second that she had died and gone to heaven. She knew full well where she was and what she was doing there and she felt like a damn fool.

After Virginia had left her bunched up against the cold paving of the house, Melody Simpson had done her best to wait with fortitude. But she had known absolutely that she was dying: even in the lee of the house the winds were bitter, and seemed to strip away not only her clothes but the layers of her flesh as well. Not that she had felt anything about it, other than faintly annoyed that death should take so long and be so uncomfortable. But obviously she had dwelt a great deal on the subject, because the next thing she knew she *was* dead, or believed herself to be, and although still chilled she was warmer, and she had climbed through the window and was in the house.

It wasn't at all neglected. In fact, it was brightly lit and furnished with familiar objects, and its only drawback was that it seemed to be recently abandoned—not unlike the Tarbish Hotel, only the day before, Melody had thought to herself. There was music wafting in from somewhere ('Roll, those, roll those pretty eyes . . . '), and Melody (remarkably spry and able, and, she noticed, in full possession of her own, original bosom) wandered through the house to find its source, calling out every so often, although nobody answered her. She was just coming to the realization that the origin of the music was God, and was feeling sheepish about not having believed in Heaven when here it was, and lovely too (if a bit empty), and was just thinking what a pleasure and a relief it was to be at last finished with the trials of life, when it started to rain, and she awoke to find herself still on the steps of the house, alone and cold and now wet into the bargain, and suffering the agonies of the damned in her horrible twisted foot. But it did make her think, and she did wonder, for the first time ever, whether on some level of her encrusted, atheistic old self, she didn't *want* to believe. It must, she thought, make the most final things so cheerfully furnished and comfortable.

Virginia had returned, in time, with two thick, surly men from the village down the way. Neither seemed versed in the medical—even in her disoriented state Melody Simpson had called them brutish to their faces, an insult which they seemed not to register. They had hoisted her between them and lugged her up to the Ford Fiesta, where she had remembered at least that the passenger seat would be wet and had laid claim to the back, although she had a suspicion that she had actually just moaned. And then one of them, a burly, bearded fellow, had driven at breakneck speed to the hospital in Portree, an interminable time during which Mrs Simpson had given in to the pain and had dozed and awoken several times, generally to find Virginia clutching at her, teary-eyed, her face wobbly

211

and too close to focus upon.

In that odd, fluid, woozy period, Mrs Simpson did realize, solidly, that she would never be able to explain any of this, the before or the during, to anyone. She felt hollowed by the tiresome old thought of how lonely life was. And death too—if her dream was any indication.

In the hospital room it didn't all seem so bad. Melody Simpson felt a damn fool, but she didn't think she was going to die any more, and with the help of the painkillers she'd been given, she almost believed she might never die at all. Only two thoughts irritated her: one was that her letter to Emmy remained in her handbag, unsent, and now, she knew, she would never send it; and the other was that, given that she had unexpectedly survived her trip to Alt-na-Ross, she was sorry to have spent twenty-one pounds on her lunch the day before. The food had not been that memorable, after all. But these were small, feathery things.

Everyone around her—Virginia, the fluttering nurses, the doctor—appeared quite concerned, but she wasn't worried. Not hungry, not tired, not in pain, not worried: she turned her head to look at her daughter, to try to convey this.

'I feel very . . . not,' she said. She could tell that this communication only caused Virginia's brow to furrow further, but Mrs Simpson could not get upset about it. Virginia looked pale to her, a ragged sack of wrinkles and bones, and Mrs Simpson felt a great, vague tenderness. She tried to speak again.

'Pale . . . bones,' was what she said. To her fuzzy and faint irritation, Virginia put her head in her hands and burst into tears.

Virginia was unutterably tired. It was still light, but late, and the nurses, deeming visiting hours to be over, had cast her out on to the street. Not knowing what to do, she made her way the short distance down to the harbour. Before going, she turned to see if she could pick out her mother's room, but no lights shone from the upper windows.

The day played back in her head in disordered snippets and flashes: the castle, their breakfast, the soreness of the cold air in her lungs as she ran—it must have been miles—for help. Her mother's tortured, bloated ankle. The doctor seemed confident of Mrs Simpson's recovery ('It could've been her hip, now, couldn't it? And when the hip goes, they're as good as gone, aren't they?'), but uncertain of how long she might have to stay in the hospital. Unlike London hospitals, it did not seem to be busy: Virginia could almost imagine that they would welcome her mother as a diversion, and might even keep her on for that purpose.

Amidst her anxiety and fatigue, Virginia, as she stood outside the bed and breakfast, was also furious. She felt she had been conned. It was as if her mother had known it all—the tongues, the hand in the vestry—since before it even happened; just as she had clearly known about what would happen at work.

As for God—where was He? Virginia could not, no matter how much she wanted to, ally her mother and the divine. Mrs Melody Simpson would have no truck with God's plan, not knowingly or inadvertently, just simply not at all. If Virginia were to forge such a link, even only in her mind and only for a minute, she had no doubt that her mother would rise from her hospital bed and descend upon her daughter in a fury. Which meant that maybe for once—just once, she promised the seagull that landed nearby and pecked at the garbage—God had no place here. Just possibly, on this one, long day, while she, Virginia Simpson, had been traversing this nasty, wet island, He had been elsewhere.

God's absence was also the only way to explain the reappearance of Kenneth Campbell. Although he put it otherwise: 'Waiting for me outside my office?' he bellowed from the threshold of the pub. 'No need for an appointment. You're expected.'

Virginia did not want to enter the pub, or she did not *neces-*

sarily want to. But she went in. And found it empty as an office but for Campbell and MacAllister, the publican.

'Whatever you want, on me,' offered Kenneth Campbell, with a slurring such that he elided over the comma. 'You're grey as the day and you look like you could use a drink.' Then he made a great, theatrical show of looking around the pub, his hand above his brow like a sailor scanning the horizon. 'And mum?' he cried. 'Where's our dear mum? Have you got rid of mum, then?'

'My mother,' said Virginia, 'has had a serious fall. She has broken her ankle and possibly worse and is in hospital. I would be grateful if you could show some respect.'

'That's a terrible thing. You'll be needing a drink then. I *am* sorry. Do you take water with your whisky?'

Because she didn't answer, Virginia was given a glass of the stuff neat. She did not protest, because it seemed a fitting tribute to her mother: 'Mother would love to be doing this just now,' is what she said to herself, not only upon accepting the first drink, but the second and the third.

She and Kenneth Campbell sat and talked—like friends—at the table by the window, as a few other customers came and went and doubtless thought them intimates of long standing. Every so often, Virginia felt the familiar prickle of fear on her neck—who was this man and what did he want of her, after all?—but it would fade as quickly as it had come. She was in no state to sustain terror, or even surprise: she was as empty and light as the husk she had been, lying out on Primrose Hill into the small hours. Only she was being weighed down and filled with words as warm as whisky.

They did not go until MacAllister asked them to leave, and by then it was truly night, or as close as it would get. Virginia Simpson had been drunk before, but not for a long time. Not since she had become the person she now considered herself to be. She was not wild with it—blunted was closer to the truth—but a burden was lifted, and when Kenneth Campbell stumbled towards his lorry and waved her with him, she said, 'No.'

'I may be drunk, Mr Campbell, and I may not know how to drive, but I do know that drinking and driving are not compatible. I think you shouldn't drive. I certainly wouldn't go with you in such a state. Which is not to say that I would go with you at all, but there we are.'

'So what do you propose I do, sweet Virginia?'

Virginia stood for a moment and thought, although nothing was very clear, in part because it was night, at last, in part because of the whisky, and in part because she felt either like a young girl or an old woman, but certainly not like the self that she thought herself to be. Then she told Kenneth Campbell he could stay in the little blue room overlooking the harbour with her.

'Mother's in hospital, but we are paying for two just the same. So you might as well. You can sleep in her bed. Or on it, at least.'

He seemed to think this a fine idea. Somewhat to Virginia's annoyance, he appeared neither surprised nor excited: he clearly had no grasp of the enormity of her concession. But she did not feel it was an offer she could retract.

They both moved with exaggerated quiet in the stairwell. Virginia thought of the two men at breakfast and wondered which door enclosed them. She wondered whether they had a big double bed, and whether they lay asleep in each other's embrace, hairy forearms entwined on the coverlet. The idea didn't seem alarming to her now, after all the cold wind, the running, the loneliness of the afternoon: it seemed warm and safe.

Just inside the room, on the blue carpet, lay a folded square of white paper. Kenneth Campbell, who preceded Virginia, stepped over it and fumbled for a light switch, but even inebriated, Virginia was meticulous, and saw it at once. It was a note from Angelica, of the day's date, marked '7pm'.

Dear Ginny,

We have had a simply beastly day. Our search has led us
to the water's edge, where we learned from a strange,
drunken man (not even a Scot!) that Nikhil's sister and
her husband have gone far away by boat and we have no
hope of finding them. Nikhil, as you can imagine, is
feeling rather black about it all, and we could both do
with some cheering up. Regale us with details of the
ancestral home over supper? Bring mum. My treat. Give
us a ring at the hotel? Love, Angel.

Angelica's handwriting was loopy and rounded, and she had
drawn and shaded in a heart between 'love' and her name. Cheerful though the note was, Virginia could sense the disappointment
behind it. She had a faint recollection that this couple—in particular this missing man—was to have held the answer, the key.

She could hear Kenneth Campbell peeing in the capsule lava-
tory. She did not come from a world where men were close
enough to burp or swear, let alone go to the bathroom, but this
man was in her bedroom, because she had allowed him to be. Virginia was suddenly shaky and had to sit down. On her own bed;
she was careful; he had already sullied her mother's sheets by
intention alone.

He himself seemed awkward when he emerged from the
bathroom, as if he had only just realized that he—or they—had
done something out of the ordinary.

'Small, ah, small facilities, eh?' he ventured, looking out of
the window. 'Must be a nice view in the day.'

Their discomfort was sobering them both up: not, Virginia
recognized, desirable. This whole sequence of events, she decided, was not pleasant, but there was a point to be proven and it
was best taken care of efficiently.

'That is your bed,' she said, pointing at the one she wasn't sitting on. 'I think my mother would be grateful if you didn't use the pillow. I mean, she likes to, and two people—it's not very sanitary.'

He went and sat on his bed. She could see in the lamp's filmy light that his cheeks were dusted with grey stubble, and one of his eyes was ticking slightly. He tested the bedsprings with his fingertips and then lay back, deftly removing the pillow from behind his head before so much as a hair had touched it. He leaned it vertically against the bed, on the floor. He did not take his shoes off, and his eyes were already shut.

Virginia didn't know whether this was an ideal or an anticlimax: she felt deprived of her fear. She sat, her body facing the room, her head turned to watch him. Long after she assumed he was asleep, he opened one eye.

'Virginia Simpson,' he said. 'You can go to sleep if you want to. I may be a flawed man but I am not a bad man and you've nothing to fret about as long as I'm here.' Then he shut his eye again. 'We're all frightened,' he said after a minute, in a low voice. 'It's just a question of degree.'

Virginia held his words to her, closer than she had ever held her Bible. She didn't mind when he started to snore, a great, gargantuan, bottomless rumble, wholly unlike her mother's piccolo whistle. She just sat there looking at him, and then out to the black water, and then back at him, until, not so long after, it began to get light again. She didn't even think to thank God.

Bali

AFTER THE PARTY, everything changed. For a start, Frank moved in. He slept sprawled on the bed in the main room and remained slumbering, imperturbable, for hours after Jenny and the others started work in the morning. Not even the pool-makers' vigorous stone-cutting could wake him.

But his objectionable presence was not the only alteration. A weight hung in the air, heavier each day; Emmy could feel it. Aimée wasn't its sole source, either: Jenny behaved differently, and so did Max (whom Aimée insisted on calling Christopher). Meanwhile, Buddy all but disappeared, and even the languid K'tut did not surface for a couple of days at a time.

Most people, Emmy knew, would take these subterranean currents as an indication that it was time to move on; but most people, she also told herself, would have something to move on *to*. Since the night of the party—since Buddy's tiny kiss—she felt that she was accepted, by those who counted, anyway, as basically one of the family. And she was determined to stay where she was until she was good and ready. There were still things to be learned in the Sparke household. Emmy continued to imagine that her future (seeing as her past was gone) might lie somewhere hidden in this place: perhaps she, too, could belong to this tight community of misfits?

That said, Emmy was growing bored. Bored of the routine, or lack of it; bored of the pointed silences that punctuated many of the goings-on; bored of waiting. That was really the source of the tension, and possibly the reason why Emmy couldn't bring herself to go: a full week after the party, everybody was waiting, coiled like springs, unspeaking. Even the slothful Frank was waiting. In the conversation she had overheard and only half recalled, Kraut had said something about 'next month'. Next month was just about to become 'this month', and now everyone was so tired of waiting for whatever it was that they were all ready to burst. Which, Emmy reflected as she splashed in the hotel pool, beneath the outlet of the mountain spring, was all very boring indeed.

Emmy stood in the shallow end, her body underwater. She loved the way the refraction of light created a disjunction between what was above and what beneath the water's skin. And she loved the way that her legs appeared to shimmer slimly in that other world just beneath her. That silvery, elusive self was much closer to the person she considered herself to be than was the matronly torso rising up out of the depths. When she lay in bed at night, in the darkness, with the cicadas singing, she was this aquatic being: invisible as it was to her, this was the body she imagined.

A fluttering at the edge of her vision made Emmy look up. Jenny was at the poolside, waving at her, with apparent urgency. Emmy swam over in a few brisk strokes.

'Where's Max? Have you seen Max?' Jenny's eyes were open very wide.

'Not at all, not this morning. Why?' Emmy had water in her ear and jigged up and down with her head tilted to try to get it out.

'It's not important. No, it is very important, but it doesn't matter.'

Emmy stopped hopping. 'What do you mean? I thought you and Max weren't speaking. Am I the only one who isn't to know what's going on?'

'Of course Max and I are friends. Do not be angry. Very good friends. It is only Aimée who does not like me. She tries to make my life very, very hard, and I worry that if she hurts me I will not go to Australia.' Jenny, who had been squatting on her haunches, sat flat on the grass at the water's edge. Her one long plait snaked across her shoulder and hung down between her breasts. She looked miserable.

'What you really mean is that Aimée will make trouble for you if she finds out about you and Buddy.'

Jenny did not look at Emmy; she did not say yes or no.

'But what hold does Aimée have?' Emmy genuinely wondered. 'She and Buddy aren't lovers any more, are they?'

Jenny shrugged. 'I only know the room I am in,' she said. 'I do not know the rooms of others. But there is also Ruby. Buddy loves his children very much. He loves Max very much.'

Facing the sun, Emmy's back had grown dry and hot. All of her that was above the water had, in the heat, regained its fixed and freckled parameters. Even her bathing-suit was starting to dry. 'So why are you looking for Max, then, in such a hurry?'

'Buddy would like to go to Komodo, for the dragons, as soon as Max is completely well.'

'Not today, surely?'

Jenny shrugged again. 'I want to talk to him,' she said, standing to go. 'Maybe if you see him you will tell him I am looking.'

She turned and was heading off when she stopped and came back to the water's edge. 'Is it easy to swim?'

'Of course it is,' said Emmy. 'Do you want me to teach you some time?'

Jenny nodded and then darted away, her plait beating time against her back.

Later, as Emmy walked barefoot up the prickly, stony slope to the house, she saw a car pull up on the road a few metres away. Kraut, who was driving, honked the horn several times and then got out, his ears more pointed than ever. He walked over to Buddy's house—with the awkward, halting gait of people wearing flip-flops—and began to shout in what sounded like German.

A vision in lurid batiks, Buddy appeared at the top of the stairs leading down from the kitchen to the road—the back way out. And in time to Kraut's shouting, he sprinted down the stairs and along to the car. Emmy had never seen Buddy run. Even coming down Abang, he had kept to a stately, if athletic, pace. The two men got into the car, honked some more, to scatter any women or children or cocks or ducks that might take it upon themselves to round the bend at that moment and then, in a cloud of dust, they were gone. Northwards. Away from Ubud, but not towards Kintamani, either. Just gone.

The world settled back into midday silence, the sounds of heat and hovering insects and the distant whooping of voices and the thud of the stonemasons. Her feet stinging, Emmy passed through the carved Sparke portal and climbed the rest of the way to the house.

Except for Ruby, the main room was quiet. Quiet, but full: clad in his linen suit, barefoot, Frank lounged on the bed, scanning a tattered magazine; at the table, Jenny, bent over a massive arrangement of flowers, fiddled; while Aimée lounged in an armchair by the veranda's edge, smoking and watching Ruby canter up and down, squealing like a banshee, naked but for a pink bow in her hair and her pink patent leather shoes.

Emmy tried to picture the scene minutes before: she attempted to rearrange the room in her mind's eye to fit Buddy into it. Had these people been conversing with each other? Or had a deeper, more peopled silence prevailed?

As Emmy crossed to the veranda, Jenny flashed a squirrely smile, but said nothing. Emmy did not look again at Frank, so could not judge his reaction to her arrival. As for Aimée, Emmy *felt* her looking, and the feeling was not comfortable. Wrapping her towel more closely around her, Emmy went to lean on the woven rattan balustrade and watch an easier world go by. No wonder, she thought, looking at the bare-backed workmen laying stones, and the waves of wriggling heat across the valley, no wonder K'tut did not come round any more.

After a long moment, Aimée cleared her throat. Not innocently, but in a deliberate way. Emmy knew this because she did it a second time and then, more impatiently, a third. Emmy turned to find that Jenny had slipped away, and that Ruby had been seized and silenced and propped upon her mother's knee. One of Aimée's hands gripped her daughter's shoulder tightly, while the other twirled a lit cigarette in a holder.

Over the course of Aimée's visit, Emmy's sense of intrigue about this woman had turned to distaste and thence to dislike. Perhaps it was contagious: the effect of watching Aimée's effect? Because there was no other cause: since the airport they had hardly exchanged a word.

'Can so much smoking be good for a child?' Emmy asked.

Aimée glowered. 'I was wondering,' she said, 'how long you are planning to stay in my house.'

'I wasn't aware that it *was* your house. I'm Max's guest, really, so I suppose it depends on him.'

'As the mother of Ruby, I am the mistress of the house,' said Aimée, adjusting the weight of her trophy child. Ruby was sucking her thumb, kittenishly tired. 'I did not invite you and I do not know your intentions. So I ask. Because I do not like what I see.'

Emmy wished she were fully dressed. Her outraged dignity would have felt more robust than it did in a Speedo bathing suit. 'Not only Max, but Buddy has asked me to stay—for as long as I want to. He has repeated his invitation. He's even invited me to go to Komodo with the family to see the dragons,' she lied, only a little—the invitation had been implicit, and he *might* have been about to ask, after all—to ensure that her position was firm. 'If you have a problem with it, surely you should take it up with Buddy?'

'With Horace? Of course, you would say that. But women are Horace's vice; they are *my* problem. And so I deal with them myself.'

'What exactly are you implying?' Emmy felt an involuntary surge of excitement: if Aimée thought that she and Buddy were lovers, then perhaps it was because of something he had said. It was, then, perhaps, a possibility.

'I cannot see what he sees in you,' Aimée said, with a disparaging wave of her well-manicured hand. 'But I also have seen what I have seen. And I am asking you to go. If you do not, then I will make it impossible for you to stay. You may not think so, but Horace needs me. More than he needs you.'

'I think you've seen too many old Hollywood films,' said Emmy. 'I really do. There is no connection between Buddy and me. We hardly speak, for Christ's sake. I'm just a middle-aged *Hausfrau* on holiday from Sydney.'

'Precisely.' Aimée stood—gracefully, considering that she was hoisting the dozing Ruby on to her delicate hip. 'You must understand my point of view. I was a child. Horace took that away from me, because it amused him. Now he owes me a life, and I must always make sure that I get it. *I* make the rules.' She shook Ruby slightly and slid the child to the floor, where Ruby tottered half awake. 'Come,' said her mother, grasping Ruby's entire forearm in her hand and practically dragging her to the door. 'Nap-time.'

Had Emmy been able to whistle through her teeth, she would have. As it was, she laughed aloud at the absurdity. It was Frank who whistled through his teeth. He had remained prone on the bed around the corner throughout. 'Cor,' he said, 'She's a pistol, eh?'

'What are *you* doing here?'

'I can ask the same of you,' he said. Then: 'I guess you know where you're not wanted.'

'These accusations are ridiculous, you know as well as I do. I won't be bullied by a girl young enough to be my daughter, just because her ex-boyfriend—old enough to be her father—has dumped her. This kind of thing doesn't happen in my world. People live by a code, where I come from. They act like civilized human beings. You know where you stand.'

'It's not the locals around here who live without a code, dearie. What kind of code have you been living by, exactly, since you landed here?'

'Speak for yourself.' Emmy looked Frank up and down: his dissipated, flabby, forgotten self, the marks of laxity all over him. 'Why the devil is that child so poisonous, anyhow?'

'Buddy worked—works—well, does business with her father. That's how they met. It's complicated. Buddy doesn't usually keep girls around when he's done with them. She knows that.' Frank licked his lips but he seemed genuinely moved by his story. It transpired that as well as the issue of Ruby, there was the question of Aimée's father. He had not been pleased by the liaison—his daughter had been, as she herself had said, little more than a child—but had bowed to it because of Aimée's stubbornness. Now that the affair was to all intents and purposes over, Aimée was too proud to let on to her father that she had not instigated the rupture, but with her silence she set certain conditions. Because if she *did* tell her father the truth—that she, and her beautiful daughter, had been more or less dumped—then he would stop doing business with Buddy. 'And that,' mused Frank, 'would leave Casanova well up shit creek.

'Not to mention,' he continued, 'that he might just break every bone in Buddy's body. Y'know? Or Buddy might mysteriously fall off the top of Abang.'

'But what does he *do*, this man?' Emmy again recalled the conversation at the party.

'He's a businessman, that's all,' said Frank. 'But you never know. Buddy always says, East and West, like oil and water. Oil and water.'

After suffering the doctor's treatment for a week, Max was inclined to agree with K'tut. 'A charlatan,' he told Emmy. He was done with his injections, and the mark on his neck seemed to be healing fine. But still the doctor made him come to his sweaty green surgery in central Den Pasar, where he loaded Max down with large, vile-smelling tablets and wads of herbs to be brewed into tea. And Max had continued to feel sick ever since the monkey bit him.

Max thought it was the various teas that upset him so badly, but the doctor insisted they were to calm his insides. And it was true that on the one day Max hadn't taken them he had suffered just the same. His father dismissed it as a bout of Bali belly. But Max worried that whatever it was might be fatal. The monkey might have had AIDS, for example. Or it might have had a strain of rabies the vaccine couldn't protect against, and the existence of which they were hiding from him. Or it might have passed on any number of unidentified viruses or bacteria. Some nights he woke up, bang, certain that his heart had stopped or was just about to: certain that even before life had begun, it was over. He didn't tell anyone about his terrors: not the doctor (before whom he feigned a sullen, superior indifference); not Emmy (who, he worried, would get all gooey and maternal and would treat him like a complete infant); and certainly not Jenny, whom he might have told under other circumstances but whom he had been avoiding since the night of the party. He would have been avoiding his father, too, except it was clear that Buddy wouldn't have noticed: business was keeping him so busy that he was hardly even around. A big day, business-wise, was coming up. A couple of trips. And a planned junket to Komodo to see the dragons. Max didn't much want to go.

Seeing as Buddy had given K'tut the bus and the day off, and K'tut had driven to Candi Dasa to look at some property his cousin wanted him to buy, Max had hitched a ride into Den Pasar with the van from the hotel next door. But it meant that after his appointment he had to take a *bemo* back up to Ubud.

It was noon, and the *bemo* was crowded and unpleasant. The breeze that blew in from the road seemed hotter even than the air inside the covered lorry. The driver took a perverse delight in bouncing over potholes and in veering madly from side to side to avoid stray dogs or wandering humans. All the drivers were known for this tendency but this one was the worst Max had encountered and, frightened, Max found he was sweating terribly. Then Max could hear his heart pounding: it was louder than the squealing suspension, louder than the spitting of gravel and the diesel-chug of the *bemo* engine. Louder even than the fare-collector's yelling. All Max could hear was his heart. And he suddenly thought: 'I must get off this bus. I am going to be sick.'

He motioned to the conductor, who, in turn, leaned off the running-board and shrieked to the four winds and the driver to pull over, and the driver obliged by slamming on the brakes. Max got off, picking his way over old men and mothers and children and, still clutching the damp packet of herbs from the doctor's office, he watched the *bemo* bounce into the distance.

Teetering in the ditch by the side of the road, he tried to retch but couldn't be sick. He sank to the ground, bent in the ditch, put his head between his knees and shut his eyes.

'Just concentrate on your breathing,' advised his reasonable self. In, out. In, out. Slower: in, and . . . out. He pressed his fingers to his temples. His T-shirt was clammy with sweat and prickled by grasses. He hunched like that for a while and started to feel better. A little. But there was no doubt in one significant part of him that this was the beginning of the end. He looked around him, and his eyes didn't seem to work properly. Transparent swirly things drifted across his vision. The road was unbearably bright.

He might, he thought, just die on this island. He wasn't sure how he felt about that: he pictured his mother, forced to fly out to join Buddy, whom she hated, for the funeral.

Considering her distress made him feel marginally stronger. He couldn't really hear his heart any more, but he still found its beating tiring, and his ribcage ached. And then he thought about Jenny. The thought gave him a quick palpitation, satisfying in its way. When he thought about Jenny, it occurred to him that the only reasonable thing to do was to confront her. To tell her, perhaps, about the true, final nature of his illness, and to insist that she make a choice—to share his last weeks, or, possibly, days. His reasonable self argued that he might not actually be at death's door, and even half-allowed the possibility that she could, in any event, choose against him. But the voice of his un-silenceable, as yet unvanquished heart prevailed. He would speak to her, now, as soon as he could get home to Ubud.

Feeling herself battered by insults, Emmy lay on her bed to consider future movements. Soon, she conceded, she would have to make a decision about the Sparkes, and then, no matter what it was, she would have to look again at Pod, at Pietro, at that utterly alien world of hers, now as unfamiliar as Ubud had been. She was letting herself slide: if she wasn't explaining things to herself then she was simply escaping. And while that might long ago have been her intention in coming to the island, things had changed. Escape was not what she had climbed the mountain for. Contemplating the opacity of truth (why *couldn't* it be as distinct as the disc of the sun, rising and setting opposite?), Emmy fell asleep.

When she awoke it was late afternoon, and she was cold,

curled on her bed in a bathing-suit and towel. Her hair was matted and eccentric, and her head thick with dense and distant dreams. She had dreamt, she was aware, of her mother and sister, an exhausting, busy dream of the world in which she would only ever be a child. Her exhaustion was born from the effort of trying to make Virginia like her: she had done something wrong, and her sister had sent her away. Their mother, a stern vision in an apron, had taken Emmy's part, but this alliance had only made Virginia shun her the more. In the dream, Emmy knew she had wept, great racking sobs of shame and sorrow, but upon waking, her cheeks were dry.

After lying for a few chilly minutes, she realized that if she remained in her room, waking would only feel like more ghastly sleeping, so she decided to get dressed and go for a walk.

She didn't bother to look upstairs for any companion for her stroll. Still smarting, she knew where she wasn't wanted, and until one of her true hosts came forward to claim her, she would keep out of the way.

She decided to follow the web of paths through the paddies on the west side of the road, to a village she and Max had stumbled upon in the early days of their acquaintance. There, at this hour, everyone would be gathering beneath the central pavilion to watch their communal television, and as the sun set, their one street light, a long, lonely fluorescent bulb, would cast its mauve light on one small patch of ground. She could return in time to witness one of her favourite quotidian moments: the duck-herder crossing the paddies in his mollusc hat with a stick on his shoulder and a half-dozen jabbering fowl marching smartly in his wake. Watching that ritual would cheer her, Emmy reasoned, even if the rest of her outing failed to.

But she realized as she set out that the sun was lower than she had thought; she would not see the ducks march upon her return. It would be too late. She even contemplated going back to her room: when night fell in Ubud, the earth disappeared and everything was given over to the realm of the spirits, a dark world of shifting shapes and unknown quantities. That was what the local people believed: it was why they made and tended their roadside shrines; it was why Gdé had so carefully prepared the ascent of Abang down to the last member of their group. And in this place that was not hers, where other people's truths held sway, the generally aspiritual Emmy was inclined to believe it too. She hesitated about going alone into the dusk—but resolved not to be hindered by superstition, not to be banned from the island's pathways as she had been effectively banned, by Aimée, from the Sparke sitting-room.

As she picked her way along the muddy barriers between the paddies, she heard the duck-herder calling to his ducks. Already the paddies themselves were black and possibly bottomless pools, their thousands of green shoots invisible in the failing light. If night had fallen fully, it would be all but impossible, she acknowledged, to negotiate a dry return. The paths between the paddies were slippery and narrow, and the mud slimed up around the edges of her sandals. But her mind was made up. As if from another planet, she heard the buzz of a motorbike on the road behind her, and the sound of voices. The light was blue, and deepening fast.

Emmy made it across the rice paddies and was into the stretch of forest that hid the village from open land when she decided she would have to turn back. She imagined she could see the light of the fluorescent bulb ahead, made to flicker by the movement on the public television screen, but she couldn't be sure. The distance and the dusk and the trees played tricks. It was dark—almost night now—and she was, she told herself, getting cold. She didn't want to miss supper. There was no point in going on. It was hard not to feel as though Aimée had triumphed: no Buddy, no ducks, and even her walk aborted. No more life here than at home, was the truth of it. 'I am a damn fool,' she said aloud to the trees, and she felt they rustled in assent. But it didn't make her feel any better.

The walk back was a nightmare. Emmy kept thinking this sentence as she walked: imagining talking about her walk, with Max, with Buddy, with Jenny perhaps. It did not make the slipping and stumbling any less unpleasant, nor did it warm the icy ooze of the paddies into which she occasionally fell, but it did take her out of the moment to a time when this would only be a faintly hilarious memory. And as the night closed in—and the moon had not yet risen—considering the experience in the past tense made it a lot less frightening.

Until, that is, Emmy heard something, or someone, alive. She was within earshot of the road, but the sounds were much closer than that. They were animal sounds—a rooting and snuffling, perhaps of a wayward pig, or of one of those craven, gaunt dogs, foraging for toads and lizards in the water. Emmy didn't want to think that it might be one of the island's famed spirits—that didn't, she hastened to add, exist—but she couldn't help but consider it. She stopped her slurping steps to listen better, and the sounds continued but did not move. Whatever it was, it was ahead of her on the path, snivelling, and she didn't much want to run into it.

'Hello! Hello? Who goes there?' Emmy called, to shoo away the dogs and pigs and spirits.

The noise stopped, as if the creature had tensed itself, was hiding.

'Is somebody there?'

The silence held. And held. And then broke.

'Aw, for Chrissakes, Emmy, leave us alone? Jesus, what're you doing following a guy around like that? Bloody hell!'

Spirits sometimes spoke in the voices of friends and relatives. Emmy started to move forward, swinging her arms back and forth crossways in front of her like a mine detector. No pig, this.

'Is that Max? Max, is that you? Max? What *are* you doing here?'

'None of your fucking business. Jesus.' His breathing was ragged. She felt from his voice that he wasn't far away, only a few steps now.

'I didn't follow you. I'm coming back from a walk. What's happened? Have you been crying?'

'I'm fine. I feel just fine. Leave us alone, Emmy?'

She was almost upon him. He was beneath her, or at least, his voice was at the level of her thighs, which meant that he was actually sitting in the mud.

'I'm glad it's you—I heard the noises and I thought . . . but it was just you crying.' She squatted down beside him, caught the luminous glow of his watch face. 'The moon will be up soon,' she said. She did not have to see Max to know he was upset. 'And you'll be caught here. It's like a searchlight when it comes. Will you help me get back to the house? I'm having some trouble, in the dark.'

Max said nothing. Emmy imagined it was Pod she was talking to, quietly, in the dark. Or rather, Portia. Someone once utterly known and now slipped away. 'I'm low myself, you know. I've had the treatment from Aimée, who thinks I'd better go.'

Max sniffed.

'Is it worse than that? Aren't you feeling well? Is it the after-effect of those shots?'

'There's no after-effect from the shots. I'm fine, really. Please, Emmy—'

It was true that at last, physically, Max felt perfectly well. He couldn't explain that when he had finally spoken to Jenny, it was as if his stomach were unclenching and his heart, so speedy, were slowing back down. There wasn't any way to explain that he felt a rage as blind as the dark night, but that his turmoil wasn't due to anything he had said or done. It was because of what had been done to him. The doctor's handful of herbs and the island's sup-

231

posed spirits—they all counted for nothing.

'Did she find you, then?'

'What are you talking about?'

'Jenny.'

'I was in town today. Den Pasar. You know, the doctor. More useless medication. I'm perfectly all right. I just want to be on my own. Please?'

With some effort, Emmy stood back up. 'You did say I was useful because I wasn't part of it.'

Max didn't say anything. But each of them listened for the other as Max rasped in his wrath and Emmy tramped off towards the road and the flickering lights of the house.

Emmy expected preparations for supper to be underway upon her return, but she didn't expect such a to-do. As she approached the house she heard a great thumping and thundering from within, and men's voices singing. The banging, she discovered, originated from Buddy and Frank leaping about, dancing almost. It was an extraordinary sight. The song was tuneless, like a football chant, like cheering. Kraut was smoking, holding his cigarette in his mouth, his eyes slitted to keep out the cloud in front of his face, and he was clapping, in little erratic bursts. They did not stop when Emmy crossed the threshold, and it was only then that she saw that they were leaping *for* something, in front of something: against the wall, on a table, sat a bronze Buddha flaked with gold leaf, shimmering in the dim light, gazing on the proceedings with an opalescent eye. Finely carved, androgynous and elegant, he was a handsome sitting Buddha, between two and three feet tall—slim, placid, and clearly adored, to judge from the number of gilt leaves, offerings from supplicants, that covered him and his small pedestal. Between his hands rested a slender cylinder in which to place lighted joss-sticks, filled, by Buddy, with flowers that Emmy recognized from Jenny's arrangement.

'Beaut, innit?' panted Frank, nodding half to Emmy and half to the statue, slowing his steps.

'Curious place for a Buddha,' she said. She crossed her arms. 'Where does he come from?'

'Burma,' said Buddy, grinning, also still now. 'Absolutely un-fucking-believable, eh?'

'Is he full of drugs, then?' Emmy felt a little sick and clasped her sides with her crossed arms. So she had been right: what had seemed too extraordinary to be lurking beneath Ubud's ordinary surface *was* true. She had half-thought that simply by imagining that they were drug smugglers—by envisioning the intrigue—she had prevented it from being so. But clearly here, too, she was subject to reality, and not the other way round. Even here she was having bad luck. Her code was not working. She got as far as thinking that perhaps it had not been Max she had encountered in the rice paddies—that it had indeed been an evil spirit—when she realized that all three men were glaring, and that Buddy was speaking in a hushed, deadly tone. He was pointing a finger.

' . . . a fool? You take me for a complete twat-brained arse-hole? Drugs! Drugs! Do you hear that?'

'I'm sorry, it's just that—'

'The penalty for smuggling drugs out here is death. *Death*. And I may not live in your tight-assed Sydney society, but I am not fucking daft. It's a fucking Buddha, for Chrissakes. Are you blind?'

'I just . . . It's a lovely Buddha, it's just . . . is it for the house?'

'Maybe it is. I don't know yet.' Buddy seemed to be calming down. He dropped his stubby, menacing finger. Frank retreated to his bed in the gloom at the far end of the lounge, where he fidget-ed like a scolded child.

'It's just odd because—'

'Because why?' asked Kraut, turning towards her and exhaling smoke.

'Because, if it's for the house, it's . . . well, nobody here is a Buddhist, are they? Nobody who lives here. They're Hindus, aren't they? Or sort of. But I mean, it's not a Buddhist island, is it?'

'And?' Kraut was staring in a tiresome way. 'It's not *not* a Buddhist island. It's not *anti*-Buddhist.'

'It doesn't seem very thought through, that's all. And I think it's possibly disrespectful—a religious icon, of that sort, here.'

'Why?'

'I don't know why. It's just a feeling. Look at the flowers—they're from Jenny's arrangement, an arrangement that was an act of religious devotion. And you've—'

'Don't get your knickers in a twist,' said Buddy, laughing now. 'This is all business. Just business. A sideline I have in Far Eastern art and antiques. Buddy here—as I like to call him—is the preview, a taste of a shipment these boys are heading over to Bangkok to pick up. That's all. He's what you might call our quality control, sent out early for us to make sure—well, to make sure we're getting what we pay for. Besides, the religious side, no offence, but it's all the same really.'

'I see.' Emmy felt deflated. Was this a relief or another shock? Was this good news or bad? Legal? Illegal? These were, it seemed, questions that could not be asked. The men were looking at her again as if waiting for her to evaporate, so they could return to their queer male ritual, clod-hopping in front of a glamorous god—but a god stripped, here, of his divine power: a displaced divinity. She longed for someone to emerge from the kitchen, or to come downstairs and through the door behind her: Jenny? Suchi? Madé? Aimée, even. She waited a moment, suspended in silence, expecting a theatrical ending to so theatrical a scene. But eventually she simply bade them goodnight and retreated.

★

By the time Max limped home, he felt like a sodden sponge. Sitting in the muck of the rice paddies had been wet and uncomfortable, but he hadn't realized that his bum had been anaesthetized by the mud until he stood up and couldn't feel it. He put his hands on the seat of his shorts and found it caked with wet slime. As he walked it was hard to tell whether his buttocks were thawing or freezing further.

At least he had pretty well pulled his head together while his body froze up. He had decided what to do, and felt that even if it was drastic it was the right thing. He would go home, first plane he could get on. He would get a place in Sydney, on his own. He would get a part-time job and go to uni. He hadn't yet decided in what. He would *not* take money from his father. He wouldn't even speak to his father once he was back home, and above all he wouldn't touch his filthy cash. Max kicked at gravel in the road. His mother was right about his father, all these years. All the things she'd said. It was all about having whatever he wanted, when he wanted. That was all.

But then—Max did not want to think the rest. He thought of Jenny, that afternoon, of how she had let him kiss her and play with her hair only then to say no, she couldn't choose to be with him here, and she wouldn't go with him to Australia; that Buddy was going to fix it, that she was counting on Buddy, that Max couldn't do it properly. He had suggested they marry. She had laughed aloud. The thing about Buddy's way was that then you never knew why anyone did anything. No motives were pure. You never knew what anybody *meant*. What did Jenny mean when she laughed and pushed him away, her face open, her teeth sharp and white? He clasped at his filthy, iced backside and went into the house.

Frank was snoring on his bed, although it was by no means

late. Neither Emmy nor Aimée nor Ruby was around, and Jenny
had, at least—Max thought—the consideration not to be present.
He went to the kitchen and took a beer from the rumbling fridge.
On his way back he noticed Buddy and Kraut sitting out on the
veranda, and he saw the Buddha.

He walked over and stood in front of it, staring. Wondering if
it were staring back. It was spookier than spirit talk: it was as
spooky as the altars in the mist on the mountainside all that time
ago, and that's what it made him think of. Because you could tell
just by looking at it—by the flowers in its hands, by its lazy glance,
by its golden glimmer—that people, somewhere, believed in it.
The way you could tell from the offerings at the shrine. And all
that believing gave it power. The beer, cold as it was, seemed to
warm him.

'Look at what the cat dragged in,' he heard his father call,
buoyant as ever. He pretended not to notice.

'Hungry, Junior?' Buddy tried again. Max shook his head,
although he was.

'Got your first delivery, then,' he said instead, his voice as
chill as he could manage.

'Beautiful, isn't he? Worth a fortune. A Burmese Buddha,
my boy. Aren't many on the market.' Buddy came up and put
his hand on Max's shoulder; Max could feel the creepy German
lurking in the background.

'From a temple, then?' asked Max, who wanted to touch the
Buddha and did not want, himself, to be touched.

'Reckon so. That's the place for them.'

'Nicked?' He turned, halfway, to look at Buddy, who
shrugged. 'Illegal, right?' Buddy shrugged again.

'Burma shouldn't be closed,' he said. 'Don't be a bleeding
heart. The country's run by a bunch of murdering thugs—I suppose you support them now?'

'Would you do it here?'

'Not much of a market for mossy stone carvings. And I reckon I've already got the batik niche well covered, don't you?' Buddy sniggered.

'More of a people place?'

'You said it.'

Max twitched free. He was looking at the Buddha, out of place, like himself. 'I'm going home tomorrow.'

'Tomorrow?' Buddy started. 'Something wrong? Did your mum call? You feeling worse?'

'Just sick of it, I reckon.'

'Out of the blue?'

'Reckon so.' When he looked at his father, Max could have sworn he saw hurt, real concern. So he looked away.

'What about Komodo? Don't you want to see the dragons?'

'Let him go home, if he wants,' said Kraut from the background. His support was almost enough to make Max change his mind.

'Is it something you want to talk about?' Buddy asked—a question which, Max knew, cost him: Buddy preferred not to talk. 'Has something happened?'

Only then did it occur to Max that Buddy didn't even know. That he hadn't the foggiest idea. That if Max had asked about Jenny, Buddy would have offered her up as a gift. He would have traded her in for someone else at once. He loved his son, in his way; he didn't love Jenny. He just couldn't see what went on in front of his face. Which of course made it worse.

'I need to get back. Earn some money before I start uni in the new year.'

'That's miles away. Is there something I can do? You all right?'

'I just need to get back. Really. I'm knackered, Dad. And my arse is all wet. Gonna wash up. We'll sort it out in the morning, OK?'

As he went upstairs, he could hear his father's voice, although not what it said. He could hear disbelief, though, and disappointment, and Kraut's sinister murmuring. And the distant thundering of hooves that was Frank, snoring.

Emmy held Jenny around the middle and put a hand beneath her collar-bones. 'Kick,' she urged. 'Up and down. Flutter kick. Up and down.'

Jenny gasped with the effort and as though afraid of drowning, although her chin was clear of the water. She wore Emmy's spare suit, and it sagged and slithered on her, loose in Emmy's hand. This was their swimming lesson: between breakfast and lunch, in the lull of the morning's work, on a festival day. Today marked the temple-naming ceremony, an annual event that involved all temples in Ubud. Later, there would be much to do: the evening would be filled with happenings.

'Is it fun? Do you like it?'

Jenny laughed. 'Difficult,' she said.

'Shall I let go for a second, and see how you do?' Without waiting for an answer, Emmy did; at once Jenny's body began to writhe and twist, and she spluttered violently. Emmy caught her up again—so light, and small—and helped her find her feet.

'You can always stand up, you know. We're in the shallow end. And you mustn't be afraid of getting your face wet. Being underwater won't kill you—you just don't breathe in. Don't panic.'

'In our culture,' Jenny said, 'people do not go swimming like this. There is great respect for water spirits—they are very powerful. To put your head underwater, on purpose—in Balinese culture, we do not do this.'

'If nobody swims here, why do *you* want to learn?'

'For Sydney,' said Jenny, as if the answer were wholly evident, and the move imminent. 'Everyone in Sydney swims.'

'Not everyone,' said Emmy. 'My daughter's boyfriend doesn't. I mean, maybe he knows *how*, but he never does.'

'Will you teach me more?'

'Now? Or another day?'

'Another day, perhaps. It makes me so tired. I am not accustomed.'

Jenny was sitting on the steps, her torso out of the water, the suit drooping and gaping, while Emmy braved a length or two with her even, middle-aged breast-stroke, when Ruby clattered along the path in a frilly white swimsuit, followed by Aimée. Aimée wore a high-cut leopard-print swimsuit, and sunglasses. She carried plump orange water-wings and towels.

'Good morning,' ventured Emmy, resolved to be polite despite everything. Ruby ran to Jenny's arms and splashed and screamed. Jenny and Aimée did not acknowledge each other.

Aimée stood at the water's edge and made no move to take off her glasses. 'You'll be going then, after all,' she said to Emmy.

'Me? Really, I don't—'

'Didn't you know, Mrs Richmond, that your host is leaving?'

'Buddy? For Thailand?'

'Did you not tell me that Christopher was your host? Or perhaps I misunderstood?'

'Max?'

'Tonight. For Sydney.'

Emmy looked at Jenny who, teasing Ruby, showed no sign of having heard.

'I didn't know,' Emmy said. 'Surely not before the festival. He so much wants to see the ceremony. We both do.'

'I'm sure there's room on the plane.' Aimée spread out her towel and summoned Ruby to her, festooning the girl's tiny arms with the water-wings. Jenny looked at Emmy and rolled her eyes and giggled. It was hard to believe, Emmy thought, that these two women were about the same age. Not much older than her Pod.

Jenny spoke almost in a whisper. 'Soon I am going to Suchi's house,' she said. 'To make ready the offerings for tonight. If you come with me, I can teach you something also.'

They both got out of the water and stood, rivulets cascading off their bodies, only a few feet from Aimée and her daughter.

'I'll be fifteen minutes, at the house,' whispered Jenny, before going, leaving small crushed grass footprints glistening in her wake.

Emmy stood dripping in the sun. Aimée ignored her.

'Seen the Buddha?' asked Emmy after a minute.

Aimée nodded once, her eyes invisible behind the glasses.

'Are you a Buddhist?'

'I was brought up that way. Why?' Aimée waved at invisible flies. Her face was scrunched up.

'What's your connection to the Buddha, then? To the "shipment"—to all the antiques?'

'You ask personal questions. I *am* Buddy's connection. Without me there wouldn't be any.'

'But what,' asked Emmy, pausing to pull her sundress over her head, 'what can you possibly get out of it?'

Aimée turned her face downwards, away from the sun. 'Ruby,' she called to the little girl, who balanced at the water's edge, preparing to jump. 'Ruby, wait for Mummy. Mummy is coming.'

When Max was woken by the morning sun and he saw the splendour of the gorge outside his window, he felt better than he had since the monkey bite. As if an evil spirit's curse had been lifted and he was ready to get on with his life.

When he remembered that he was now committed to going home, the realization crushed this sense of well-being. He sat on his bed in his shorts for some time, his fingers playing, out of habit, at the place on his neck where the bite mark had all but disappeared. He contemplated grovelling to his father, saying he had changed his mind. He even toyed with the idea of trying to explain the whole Jenny thing to Buddy—before he acknowledged that to do so would only ruin Jenny's already slim chances for Sydney. He thought of bartering on the Komodo trip. saying he had done an about-face for the treat of going with Buddy to see the dragons.

But Max knew it was probably too late. The sun had climbed well above the rim of the gorge, and although there were no clear sounds, Max could sense activity—activity bent, he knew, on sending him back to Sydney.

Aimée was in the sitting-room, in her leopard-spotted bathing-suit, smoking one of her extremely long cigarettes, when Max came in. Ruby, also dressed for swimming, was playing on the floor in front of the Buddha. The Buddha held fresh flowers. On the table, for the first time since he arrived in Ubud, lay a prepared breakfast: a sliced papaya on a plate, with a lime wedge; a glass of juice; some cold toast and a dish of murky guava jam.

'Good morning, Christopher.' Aimée waved at the breakfast with her cigarette, sending a billow of smoke over the toast and fruit. 'That's for you. Your father made it.'

'Wow.'

'I understand you're leaving us,' she said, as if she were closer to Buddy than Max was. It was particularly annoying because she was not much older than Max, and he did not consider her to be family. She was just another in a long line of his father's ex-girlfriends, only still around because she'd had a baby, because Buddy was a sucker for kids.

Max didn't say any of this. He tackled the papaya and said, 'I guess so,' loathing her for making it a final decision in such an offhand way. She was one person he definitely couldn't lose face in front of. He hated being called Christopher.

'Your father sorted out your ticket this morning. He got through to Garuda on the phone—imagine!'

'Yeah. Imagine.' The papaya was very slippery, and the slices kept sliming off Max's spoon.

'He sorted out his own ticket at the same time,' she said, with a small smile, patting absently at Ruby's head.

'Yeah?'

'Yes. He's decided, since you won't be here, to come with me and Ruby and Kraut to Bangkok.'

'For the shipment, then?' Max said this because he knew it would bug her; she would want to believe that Buddy was chasing after her. Like he could care less.

She didn't say anything.

'What about Komodo?'

'What about it? He's gone into town with K'tut to cancel Komodo. For the time being. That's all I know.'

'When?'

'When what?'

'When are you going?'

'My ticket is for a couple of days from now,' said Aimée. 'But as far as I know, Buddy's hoping to fly out tonight. This afternoon, maybe.'

Max knew that he must have upset his father a great deal for him to take off in such a rush. Either that, or there was some question of sweetening the Burmese antiques deal if he went to Bangkok. The cold toast tasted like sawdust; the guava jam was sickeningly sugary. He ate half a slice and put it down.

'You haven't seen Jenny this morning, have you?'

'The servant girl? No.' Aimée picked up a pile of things from the sofa, which was mottled by sunlight: towels, sunglasses, shiny water-wings. 'We're going for a swim,' she said. She hauled her daughter to her feet with her free hand. 'Come along, Ruby, my treasure. Swims. Swims.'

'Sims!' cried the little girl on the way out of the door. 'Sims!'

Max smacked at the gooey guava with the back of his spoon. Too late. It was done, irreparably, tiresomely, done. And where *was* everyone? Why was Jenny not around? Or Emmy, even?

He walked down the hill to the hotel reception next door, to ask if they had seen Jenny, but they hadn't. The young woman at the desk did remind him, however, that it was the day of Ubud's temple-naming ceremony, and she suggested that Jenny might be at her home, involved in preparations.

Max did not really know where Jenny's home was, but he knew that her parents' house—where she formally lived, although she often stayed with her girlfriends, or, of course, in the Sparke house—was not in town. It was several tiny villages to the east, and not on the main road. He did not know how to find it. This, though, was a case of necessity, and there was not time to delay. At the bottom of the hill, by the *warung* Emmy so loved, just on the far side of the bridge and before climbing the slope into town, Max turned left, eastwards, on to a road he had often seen and rarely followed, and set off in urgent search of his beloved.

Emmy didn't know what to think about Max, much as she didn't know what to think about the Buddha. She didn't have time to look for him before meeting Jenny—who seemed, outwardly, strangely unperturbed—and she didn't know whether or not to believe Aimée. If Max *were* going, in such haste, Emmy was unsure of what effect this might have on her visit. Perhaps it would be time to move on? Back to Candi Dasa, or to Lavina Beach, with its flush toilets? As honorary mother, her duties would be over, and as anything else—well, she would just have to wait and see.

And the Buddha: maybe the Buddha, Emmy reflected, with his enigmatic smile, the Buddha so out of place in Buddy Sparke's Balinese Hideaway—maybe he held all the answers to the riddles she confronted? If she could make up her mind about the Buddha, it would be time to go—time dictated from inside herself, not by Max's whim. Emmy was fed up with how little she seemed to control in this supposedly most controllable of environments. She was aware that she had ceased, at some unmarked moment, to be a tourist, but what she was now she hadn't stopped to think.

Jenny was already waiting, dried and dressed, when Emmy reached the house. She carried a basket filled with frangipanis, lilies and orchids. They set off at once for Suchi's parents' house, where the increasingly pregnant and—since the arrival of Aimée—rarely seen Suchi was preparing for the evening's ceremonies.

The most efficient route was through town, past the clusters of tourists in the main street, past the rows of shops and stalls including the one belonging to Nyoman's mother, the tailor, who noticed them and waved. Her daughter was not in evidence, but Emmy could see that all households were busy preparing their offerings even as they tried to get on with the business of the day: pyramids and cones of flowers, like extravagant wedding-cakes, were forming everywhere, and great oval platters of fruits and sweetmeats were piled alongside the flowers, attracting the interest of curious insects.

The sun was high, and the air warm and singing; as they walked through the bustle of town, Jenny and Emmy moved in companionable silence. It was only when they turned on to the quieter Monkey Forest Road, the canopy of trees looming at the dip in the land ahead, that Emmy spoke.

'Is this the only way to Suchi's?'

'The other way is very far, and we have not much time.'

'Aren't you afraid? After what happened to Max, I'd almost rather—'

'He was bitten,' Jenny explained patiently, 'because he was not respectful. Because Nyoman was too young to know how to placate the spirits. The monkey spirit is mischievous, but not—not *evil*. Sometimes good, sometimes wicked. You see?'

'So you are basically saying that the monkeys might bite us, but then again, they might not?'

'They will not bite us, because we are respectful and wise.' Jenny reached into her basket, beneath the profusion of flowers, and brought out two paper packets of peanuts, the sort sold in the main street to tourists.

'Offerings to the monkey spirits?' Emmy took one of the packets and slit a peanut open with her fingernail. They were dusty nuts, shrivelled, their shells flimsy as rotted tree bark.

'The monkeys expect it. The tourists have made the monkeys expect.'

'Devotion has to be flexible, I suppose. Does Suchi do this whenever she comes to town to see Buddy?'

'She comes in a car, or on a moped. But not now: it is bad luck for the baby in the Monkey Forest. Shall we go on? There is not much time, when there is so much to do.'

Armed though she was, Emmy was apprehensive, tingling with adrenalin: the same feeling as when, several months ago, in Double Bay, she awoke to hear a burglar—only to discover that it was Pod, key-less, trying to jemmy the back door with a credit card. Jenny kept up a patter as they followed the road into the canopy of trees. 'Do you know the Indonesian word for monkey? No? Say after me: *monjét*. The word is *monjét*.'

Emmy, her eyes veering crazily around, caught sight of monkeys gathering in the shadows. Ears and noses, outstretched hands, waggling thumbs. So *human*. She checked the branches overhead and saw a couple scampering from tree to tree above her, calling to their friends.

Jenny deftly tossed a peanut here and there, not stopping, not looking at the monkeys. Where the nuts fell, the monkeys swarmed and batted at each other.

'Say *monjét*. The word is *monjét*.'

'This is horrible,' whispered Emmy, feeling her bare shoulders prey to the greedy monkey hands. She was prepared to scream, her throat clenched.

'Say it,' said Jenny. 'And throw one, now, to the right. Go on.'

Forcing her frozen limbs into motion, Emmy raised her arm, threw overhand: her nut made a 'pht' sound as it landed, on leaves, three or four trees back from the road. At once, a patch of the path cleared, as with great chattering and rustling several monkeys pursued the gift.

'You see?' said Jenny, still looking straight ahead, not pausing, not smiling. 'It is not so bad. The spirits can be controlled.'

'Up to a point.' But Emmy unclenched the sweating fist that clutched the nuts and proceeded to lob her share, intermittently, into the undergrowth.

'And the word?' asked Jenny again.

'The word is *mun-jette*.'

'*Monjét*,' Jenny corrected.

'*Monjét*.'

'Good. Now, the word for tree is *pohon*.'

Afterwards, Emmy did not measure the distance of the forest in minutes (it seemed an eternity), or in distance (to the very last, each step was an effort: it was like being stuck in a child's nightmare, unable to wake up); she measured the distance in words. By the time they reached open land again, Emmy had learned the Indonesian words for monkey, tree, forest, bird, duck, pig, dog and baby. She had learned the words for friend, mother, daughter and sister, not just in Indonesian but in Balinese as well. And she had learned a Balinese expression that moved her, in the soft, certain way Jenny spoke it. It was the phrase for the island's time of origin and peace, when all was right with the world; the time before the white men came. The expression was '*dugas gumine enteg*', and it meant 'when the world was steady'.

'How will we get back?' Emmy asked, holding up her few remaining peanuts. 'Do you have more?'

'Going back we will be carrying offerings, for the temples.'

'So we'll go in a car?'

'So we will walk the long way around.'

'*Monjét* would eat anybody's offerings, I suppose?' Emmy asked, laughing.

Jenny's reply was serious. 'They do not eat flowers,' she said. 'You see, the basket is untouched.'

Emmy had not realized that preparing for the ceremonies was an all-afternoon activity. When they arrived at Suchi's parents' house, half a dozen girls and women were already there. Several of them Emmy recognized from Buddy's house, and two who were unfamiliar were introduced as Suchi's sisters. Each woman was busy with a clearly defined task: with flowers, or food; with initial trimmings or twistings, or with the final formations of elegant and eloquent devout display. The women worked in the shade of a porch, overlooking a swept courtyard where younger girls entertained small children, and chickens strutted and darted about. Several cocks, preening within their bamboo cages, placed out of the sun with the finest view of the yard, ruffled their feathers disdainfully and blinked at the proceedings.

The women's voices rose and fell: for a while, Emmy listened for the few words she had just learned, but not hearing them, she gave up, relying instead on periodic English commentary from Jenny. The afternoon was hot and sleepy despite the vigorous activity. It wore on, and on, and on, uninterrupted but for late arrivals and pauses to sip tangerine juice or to admire finished handiwork.

Amid the placid hum, Emmy's eyes settled on two little girls playing with tattered dolls in the corner of the yard, rocking them, walking them, throwing them in the air. The girls were clearly alive only to each other and to the engrossing fantasy world they had created for their inanimate charges. Their entire bodies laughed with the pleasure of the stories they shared, and when one of their dolls apparently fell ill, they both grew solemn and all but wept. Watching them, Emmy felt that she and Virginia, too, ought to have had such a shared world. She marvelled at the completeness—however temporary—of the little girls' union, and she wondered, wistfully, whether being born in this paradise island might have allowed her and her sister a similar freedom, a similar joy. But it was pure fantasy, this notion, just like the girls' doll world, and it passed back into the rhythm of the women's weaving fingers and the mounting towers of thanks to the gods.

Emmy did not have her watch, but she could tell from the lengthening shadows that it was well past three. The work showed no sign of slowing or of nearing completion: several new towers were just being begun. She worried about Max, about what Aimée had said. Unaware of its truth or falsehood, she didn't want to disrupt the pre-ceremony rituals she had been invited to observe, but it was suddenly clear to her that Jenny was not going back to the house before the event and, therefore, that it was not intended that she, Emmy, go either. She wondered about making her own way back, but had only to think of the monkeys' eyes and their grasping fingers to reject the idea.

Fretting spoiled the peaceful pleasure that the afternoon had been bringing her, the delight in the women's deft hand-movements, in the economy of their bending bodies. Just the sight of Suchi, so exquisitely beautiful, had seemed a gift after the terrifying journey she and Jenny had endured. But as the afternoon wore on, Emmy's gratitude shrivelled like the discarded leaves that gathered on the porch. She wanted to get back to the house.

'Do you plan,' she asked Jenny eventually, 'to go straight to the temples?'

'We will all go to one temple,' Jenny explained. 'Only to one. Others will go to other temples.'

'Buddy?'

'Maybe to ours, maybe to a different one.'

'But you'll go from here, without going back to the house?'

'Of course.' Jenny seemed surprised that there was any question.

'But what about Max?'

'Yes?'

'Well, if Aimée's right and he *is* leaving on the plane for Sydney tonight, then shouldn't we both get back to see him?'

'I do not think he will go,' said Jenny, imposing origami-like contortions on a banana leaf without looking at it.

'I agree it seems unlikely, but if he does—surely you of all people would want to say goodbye?'

Jenny looked hard at Emmy, her fingers still twitching over the leaves, making boats of them, baskets. 'If he does go, and I do not say goodbye, then I will see him very soon in Sydney. We can be together in Sydney.'

'You really believe in it? You believe Buddy actually has the power to get your visa sorted out? You believe he'll pay for your course in advance, make sure you have somewhere to live, all of it?'

'He promises me.'

'Look at Aimée. What did he promise Aimée?'

'It's different,' Jenny said, taking a sudden interest in the folding of fronds. 'She is—she was his girlfriend. I am a true friend. Suchi now is Buddy's girlfriend.' She smiled across the room at Suchi, whose gaze was elsewhere.

'So you wouldn't even want to say goodbye to Max?'

Jenny was silent.

'Well I *have* to go back to the house before the ceremony,' said Emmy, standing for emphasis. She had been kneeling for some time and her joints were unpleasantly stiff. 'I can't possibly go to a temple dressed like this.' She gestured at her sundress, beneath which the straps of her bathing-suit could be discerned. It was, frankly, inappropriate: even Jenny's tactful once-over could not conceal the fact.

'But I cannot go now.'

'I could go alone.'

'Through the forest? No. You are not good with the spirits.'

'The other way, then?'

'It is too difficult. One turning wrong and you would be halfway to Den Pasar. It is the little paths, the little villages. And you do not have the language.'

Here I am, thought Emmy, trapped between being a tourist and something else. Most annoying.

'I have an idea.' Jenny was genuinely excited. She turned and spoke to several of the others, who stopped their work and looked Emmy up and down. One woman laughed. Another stood, came over to Emmy, indicated that she should lift her arms, and reached around her bust, embracing her. The woman said something to Jenny. Something noncommittal. Jenny was insistent. The woman did not change her tone. Suchi called something from across the porch, where she sat, and several of the women burst into peals of laughter. But Jenny was stern.

'We know what we will do,' she said to Emmy. 'So you will not have to go back to Buddy's house. We will make you a Balinese woman, in the proper clothes. In a sarong. It is very easy.'

Emmy looked around the group and understood why they had tittered. 'You can't,' she said. 'There wouldn't be a top to fit me.'

'We'll see,' Jenny said. 'I know that Suchi's *Bibi*, her father's sister, she is big like you. We will send K'tut.' She called to one of the girls in the courtyard, who laughed, nodded and ran off down the path beside the house.

But this did not solve everything. Emmy turned to Jenny, but Jenny anticipated her question.

'Max will not go,' she said, as simple as fact. 'I do not care what Aimée says, I know that Max will not go. He cannot go.' Jenny spoke not with Buddy-will-fix-it certainty, but with the confidence of one in love, who knows that she too is loved. And Emmy was convinced.

'You will be a Balinese lady,' Jenny said. 'Come.'

Max's search for Jenny was fruitless. He walked miles before giving up. His inability to speak the language hampered him in the smaller villages, where only Balinese and not even Indonesian was spoken. The name 'Jenny' didn't seem to mean anything to anyone, and only as he conceded defeat did it occur to Max that her real name might actually be something else—something less clearly English. He wondered whether she was a Wayan or a K'tut or something in between.

When, in the late afternoon, he eventually returned, sweating and exhausted, to the house, Max found K'tut waiting for him, in a very bad humour.

'You are going tonight,' K'tut said, as if this were a distasteful rather than a disappointing fact. He ran his hand through his hair as he spoke, revealing his high, veined forehead.

'Where is everybody?'

'I am here to take you to the airport.'

'And my father?'

'Gone.' K'tut gestured limply, a cynic's dismissive wave. 'With the German. This afternoon.'

'Shit.'

'Today it is the day of our temple ceremonies.' K'tut's voice carried reproach, but Max did not hear it. 'You may want to eat something before you pack your bags. Possibly I could cook.' K'tut sounded doubtful.

'No worries.' It was after six. It was a blow that his father had left, but Buddy's behaviour was not out of character. Getting the last laugh, thought Max. Besides, neither was any good at farewells.

K'tut had removed himself to the bed and was watching an old kung-fu film with the volume turned down.

'Bruce Lee?'

K'tut nodded.

'Just two quick questions for you, mate?'

K'tut turned a weary eye.

'One, where is everybody, aside from Buddy and Kraut? And two, do you have any idea where Jenny might be? Then I swear I'll bugger off.'

'Frank is at the hotel,' said K'tut. 'Aimée is with Ruby, to get chocolate cake at the *warung*. Your Australian woman, I do not know. But Jenny is probably at Suchi's, preparing for the ceremonies.'

'Where's that, then?'

'On the other side of the Monkey Forest. Far away. I do not think the spirits would want you to go there. Also, there is not time.'

Max thought for a moment and spoke again, even though K'tut had already turned back to the film. 'We could go, if you would take me in the bus. We'd be really quick. It's just that— you've got to understand—' Max stopped because even preoccupied as he was he could see the curl of K'tut's lip.

'No,' said K'tut, crossing his legs tidily beneath him. 'It is not possible. It is too late.' His eyes settled once and for all on the flickering movements of Bruce Lee.

Upstairs, on Max's bed, he found an envelope from his father addressed to him in his familiar, hasty hand. Inside there was a note, a wad of Australian dollars and a fat joint.

Junior,

Sorry about the monkey. That's what spoiled it for you I

reckon. We'll do Komodo next winter. See you in Sydney—don't know when. The cash is for having a good time till we next meet. Smoke the j before you go, or leave it here. Not cool with customs. You're a bonzer kid. Cheers, B.

Max stuffed the money into his pocket and walked out on to the terrace, holding the joint and a book of matches. He didn't know whether to light it or not. Night was falling, and he stood watching the colours and shapes change: the outlines of objects took on a dark thread, which was then filled in, till there were only silhouettes against the sky. And then the night advanced further, as if a divine sewing project were embroidering the whole globe with black silk—deep, soft, impervious, alarmingly swift.

As he stood, Max realized he was listening for the tinkling laugh that would mean Jenny was next door, in Buddy's room: unattainable, but near at least. Instead he heard the distant sounds of the procession, remote drumming rhythms from all sides, approaching different temples from different directions, all the beats faintly out of kilter with each other and out of touch with the singing cicadas. The music of the night did not delight or enchant Max: it flattened and saddened him, confirming as it did that he would not see Jenny again, that she was out in the darkness that could not include him, proceeding into another world and away from him. Not knowing what else to do, Max slumped in the balcony's wicker chair and lit the joint.

He was still sitting there when K'tut came to pick him up. They were forced to throw Max's belongings together with uncomfortable haste, and K'tut—furious in any event at having to miss the ceremony—could barely restrain himself from slapping his young charge's face.

By dusk, when the offerings were finally ready, and the proces-

sion from Suchi's house to the temple was set to begin, Emmy
no longer felt like herself. Like an offering of another kind, she
had been dressed and preened and oiled and poked into a shape
and personage she could not see (there were no mirrors in
Suchi's house).

Her boundaries and movements had been altered, as had the
weight of her eyelids and the shape of her head. She stood
among the younger Balinese women like a mascot. They still
giggled to look at her, but Suchi's *Bibi* and her mother, women
of Emmy's own generation, greeted her with solemnity and
grace before taking their places in the procession.

Around her middle, Emmy wore a crisp blue sarong with
swirls of green and golden yellow, tucked and draped into a long,
straight skirt that fell to just above her ankles. *Bibi*'s blouse was of
fine, cream-coloured lace with a low-cut neck and long, fitted
sleeves, and many buttons down the front. Emmy's arms and bust
matched *Bibi*'s admirably, and the blouse was slightly constricting
but not too snug. Beyond the waist, however, where the blouse
could have fallen full to the hips, there was no buttoning it across
Emmy's breadth, and the two sides fell away unattached, revealing
a tiny triangle of midriff above the sarong. In spite of this gap,
Jenny had deemed the top suitable—had even waxed enthusiastic
about it—so Emmy had to believe she looked presentable.

Jenny had not stopped there: she had perfumed and oiled
Emmy's hair, combing it repeatedly until it slicked back against
her skull, around her ears, in heavy, oleaginous ridges. She had
painted and powdered her face, kohled her eyes around the rims
and corners, coaxing them into an almond shape, and had rouged
Emmy's freckled brown cheeks. She had perfected the line of
Emmy's lips and had coloured them in scarlet. And she had
slipped a frangipani behind the older woman's ear.

Only Emmy's feet, still in the flip-flops she had put on that
morning, reminded Emmy of herself. The rest was new, another

woman's creation, to which she had attended only passively. Emmy's nose was tickled by the various odours that emanated from this self of hers: the sweet smell of the perfumed grease, the vegetable scent of the frangipani, the pungent wafting of *Bibi's* sweat from the armpits of the blouse, held like a memory in the lace since its last wearing. Emmy, too, was perspiring, unaccustomed to layers and films against almost every inch of her skin.

She wondered what she looked like, and looked at Jenny, beside her, to get some idea. Jenny's eyes and mouth were painted, her hair back from her face, in thick coils at her neck. Her pink silk top accentuated the strength of her arms and the delicacy of her waist, and her sarong fell in folds to the ground. As they set out in the dying light, Jenny carried on her head one of the great, intricate towers that the women had constructed in the shade of the porch. It wavered above, luminous and fragrant, surrounded by other such monuments, gliding through the sky as the people below shuffled in near silence towards their destination.

The walk was long, and after a while Emmy grew claustrophobic in the crowd. She could only take very small steps in her sarong, and she worried—irrationally, given the pace—that she might trip and then be trampled. It was getting dark. She stepped a little to the side, craning her neck to try to see to the front of their train, but the procession from Suchi's house had joined others and had swollen to a human river that seethed and surged peaceably along, winding this way and that without pause or question, and eventually, every so often, stopping still for short periods. Far ahead in the distance, Emmy could now hear drums and cymbals, and the discordant music of the *gamelan*.

Fascinated by the unfolding of events, she was also slightly alarmed (she did not like crowds, or at least didn't like being trapped in them: she *always* drove or took a taxi rather than travelling by subway in Sydney), faintly uncomfortable (the blouse, in its last fastened buttons above her navel, was cutting her in two, and she was aware that she was sweating profusely, even in her oiled scalp), a trifle bored (they had been walking for a very long time, it seemed, and she was unable to see anything besides the backs of the people in front of her and the profiles of those on either side), and even remotely anxious (where would this marathon march end up? would it then disperse? and where would she be? and how would she get home? not to mention the question of retrieving her swimsuit and sundress). She also became aware that her eyes were not seeing as Emmy felt they should: they were narrowing their vision in a lazy way, focusing on one thing, then another—a flower in a woman's plait, the rhythm of her own feet on the road—unable to take in the whole picture. It was a feeling she recognized from having taken valium, in certain quantities, at the time when William left her, and, insofar as it recalled that period, it was not a pleasant experience. She put it down to hunger: she had had no supper the night before, and no lunch that day. Had anyone asked, she would have said, 'I am not feeling quite myself.'

Eventually, they reached the stone gates of a temple and filed in. It was now darkest night. People arranged themselves around a central, altar-like area, beyond which lay an inner sanctum, to which only the priests had access. Braziers burned and lit the faces of the crowd with their flames. The *gamelan* and drums ceased.

The ritual which followed seemed to Emmy to last as long as the interminable walk. It was also fearsomely dull, difficult to follow and, frankly, an anticlimax. There were extensive periods of silence, and then of chanting, during which Emmy scanned the crowd for familiar faces and found none. There were many tourists mixed among the Balinese—in lurid polo shirts or cotton T-shirts—and Emmy was glad not to be recognizably among them; but was less pleased not to see a single soul that she knew.

The ceremony clearly involved the giving of gifts to the temple, and at long last a few large, extravagantly wrapped parcels were delivered by the priests to the inner sanctum, whereupon the event appeared to be officially over. All the food and flowers, however, were to be left outside the temple, against its walls, and people milled and loitered both inside and out, preparing to make their offerings to the gods. Only a few could trickle through the temple gates at once, and groupings were jostled and broken apart. Which is how Emmy found herself spat on to the road in front of the temple alone, with nobody she knew in sight: no Jenny, no Suchi, no *Bibi*, no anybody.

Searching for her companions was hopeless, in part because Emmy did not want to go back into the temple. Instead, she attached herself to a clutch of young Australian tourists and slunk along behind them, catching fragments of their chatter. En route to their hotel, they led Emmy back to known territory, to the main street of Ubud, where the stalls were now all closed and shuttered, and where it seemed she had not been for an eternity.

She made her way towards the valley, towards the bridge and her favourite *warung*, thence to climb, exhausted, to the Sparke house. Emmy had to navigate a patch of total blackness peopled at intervals by whispering shadows, between the centre of town and the Tjampuan crossroads, and hampered as she was by her attire, she minced through it at a wretched pace. But the worst was past, and the bridge was visible ahead, beneath her, lit by the rising moon, when there came a sudden glare of light and a blaring of horns. People Emmy had not known were there emerged in the oncoming headlights and scattered in panic. Amid the commotion, the monstrous white bus came rollicking and fuming up the hill and past her. As it roared by, Emmy caught sight of K'tut's face, set tight, at the wheel high above.

When, just afterwards, she spotted Frank outside the *warung*, she scurried up to him. He did not immediately recognize her, and then was amused by her costume.

'Gone native?' he smirked. His face was clear to her: they were away from the trees and the full moon was rising in a starry sky.

'He went, didn't he?'

'Who?'

'In the bus. Max. Aimée was telling the truth—Max has gone back to Sydney. Am I right?'

'He's not the only one.'

'What do you mean?'

'Were you at the ceremony, then?'

'Wasn't everybody?'

'I was,' said Frank dolefully. 'Bloody boring.'

'It did have *meaning* for some people,' said Emmy. 'So if it had meaning, it wasn't boring. But what do you mean?'

'What I said.'

'Who? Who has gone where?'

'They've gone and left me. Buddy brings me out to do a job, and then he bloody well takes it away again. Want a drink?'

'No thanks.'

'There's a real English pub here,' he said, pointing at a house that just looked like a house by the side of the road. 'They make gin and tonics. It's run by the hotel. Very nice place.'

'No thanks.'

'I'm going.'

'Tell me what you're talking about first?'

'Buddy's gone to Bangkok, hasn't he?'

'Today?'

'Today.' Frank was very glum.

'But why? With Aimée?'

'That she-devil's still here, lounging around up at the house, somewhere. No, he took Kraut and went.'

'Whatever for?'

'Wanted to oversee the shipment himself, he said. Got worried that what followed wouldn't be as good as what came before. Thought I wouldn't know the difference.'

'I see.'

'I wouldn't, either,' Frank confided. 'Are you coming?' He gestured at the house. Music—pop music—was drifting out on the night air. Perhaps it was a pub of sorts.

'Tell me something—where does this stuff, this shipment, come from?'

'Easy. Known route,' said Frank. 'Across the border from Burma, down from Chiang Mai, out through Bangkok. Easy as wink.'

'But before that?' Suddenly it seemed to Emmy a question of the utmost importance. 'Whose antiques are they?'

Frank made a grunting noise and rubbed vigorously at his nose with his fist, like a fat schoolboy. 'Dunno. Never thought. Have to ask Buddy.'

'But the Buddha, for example?' Emmy insisted. 'The Buddha in the living-room?'

'That's easy, innit? The Buddha's from a temple somewhere. Got to be. That's where Buddhas sit, innit? In temples.' Frank was satisfied with this reply and turned towards his gin palace. A few tourists seemed to be drifting into it. 'Sure you won't have a drink?'

Emmy shook her head and felt the weight of her oiled and pinned hair. It did not feel like her own. As Frank went, she called out to him, 'It's not . . . well, it's just not *legal*, is it?' As if hoping that legality might redeem it. If legal, it would be part of someone else's code, not up to Emmy herself to judge.

'Do I look like a lawyer?' Frank called back above the music, before he disappeared.

The last climb from the valley to the house was wholly peaceful, illuminated by the vast, cool blue of the moon. Encased in the peacock sarong, Emmy walked with another woman's footsteps, amid another woman's smells, weighted down by lives in which she had no place. She hardly felt the kisses of the evening air, so much softer and more welcoming than other kisses, hoped for or

259

received. It was so suddenly over, the life and the self she had made unravelled on the night air in a matter of hours. All that was clear was that it was time to make a decision, time to take up her own truths again. Truth was not ever, she sensed, where she expected it to be; and luck, as a code, perhaps did not exist. Who she was was no clearer; but she did know where she ought to be.

Emmy caught a perfume on the breeze—of earth and wet, of the paddies, of an invisible mist—and it was the odour of Abang, of the shrine on the mountainside, of the moment after which the summit had been, perhaps, irrelevant.

In the Sparke house, only Ruby slept, her thumb stuffed into her mouth, and dark tendrils of her hair webbed across her flushed cheeks. She was tiny in the big bed, a minute hummock abutting the dip in the mattress where her mother would lie. But for now, Aimée sat in the darkened sitting-room, her eyes meeting the opalescent glow of the Buddha's, she smoking, he sitting, half-smiling, the two of them waiting there together, far from home—whatever that meant—and, unlike Emmy, unable ever to go back.

EPILOGUE

SITTING IN HER sister's living-room, Virginia could hear the waterfall din of the bath emptying upstairs. Even with the divorce, she had imagined that Emmy's house would be grander than this, a cluttered two-bedroom cottage, really, albeit in an expensive part of the city. She, aching still from an interminable and intermittently terrifying plane journey the day before, would have been grateful for the first turn in the bathroom, but while Emmy had offered politely, it was clear to Virginia that on this, Portia's wedding day, her sibling's maternal responsibilities took precedence over the discomfort in her own joints.

Perched on the edge of an armchair, surveying her surroundings, her bathrobe tightly clamped at her waist, Virginia was already too warm. Although the room was in shade, the breeze that wafted in from the street bore the warning of formidable heat to come, and the glimpse of sky that her view encompassed glowed an electric, pristine blue. It was just as everyone who knew had alerted her, and she was grateful for their advice: upstairs, on her bed, she had a large, straw hat to protect her from the wedding day sun.

Virginia did not mean to snoop while she waited, but she could muster no interest in the morning paper and she was too restless simply to sit and think. She rose from her chair and ambled about. She noted that the profusion of artwork on the walls was modern and looked 'genuine'; that the furniture, while elegant, was on a scale disproportionate to that of the room—clearly remnants of a former solidity, salvaged from the wreckage of Emmy's marriage. The bay window at the front of the house gave on to a quiet side-street, but if Virginia leaned forward she could see the corner where the urban bustle began, and could hear, faintly, the growling of cars and the occasional horn. To the rear of the house lay the kitchen, with its open dining area (a table, again, too substantial for its space); and beyond, the exuberant, semi-tropical tangle of Emmy's tiny, neglected garden.

Virginia tried to imagine what it would be to have such freedom, to glance across even such a modest expanse and know everything was in its place because she had put it there herself. Not only her body but her spirit would have the run of the house, without being answerable to her mother, a lame, difficult old woman whose personality seemed to stretch by force of will into the corners of the London flat where her legs now refused to take her.

Such freedom seemed at once the thing she had most envied her sister and a dread emptiness, the desolate unfurling she foresaw for herself when their mother would at last be gone, the one thing that everyone else seemed so zealously to guard against. From this perspective, she felt pity, almost, for Emmy who, like all the others, had so tried, and yet had failed. And yet—Virginia's eye fell on a cluster of framed photographs of her niece at a variety of ages and in various poses—Emmy had Portia.

Virginia's train of thought was interrupted by the sight of two surprising photographs, one old and one new, tucked forgotten amid the myriad representations of the elfin Pod. In an elaborate silver frame that dwarfed the blurry black-and-white print, Virginia suddenly saw herself, a skinny, long-necked child, her hand firmly entwined with that of her younger sister. Their mother, slight and careworn, but so young, stood half-crouched behind them, an arm around each child's shoulder. What struck Virginia was not the serious, vaguely concerned visage of Melody Simpson (who did not look at all as powerful as she remembered) but the glee on her own crinkled face, a pure pleasure mirrored absolutely in that of her sister. Where was it that they had been so happy? What moment—erased till now from her memory—had seen these two eager little girls so linked in their common delight?

She heard Emmy's tread on the stair and swiftly replaced the picture in its corner, taking up the other, almost new, which lurked beside it behind the rest. It, too, was slightly out of focus, and misty, a photograph snapped in haste of a group of sweaty men and women amid some mossy stones. Emmy was among them, looking pale, her hair lank about her face. Her expression was inscrutable, somewhere between fear and triumph. She was smiling.

'That's in Bali,' volunteered her sister, suddenly behind her in the room. 'About six months ago. I climbed a mountain—I think I wrote to you about it. Not the most flattering shot, is it?' She laughed, quite formally, Virginia thought.

'Who are the others?'

'Just a bunch of other climbers. The older fellow, in the batik, he's the one whose house I stayed in. Extraordinary man.'

Virginia nodded and put the photograph down. 'Do you miss it, ever?'

'What?'

'The island.'

Emmy was busy checking in her handbag, which was tiny and expensive-looking and matched her suit exactly. 'Oh,' she said after a moment, 'You know, it was a holiday. You can't stay on holiday forever.' She looked up and smiled, a controlled smile, not like the innocent eruption Virginia had recently seen on her childhood face. 'Ginny dear, I'm in such a state. You *will* forgive me if I go on ahead, won't you? I promised Pod I'd help her get ready, and I'm running late as it is. I feel terrible leaving you'— Virginia shook her head slightly to dismiss her sister's guilt—'but you know how it is. The number for the cab company is by the phone in the kitchen, and I'd allow about twenty minutes, if I were you, just in case.'

Car keys in hand, Emmy fumbled at the front door and turned back. 'I hope you're not disappointed that it's a registry office do,' she said, blushing visibly beneath her tan. 'When you've come all this way and . . . well, you know. But the reception should be an event.'

'Yes, of course.'

'See you there, then.' With a vague wave, her sister was gone.

Virginia stood for a while in the centre of the little living-room, conscious of an ache at the base of her spine, puzzling over Emmy's parting comment—a reference, she took it, to the absence of religious ritual in the forthcoming proceedings. In a different world, in a different time, she might have tried to explain to Emmy the complexity of her own current relationship to the divine, but her sister, she knew, would not have under-stood. Virginia was momentarily overwhelmed by the loneliness of this sororal isolation, her own greatest human failure, and her sister's.

Since the summertime, since the awful cataclysm of their mother's fall and all that came before and after it, Virginia had not settled back into easy conversation with her God. Citing her mother's greater need, she shunned the comfort of the prayer group (which no longer met at Angelica's, since she had aban-doned her faith, but gathered instead in the fiery bosom of Frieda Watson's house), and she could no longer face the sermons that Reverend Thompson continued, so fervently, to declaim. She felt that the church, but not God, had deserted her in her time of greatest need, and yet she was uncertain of where the blame lay:

with the Reverend? with St Luke's? with the blind joyfulness of evangelism itself?

When Angelica revealed her faithlessness, Virginia had concurred, falsely, that God might Himself be in the wrong, or at least, might be cruel. But for herself, she attributed fault to human inadequacy and she continued to try to believe that He Himself could not disappoint. Almost behind the back of her quavering, invalid mother, Virginia tiptoed from church to church, three Sundays here, a couple there, the larger the congregation the better. She sat quietly in the back corners of these churches, behind pillars, near exits, and learned how to slip away from even the friendliest gatherings without meeting anyone or shaking the minister's welcoming hand. Her former solace had become a terrifying covert expedition, an addiction almost, that she would have abandoned altogether, even temporarily, if she had been able.

But out in the world, in the London that looked ruthlessly and exactly the same since her return from Skye (except for the promotion of Martin to Selina's post when Selina left unexpectedly to marry a wealthy man), she could discern only emptiness and terror, a morass of humanity's failure masked only by its transparent illusions of meaning. And she felt that the only way open to her was to keep searching for the warm arms of her God. If she had had one wish, it would have been for the restitution of her own all-consuming certainty: never to have seen, never to have known, never to have doubted.

Under the circumstances, however, she thought as she ran the lukewarm bathwater, she could hardly blame Emmy for holding her daughter's wedding in a registry office. It would be a quicker ceremony, more impersonal. More honest.

The Saturday morning traffic crawled across town, and although Emmy was only going as far as Pod and Pietro's flat in Paddington, she found her anxiety mounting as she inched away minute upon minute. She had a terror that Pod would go ahead and dress without her; that she, Emmy, would be denied that symbolic mother–daughter wedding ritual as she was being denied all the others: for obvious reasons, the reception was to take place on William's vast lawn, rather than in her own minute garden. She tried, as she stopped and started in the fug of exhaust smoke, to look ahead at the day with an open heart, but she found her mind straying to the photograph Virginia had held in her bony hand, of Emmy—another Emmy—on top of Abang.

It was Jenny who had sent her the picture, only a couple of months before, with a long and slightly incoherent letter. Buddy, it seemed, had then recently left Bali for good, escorted to the airport by his former friend, the Ubud Chief of Police, and forbidden ever to return. Jenny did not make clear what had occurred, and Emmy could only guess, but the final Sparke departure had evidently been as abrupt as the one she herself had witnessed.

The house, its swimming-pool completed, had been left open and unchanged, as though Buddy might resurface within hours from one of his periodic junkets. It was Jenny who had scrubbed and washed and folded and pulled the shutters down; it was she who had taken the abandoned photograph of the climbers from on top of the television and had thought to send it to Emmy. She did not speak openly of disappointment in her letter, but nor did she speak of coming to Sydney: her last chance had flown away, like all the others, in a silver 747.

When she received this communication, Emmy had been moved to a frenzy of remembering, to a nostalgia for a self she had really believed to be truer than her Sydney one. (She had said so, upon her return, over lunch with her friend Janet, but Janet had scoffed and said no self was truer than any other, that they were all the same really, and that it was merely a sign of how unbalanced

Emmy had been that she had even considered staying in Indonesia.) Remembering, Emmy had sworn to herself to do for Jenny what Buddy had not: to send her application forms for accounting courses, to look into visa requirements, to try, if necessary, to pull strings to ensure her a place and a future. But then Pod had announced her sudden plans to marry Pietro, and amid the whirlwind preparations the photograph had slipped from sight, and Jenny with it.

Emmy felt ashamed, in her elegant silk, on her way to see her daughter married; ashamed that Jenny had been so easy to forget. The self Emmy wanted to be, the innermost self she thought she truly was, would not have forgotten. It was as though, by going out into the world, that self had been encased and mummified by all the other selves she was to other people, until it was impossible to remember, or even to be certain, that there was a truth beneath the skin.

This was her way of being, she recognized, and her way of not suffering too much, which was why she had come home to the mantles—however tattered—that she knew how to wear. And it was a condemnation of this way that she felt she had seen this morning (felt, indeed, that she had *always* seen) in her sister's eyes, her sister who had always found meaning and merit in suffering, even for its own sake.

As she neared her daughter's house, Emmy wished she could be certain that after the fuss of the wedding was over, she would think again of Jenny and fulfil her earlier promises to herself, but she found she could not. In all honesty, she did not want to be naked to the world, and wounded, even if that nakedness made her a nobler person. She did not want to remember everything. But she had thrilled to her illusions of honesty and freedom, and even if she forgot Jenny's future she would treasure her walks in the dream landscape the Sparkes had offered her, and would cling to the few, magical words Jenny had taught her in the Monkey

Forest, and she would believe that somewhere, at some time, she had truly been herself.

And as she ran from the car to Pod's front door, catching her heel in the pavement on the way, Emmy Richmond hoped more passionately than ever that her daughter had not got dressed without her.

Virginia accepted a glass of champagne from the passing waiter's tray and stood observing the crowd on the lawn. It was terribly, very un-English-ly hot, and she was grateful again for the broad brim of her white straw hat. That aside, the day could not be faulted. The Australian summer sky had remained impeccable, and both the elegant and the less elegant had dressed in their finest for the occasion. Virginia held her champagne flute with both hands.

'Of course she's too young,' she heard her sister say, in a falsely gay voice, 'but isn't anyone, anytime? Aren't we all? Whatever makes her happy . . . Yes, she does look beautiful. She does. Originally, I wondered about the red and gold, but you know how they are, and now I see it . . . ' Emmy drifted over to Virginia, her mouth fixed in a crimson hostess's smile.

'All well, sister mine? Can I introduce you to some people? I know the service wasn't much, but isn't this lovely? It is so wonderful that you could be here!'

Emmy said this, Virginia thought, with exaggerated enthusiasm.

'It's a lovely wedding,' she volunteered.

'Trust Portia to choose the week after Christmas, that's all I can say.' Emmy's eyes were darting around as she spoke. She winked or blinked at someone, raised her glass to another, nodded to a third, grinning furiously.

'He's got a lovely place here, hasn't he?' said Virginia. Emmy

268

flashed her a glance, aware in the midst of her formal responsibilities that Virginia was not acting her part: that she either knew nothing at all about her sister or was deliberately trying to wound.

'William? William and Dora? Mmm, lovely.' Her smile was brittle.

'You do too, of course. I love my room.'

'Pod's room.' Emmy said this rather sorrowfully. 'She does look beautiful, doesn't she, my baby, going out into the world?'

'Yes, my niece is really very beautiful,' said Virginia. It sounded strange coming from her, like a sentence in a French lesson.

Emmy looked her sister up and down, Virginia who had come all this way (first time ever) for this niece she hardly knew. She would almost have said Virginia looked pretty, if Virginia had been someone else. At least she was wearing lipstick, and her dress, while somewhat old-fashioned, was not painfully dowdy. Emmy, in spite of the heat and the hectic to-and-fro of the wedding, continued to look good and knew it: on William's lawn, among Pietro's relatives, this was her only armour. It was armour that Virginia, Emmy felt once again, with some exasperation, was looking right through.

'Why did you come, anyway?' Emmy asked. 'After all this time?'

'I thought it was important,' Virginia said. 'I knew Mother wanted me to. It was important to her.' She paused. 'This is an ordeal for you, isn't it?' she said, which really made Emmy hate her. In this garden, among these people, wreathed in failure as Emmy felt herself to be (Dora, her ex-friend and ex-husband's wife, was only a stone's throw away), the largest part of the effort lay in making it seem effortless. Only an enemy would expose her.

'Such a shame Mother couldn't be here, no?' she offered by way of reply, raising a glass to a small, dark, plump woman in stifling-looking purple velvet. 'The mother-in-law,' she explained between her teeth.

Virginia wanted to turn and walk away from her sister. Or to hit her, or something. 'Mother couldn't possibly have come. She finds it extremely difficult even to walk, you know. She almost never goes out now.' She wasn't sure whether Emmy was listening or not. 'I told you last night, if my friend Angelica hadn't moved into the flat to take care of her, I couldn't have come myself.'

Emmy clucked in a superficially sympathetic way.

'After the fall, the peculiar thing was, she wanted to stay on Skye,' Virginia continued. 'She went on and on about it.'

'Good heavens. How horrible.' Emmy and Virginia's eyes met. 'Was she delirious or something?'

'I don't know. She never mentions it now.'

William's elegant outline loomed into view at the edge of the gathering before them.

'William, darling,' cried Emmy, lunging for his arm, 'You remember my sister Virginia, don't you? Haven't seen each other in decades. Do us a favour? Take Ginny along to congratulate Pod and Pietro? I don't see how she's to make it through the crush otherwise. There are some new arrivals over there I just must say hello to before they're swallowed up.'

Both women were grateful for Emmy's desperate act, although only Virginia had the luxury of feeling superior to it. As they forged their separate paths through the swelling, ever-tightening mass of the party, each woman held up her escape from the other as a tiny, shining trophy, even though both knew that their joy in such freedom could only last moments.